LITERARY & OTHER FICTION

DO NOT WITHDRAW

To Headquarters Store

DORSET STORIES

Sylvia Townsend Warner

Foreword
Judith Stinton

BLACK DOG BOOKS

Published in 2006 by Black Dog Books,
104 Trinity Street, Norwich, NR2 2BJ

Text copyright © Susanna Pinney.
Illustrations copyright © the estate of Reynolds Stone.

ISBN 0-9549286-3-6

All rights reserved. No part of this publication may be reproduced, stored in a retrieval system or transmitted in any form or by any means, electronic, mechanical, photocopying, recording or otherwise, without the prior permission of the publisher.
Whilst every effort has been made to ensure that the information given in this book is correct at the time of going to press, no responsibility can be accepted by the publisher for any errors or inaccuracies that may appear.

Printed in Great Britain by Biddles Ltd.
King's Lynn, Norfolk

FOR JANET

Acknowledgements

In 1960 Chatto & Windus published *Boxwood*, a collection of twenty-one engravings by Reynolds Stone illustrated in verse by Sylvia Townsend Warner. Both lived in Dorset, Stone at Litton Cheney and Warner just over the hill in Maiden Newton. This joint venture grew out of their friendship and their love of Dorset and so it seemed fitting, with the agreement of Humphrey Stone and Susanna Pinney, that this collection of Dorset stories should reflect that collaborative spirit. The collections in which most of the stories originally appeared have been out of print for some time but several stories are reproduced for the first time since their appearance in *The New Yorker*.

'A Bottle of Gum' (*A Chatto & Windus Miscellany* 1928), 'Early One Morning' & 'Over The Hill' (*The Salutation* 1932), 'A Village Death' (*More Joy in Heaven* 1935), 'An Unimportant Case', 'The Mothers' & 'Rainbow Villa' (*A Garland of Straw* 1943), 'Poor Mary', 'The Cold', 'English Climate', 'Major Brice and Mrs. Conway', 'Boors Carousing' & 'Bow to the Rising Sun' (*The Museum of Cheats* 1947), 'Evan' (*Winter in the Air* 1956), 'A Dressmaker' (*A Spirit Rises* 1962), 'Folk Cookery', 'Dieu et Mon Droit' & 'A Queen Remembered' (*Scenes of Childhood* 1981), 'A Breaking Wave' & 'The Proper Circumstances' (*One Thing Leading to Another* 1984), 'Flora' (*The Music at Long Verney* 2001); reprinted by permission of The Random House Group Ltd. 'Love Green' (*The Nineteenth Century* 1932), 'I am Come into my Garden' (*Time & Tide* 1932), 'The Jenny Cat' & 'Two Minutes Silence' (*The New Yorker* 1936), 'If These Delights' (*The New Yorker* 1938), 'The Family Revisited' & 'England, Home and Beauty' (*The New Yorker* 1942), 'It's What We're Here For' & 'Tabbish' (*The New Yorker* 1943), 'Such a Wonderful Opportunity' (*The New Yorker* 1948); reprinted by permission of Susanna Pinney, the estate of Sylvia Townsend Warner.

Peter Tolhurst
Black Dog Books 2006.

CONTENTS

FOREWORD	vii
Love Green	3
A Bottle of Gum	14
Early One Morning	18
Over The Hill	26
I am Come into my Garden	33
A Village Death	40
Folk Cookery	44
The Jenny Cat	49
Two Minutes Silence	56
Dieu et Mon Droit	59
If These Delights	67
The Family Revisited	77
England, Home and Beauty	82
It's What We're Here For	89
Tabbish	99
An Unimportant Case	105
The Mothers	117
Rainbow Villa	126
Bow to the Rising Sun	136
The Proper Circumstances	143
Poor Mary	154
The Cold	165
English Climate	175
Major Brice and Mrs. Conway	184
Boors Carousing	191
Such a Wonderful Opportunity	201
A Breaking Wave	206
Evan	218
A Dressmaker	226
A Queen Remembered	244
Flora	250

FOREWORD

Sylvia Townsend Warner spent the best years of her life in Dorset. Her discovery of the county – little-explored in those days – and of the remote village of Chaldon Herring, came in 1922 when she was taken to meet the writer Theodore Powys. Powys lived with his family on the edge of Chaldon in a boxy, brick house. A self-proclaimed hermit, on his solitary walks he observed the daily lives of ploughman, shepherd, road-mender, in field and flinty lane. Their lives were simple, but as characters in Powys's fiction they became simpler still: allegorical figures, stiff as winter trees against the poverty-stricken grandeur of the chalk downs. On her visit, Sylvia was immediately taken both by the village and its interpreter. She continued to go to Chaldon, staying with Theodore and his wife Violet (of whom she was also fond) or renting a room in one of the cottages. Her affection for the couple is evident in the extract, here entitled 'A Bottle of Gum', from her ostensibly factual 'Study of Theodore Powys' which ran to over eighty entertaining pages and was only abandoned when she discovered how much Theodore disliked the enterprise.

Warner's first book, a volume of verse called *The Espalier* (1925) includes a number of poems set in Chaldon, and haunted by some of Theodore's characters.

Her second book, the novel *Lolly Willowes* (1926), is a gentle tale of witchcraft in the Chilterns; witchcraft was a theme to which she returned in a Chaldon short story (originally planned as a novel) called 'Early One Morning'. Old Rebecca, a retired lady's maid, lives in a cottage close to the church and keeps a feathered flock of contented hens. She is envied by the ineffectual new priest, Arthur Clay, who is unable to manage his own parish flock. One morning he hears the voices of some of them, coming from the henhouse. They have been transformed into fowls, while Rebecca has become a young greyhound bitch. She persuades the puzzled cleric to toll the bell – for the old Rebecca, who is dead.

'Quite Early One Morning' was collected in *The Salutation* (1932), along with another Chaldon tale. 'Over the Hill' tells of grandfather Jacob, moved by his family 'from the east side of a hill to the west', to a house which reminds him of a station waiting-room. The only way out for unwitting Jacob will be to the infirmary. This bleak account of a declining life finds echoes in Sylvia Townsend Warner's essay on Chaldon, 'Love Green', which also appeared in 1932 and is reprinted here for the first time. Such pieces provide a tart corrective to the usual urban vision of the rural idyll.

In 1936 Sylvia Townsend Warner began contributing to the *New Yorker*. During the next forty years more than one hundred and fifty of her short stories were published in the magazine, providing her with a valuable and regular income. Among them were three early stories which show a lighter, more humorous side of Chaldon life. The whimsical grimness – the shade of Theodore – has vanished. The main character in 'The Jenny Cat' is Lucy, a beautifully amoral housemaid who can run like the wind

FOREWORD

and lie like a trooper. 'Two Minutes' Silence' is the story of a humble, bumbling Remembrance Day ceremony in Chaldon. And, in 'If These Delights', an incoming couple are foiled in their programme for the village by the undertaker's practical jokes.

Chaldon was a 'holy ground' to Sylvia from the start. Above all, it was there that she met the poet Valentine Ackland, who became her life's love. They lived together in Chaldon: first in 'the late Miss Green's cottage' opposite the East Chaldon inn, and later at 24 West Chaldon, a house on the winding road between the two settlements. Both buildings are gone now, the one destroyed by a bomb in 1944, and the other, a near-ruin, demolished in the 1960s.

Indeed, the decaying condition of No 24, with its rats and mildew, was one reason why the two women moved to Maiden Newton in 1937. Another was the deaths of two of the people they loved best in Chaldon: 'Grannie' Moxon (heroine of Warner's epic poem 'Opus 7') and Mr Dove, the East Chaldon shepherd, whose cruel end is mourned in the elegaic story 'A Village Death'.

Although only fifteen miles north-west of Chaldon, Maiden Newton is a very different sort of village: large, sprawling and untidy. Today it has the vitality of a place free from the arid gentility which afflicts so many Dorset villages (and from which Chaldon, alas, has not entirely escaped). Chaldon was an estate village, its land, farms and cottages owned by the Weld family of Lulworth Castle (Warner remarked that she had bought Miss Green's because it was 'the only freehold cottage in the village'). Though much of the land in Maiden Newton was held by the neighbouring Frampton estate, the estate did not own many of the houses. Also, the villagers were not nearly so tied to farming for a living as were the cottagers of

Chaldon. Maiden Newton was a railway junction; there was a milk factory, a corn mill – and four pubs. Estate villages like Chaldon, common in Dorset, bred a fatalism of the kind portrayed by Hardy. The people in Maiden Newton were more independent.

In a way – although she lived there for most of the next forty years – Warner never really took to Maiden Newton. From the start she loved the house, which she found 'most accommodating'. The river, too, was charmingly full of trout and moorhen, plus a water-rat 'like a half-submerged bulrush'. But she continued to be disparaging about most of the village's inhabitants. Her attitude may have been partly due to geography: the house was just over the boundary from Maiden Newton, and 'isolated from it by a field' (which she eventually bought). The house was called Riverdale; Sylvia and Valentine always referred to it as 'Frome Vauchurch', the name of the separate parish – and place – in which it stood.

It took a war to engage them with the natives. In 1940, Sylvia Townsend Warner began working for two days a week in the Dorchester office of the Women's Voluntary Service, a job which was to provide her with much raw material. Dorchester – or 'Dumbridge' – is the setting for several wartime stories. There was a serious shortage of paper at the time, and Dorchester had its own Book Mile of volumes donated for salvage, a novelty which features in 'English Climate'. (Prayerbooks and Bibles were allegedly pulped in a separate vat.) The WVS also dealt with evacuees from big cities, who were bored and lonely in the country and reacted badly to their new surroundings. In 'What We're Here For' an especially difficult evacuee succeeds in eluding the persistent kindness of the WVS ladies. The owner of 'Rainbow Villa' (the name of an actual house in Maiden

FOREWORD

Newton, variously a Dame School, a bed-and-breakfast and a nursing home) returns from a long absence to find the house wrecked. Dismayingly, it has become 'the mammocked billet of thirty-five freezing soldiers, that Aunt Sally of evacuee children, that doss-house of tramps . . .'

In the summer of 1942, measures had been taken to protect the Dorset coast against invasion. Tank traps were built in the village – which is fifteen miles inland. More unofficially, Colonel Barnes of Maiden Newton House (grandson of the poet William Barnes) started a Ladies' Shooting Club. The ladies were taught how to load, aim and shoot, and how to throw hand grenades. In 'England, Home and Beauty' they are also trained in the use of the machine gun which sits 'like a pet alligator' on the hearthrug. At the end of this drawing-room comedy, the ladies reluctantly surrender their weapons; in fact – according to local residents – they continued to keep them ready to hand. Truth here is cheerfully outdoing fiction.

Warner went on writing about the war effort. 'An Unimportant Case' tells of long-term unemployment and its consequences. 'Bow to the Rising Sun' is, as Warner said, a study 'of the young clerk in the Dorchester Fuel Office who was replaced by Valentine and [of] local gentry of 1943-4'. 'The Cold' is another study: of the Maiden Newton rector's wife, who was 'ill-acclimatised to wartime circumstances'. The shifts and displacements, the hardships, of rural wartime existence are subtly observed in the many and varied stories she succeeds in drawing from this necessarily narrow experience.

Tales about Maiden Newton dwindled after the War, and those which did appear – such as 'A Wonderful Opportunity', 'Poor Mary' and 'A Dressmaker' – hark back to those times. A further, fine story, 'Boors Carousing', takes place in the watery Frome landscape of willow and alder. 'Our river,' Sylvia Townsend Warner noted, adding that its main character, Mr Kinloch, was 'studied from myself'. Mr Kinloch is distracted from his novel-writing by a call from a maiden lady with a weakness for drink, and dutifully rescues her rabbits from the floods. Afterwards, he wonders whether he ought to become more neighbourly towards her. He imagines the situation, the pair of them enjoying a quiet evening tipple . . .

What a story she would make!
'You to the life!' he said aloud. 'Do nothing for her, but put her in a story.' The admission released him. He quickened his pace, he bounded up the steps to his door, he let himself in, he threw off his wet coat, he glanced at his wrist-watch. It was four o'clock. It was still raining. With a long sigh of relief he walked sedately into his library, sat down, and pulled a writing-pad towards him.

Mr Kinloch is forced to abandon his novel and write short stories instead. He has become 'a prey to human nature – which is poison and dram-drinking to the serious artist'.

Here he differed from his creator. Human nature was food and drink to Sylvia Townsend Warner. Her characters come from many different worlds – feline and fairy as well as human – and are observed in stories which are elegant, individual and witty. Dorset provided the material for a satisfying number of these tales, collected here for the first time. They are Dorset 'to the life'.

Judith Stinton
Maiden Newton

CHALDON STORIES

LOVE GREEN

Described in the county directory as a hamlet, Love Green lies among the seaward-swelling chalk downs, approached by a lane that leaves it only to scramble round a green hill and rejoin the main road. It is an agricultural village, and this may be seen by the architectural predominance of its barns, that rise stone-built and massive among the cottages. Even the ricks and haystacks overtop the roofs of thin slate or threadbare thatch. Being an agricultural village, it is a poor one. Year by year husbandry decays, and the large squares and oblongs of arable that look like carpets tightly stretched upon the contours of the downs show by their colour the invasion of thistles and sorrel and the resurgence of flint. Year by year fewer men are employed upon the land, and the physical standard both of labourers and draught horses grows lower. Upon one farm in Love Green a mule is used; another, for cheapness sake, is worked by old men and boys.

At one end of the village is the church, at the other the inn. Here, two years ago, a badger-baiting was held. From one of the few badger earths in this part of England – a ruinous city of earthy tunnels – a female badger was dug out and carried in a sack to the inn. News of the proposed frolic went round, and every man who owned a dog or loved sport went up to drink that evening. A ring was made and the badger loosed into it. As it turned this way and that from the dogs a kick and a shout stopped its escape, till, fighting sullenly, it met its end.

The inn provides other traditional games, though not such stirring ones. Shove-halfpenny and rings are played there, and, if someone can be found to put up the money, Will Francis will perform his celebrated feat of drinking eleven pints at a sitting. This achievement is interesting as a rarity; but Will Francis is not an enlivened drinker, even upon eleven pints. Intellect tells, even in a country public; and Jimmy Matthews, the 'enlightened man' of Love Green, is by far the best company among those who visit the inn. Jimmy is a reader, one who enjoys, as he said himself, 'books of any nature, poetical, historilolical, or Scriptural,' and being lent Lecky's *History of European Morals*, found it much to his taste. He also spent a whole day sitting on the green reading Marcus Aurelius, but did not think so much of him. Theology is Jimmy's forte. When on March 23 he wished me, with every cordiality, a Happy New Year, he added that if I had any religious doubts I had only to apply to him; and if my religion were substantial enough to support doubts, I daresay I would do so. On this occasion he was about half seas over; but I have been assured that when Jimmy is thoroughly glorious he begins to recite the Bible by heart, and cannot be stayed, however urgently his fellow-drinkers protest at this interruption upon the ordinary tavern conversation of scandal, bawdry, the weather, and social injustice.

Few women visit the inn. Those who do so are of the old school. The remainder, who either have pretensions to

LOVE GREEN

gentility or ape such pretensions, send there for beer or whisky and drink it at home. It is common too, to make home-made wines – carrot, mangold, elderberry, parsnip – and, more rarely, mead for domestic drinking. These home-drinkers certainly do no drink less than the inn-goers, and from the point of view of social pleasantness the custom is to be deplored, since it increases the suspicion and narrow-mindedness which are cankers of village life.

During the winter Love Green joins with the next village in fortnightly whist drives. But these, since prizes are awarded, cannot be classed as anything so light and trivial as mere social relaxation. They are attended in a spirit of religious cupidity, and on the morrow the winner of a set of pink-handled tea-knives, a china biscuit-barrel, or a cigarette-case walks out with the strained simper of one who has roused the envy and fury of mankind. So solemn, indeed, are these orgies that the unfortunates whose station exposes them to the levy of fortnightly prizes dare not give below the level of expectation; and the level is a rising one, since it is known who gave what, and to give the handsomest prize is equal in glory, if not in satisfaction, to being its winner. A member of the prize-giving class in Love Green pays, I suppose, anything from £3 to £4 yearly upon this score - a ridiculous and unprofitable mulct, since the convention of good manners demands that the prizes should always be of a completely useless nature.

There is, of course, the expedient of giving the booby prize. Once, some years ago, this was awarded to a girl in the neighbouring village, who took the matter so much to heart and was so badly teased about it that she drowned herself.

Such are the diversions of Love Green. The games of its

children are even more closely in touch with real life. The smallest among them play, as all very young children do, by pretending to be their elders; but once infancy is outgrown they turn to the traditional rural sports of harrying strangers, teasing the half-wit, and tormenting animals. The nature study learned in the school has put a slightly different complexion upon this last sport. But whether the victim be called a stickleback or a 'minnie' it meets the same underheel end. Meanwhile, in the economy of Nature, the elder boys harry, tease, and torment the children and any half-grown girl they can lay their hands on.

Yet, among the older folk of Love Green, there is a legend that its children were once well-behaved. That was thirty odd years ago, when Mr. Pagan was parson here. In Mr. Pagan's days every family received at Christmas beer, a joint of beef, and a plum pudding. Each new-born child was inspected and a half-sovereign wedged into its small grasp; any older child who, playing, chanced to butt itself against Mr. Pagan's legs or muddy his broadcloth trousers with a hoop was likely to get half a crown, and those who had come to a competent age and attended the confirmation classes were refreshed with chocolates. In Mr. Pagan's day no one who went to the parsonage for succour was ever turned away, and the church was always full, for a score at least sang in the choir, and those who were not qualified to do this attended in order to hear the singing and watch the children parading the church behind the gold cross with a crimson jewel in it. Nor did Mr. Pagan neglect that most important part of a parson's duty – to give his parish something to wonder at on weekdays; for it was his custom to drive through the village in a swift gig, preceded by eight black dogs leashed together in couples.

LOVE GREEN

A materialistic Eden, no doubt, in the light of present-day use, when few people of Mr. Pagan's mind or means go into the church, and when flocks are chiefly edified by the gifts of the spirit. Nor, from those who remember him, have I heard a word breathed that might suggest that Mr. Pagan had quickened their spiritual life. He is remembered as a generous man and a stout drinker, just such another shepherd in his own line as is Mr. Kid of Love Green – Mr. Kid whose sheep always fetch good prices, who never nicks a ewe at sheep-shearing, whose dogs cringe at his enormous bellow, and who, on summer evenings, may be seen in his garden trimming the heads of the Love Green labourers with a pair of sheep-shears. Yet Mr. Pagan's influence is still discernible in those who grew up under his regiment. They preserve a certain good humour and natural self-respect which not even the acrimony, vanity, and squalor of village life has quite obliterated. They themselves are well aware that things have changed for the worse. Love Green was different in old Pagan's time, they say, in the days when it had a parson of its own. Actually, Mr. Pagan had a successor before the parish was amalgamated with its neighbour, and so lost a resident cleric. But he, being a poorer man, giving away less and keeping no retinue of dogs, counts for nothing in the village memory; not even the fact that he went mad at his wife's funeral has endeared him to posterity.

Now, once a Sunday, the three church bells jangle their ditty for a formal minute or two, and the churchgoers walk up the road. It is a slender congregation. The old guard, Mr. Pagan's remnant, attend pretty regularly, still holding to the belief that to put on their best clothes and join in the hymns is in some way a right and proper proceeding. The remainder attend only when they feel some special call to do so. Their reasons are various: a new pair of boots, a well-combed child to exhibit, a recent death in the family, or a smoky chimney. It is only for harvest festival that the whole village turns out to admire the decorations, the pulpit with straws in its hair, the font wearing moss gaiters, the phenomenal cabbage before the altar, the vegetable roasts of apples, marrows, and potatoes balanced along the hot water pipes, and to listen to the anthem – a yearly hazard, like the Derby. Deeply and contentedly excited they throng creaking in, and crowd the pews and sing, whatever the season, 'Now thank we all our God' with enthusiasm. The offerings go to the local hospital; and on the morrow everyone agrees that they are wasted there, thrown away or eaten by the nurses, with chapter and verse of how, when our Sheila was in, she never so much as set eyes on an egg or a good plateful of greens. But that is no bar, when harvest festival comes round again next year, to giving the crispest savoy or the finest beetroot, for the offerings are made to nothing so immaterial as a God or so concrete as an institution. Love Green is incapable of worship; but somewhere in their world, perhaps under the green hill, lurks a deity or demiurge, and it is this being, curiously compounded of manure and the weather, that they propitiate.

If the religion of Love Green is a trifle behind the times, its politics are up to date. Those who bestir themselves to think at all are Communists, and the rest, who know at any rate that something must be wrong with a world where wages are so low and summers so rainy (though the wireless is the likeliest cause of that), follow their lead. Every village has its Robespierre, and the Robespierre of

LOVE GREEN

Love Green is Mr Taddy, who understands everything. Mr. Taddy is a small man, reddish and diligent, like an ant. So deep is his scorn for a capitalist society that it is his boast that he will beat his children within an inch of their lives if ever he hears them use a servile 'sir' or 'ma'am'. Meanwhile, by exemplary industry, enterprise and thrift, he has become the richest man in the village, and will shortly buy a car.

Mrs. Taddy is a Communist also, noticeably whenever her rival, young Mrs. Trey, appears in a new dress or buys new household gear. For the discontent of Love Green, that might seem so well justified by what people lack, is in truth aroused by what other people have. In the years since the war a new standard of living has been imposed upon the old, but imposed as paraffin upon water; it is the upper layer only that is kindled by discontent and flares up in anger and threatenings. In Love Green there are only outdoor privies; water has to be caught from the roof gutters or drawn from wells liable to contamination; the cottages are small and inconvenient, some barely weatherproof, and infested with vermin. These conditions are accepted without a murmur. No one minds the prospect of living for ever without a vestige of plumbing, or packing three into a bed, but not to be able to afford a wireless fills them with fury and resentment. When young Lucy Mendicott came back from the sanatorium to die of tuberculosis, the fact that the one place where she could sleep apart from her family was the larder-cum-pantry was taken for granted, calling for no comment unless it were the remark that now she could get at the sugar whenever she pleased; but even down-draggled Mrs. Mendicott, the poorest woman in the village, so poor that her children are fed upon biscuits and bottled lemonade, has spirit left enough to rail at a social scheme which denies her a string of imitation pearls and a fur coat.

This deep feeling for superfluities is not a new thing in village life or in human nature. But it is now of such rampant dimensions that it must be counted as a new social factor. At the level of life in Love Green materialism is inevitable, for in the pinch of not-having the lust for possession is biologically quickened as a compensation. Winter sets squirrels hoarding, and the cottage living-room, unwieldy with belongings, is as sure a sign of poverty as the room poverty has swept bare. But now the Love Green appetite for possessions is fed, like the young Mendicotts, upon biscuits and bottled lemonade, and is fast losing the taste for anything more solid. If proof be needed as to how this passion for rubbish is sweeping the countryside, the reader has only to visit a London Woolworth's and one in a country town and compare the wares sold in one and the other. The very cheapness and accessibility of these toys inflame the breasts that pant after them. When the Mrs. Taddy of a previous generation outpaced her Mrs. Trey it was by something solid – a marble-topped wash-stand or a set of grand fire-irons; and, however sternly Mrs. Trey resolved to get even with Mrs. Taddy, a certain time must elapse before enough money could be saved up for the riposts. But in this warfare of trumpery there is no time for desire to settle down into intention, or envy grow tired of watching the rival.

Meanwhile Mrs. Taddy and Mrs. Trey continue to fetch water from the same dubious well. The open quarrels and clapper-clawing that might have eased their ancestresses are not possible to them. Love Green has long known that it is low to quarrel – such doings may be left to the gipsies. So Mrs. Taddy and Mrs. Trey commend, with distant civility, each other's wall-flowers, or inquire, with pale, set faces, after each other's cats. Not even the intimacy of open hate is allowed them by their code of respectability. Their husbands stand apart from these dissensions – such things are women's work. But in such a community as Love Green any social relationship is women's work. The labourer, a-field for eight hours, walking perhaps two or three miles to his work, only knows his village as the place where he sleeps, breakfasts, sups, keeps his wife and children, and visits the inn. At the inn he meets other such tired animals as himself, and treats with them with an animal gregariousness, the comradeship of a team of cart-horses.

The fate of Love Green as a village – that is to say, as a compacted unit in English country life – is in the hands of its women. If they fritter away that feeling of community which has bonded village life since first men built their mud huts neighbourly together for the mutual society, help and comfort that they looked for and were even, in the necessarily slighter degree, prepared to give, there is nothing to save it from disintegration, from falling away, like an old lavender bush, from its dead centre. The church is powerless; the inn, under the attacks of respectability and refinement, is fast losing what power it had. Even badger's blood gave but a temporary fillip; and now the badger's earth is forsaken. Of the three sizable houses in the village, whence one might expect some show of leadership, two belong to farmers who cannot manage even their own affairs; the third is let to a lady who is so busy organising county uplift that she scarcely knows the names of her neighbours. And even if one rose from the dead, from the extinct class of the squirearchy that produced Mr. Pagan, it is doubtful if it would be of any avail. The atavistic feudalism of Love Green is worn very thin now, cadging old Mrs. Tibbs with her curtseys, and a general aptitude to toady, its last manifestations. Yet the feeling of a common lot is still in existence among the Love Green women, however it may be smothered under a desire to seem superior to one's neighbour – so superior that one would prefer to having nothing to do with her. Women, by nature so much more susceptible to change than men, are by circumstance much more deeply tethered to permanence; and, confronted with a really rousing scandal or a saliently unfortunate childbed, Mrs. Taddy and Mrs. Trey will cast off their touch-me-not civility, gossip heart to heart at the well, or hurry up the road together to offer their services.

Such puffs of accident will rouse up and flame from the core of the old fire. But it seems doubtful how much longer it will last under the steady drench of new influences. Indeed, Love Green is now so little a true community, so increasingly a fortuitous collection of dwelling-houses, that perhaps it is idle and epimythean to look for saving virtue in anything out of the past, With the decay of farming the labouring class is becoming migratory – people come to the village, stay for a year or two, and then are dismissed or move off in search of something better; motor transport brings town commodities and town novelties to the cottage door, education and the newspaper direct attention away from the village to the advantages of genteel professions or what is being worn on the Lido; and if any commendation of rusticity reaches Love Green it is of the folk-dancing, rustic pottery, sun-bonnet-rural kind –

LOVE GREEN

so many hand-made nails in the coffin of rural life. An adjunct to its tall barns and rickyards, Love Green waits upon tillage, and from the very decline of the old order draws a certain outward permanence – the little-changing aspect of something too weak to register change; but if ever there should come a revival of agriculture the facade which yet screens the change of heart must crumble, and Love Green be a village no longer, but instead, what even now it harkens to be, a small west of England Middletown.

A BOTTLE OF GUM

In December 1923 Theo's elder son left home for Africa, where he was going to work on a stock farm belonging to his uncle. All through the autumn Violet had been busied in getting together his outfit and preparing for the departure. For many years her duties had not taken her further than to Weymouth or to Dorchester, but now her mind had to make a longer journey and acknowledge a continent which imposed upon her shopping list such items as a rifle, a sun-helmet, and a ticket costing £80. However, though the purchases were new, there was nothing new in the responsibility for making them, for Violet has always conducted the family affairs, and has always conducted them with the same unflurrying, unpretentious ability. Theo is disabled for any practical dealings by two grave faults: an unappeasable imagination and an insatiable carefulness. If he had taken a hand in preparing Dicky's outfit his proceedings would have been somewhat after this fashion. Whilst adventuring himself to Dorchester in the carrier's van (equipped, I need hardly say, with a shopping list that summed up the labours of days and the second thoughts of nights, and mentally practised in every wary artifice by which man might hope to outwit what an inscription in the church of Steeple Ashton calls 'the uncountroulable Providence of God') his fancy would conjure up some concatenation of chances which would make it absolutely essential for Dicky in Africa to have at hand a bottle of gum. Gum accordingly must be sought for: not unadvisedly, lightly, or wantonly; no! but reverently, discreetly, advisedly, soberly, and in the fear of God; duly considering the causes for which gum was ordained. A search conducted in this spirit cannot be the work of a moment. One must be careful to buy the right kind of gum, in the right kind of bottle, and to ascertain that it is rightly secured by a suitable God-fearing cork. Moreover, one must be careful to buy it from the right kind of shop-keeper: not one of those loose-living fellows at W. H. Smith's, who dally in all manner of merchandise and would be as likely as not to sell one green ink or an evening paper by inadvertence, nor yet a lean woman whose back parlour smells of rats: and finally, one must be careful to pay the right price for it. Weighed down with so many cares one cannot walk fast. Indeed, under no circumstances does Theo approve of haste, and of all the axioms of good living laid down by the philosopher Chilon, that which pleases him best is: *Never let yourself be seen in a hurry*. The gum being purchased Theo, pulling out the watch which is tethered to him by a finely-wrought old chain, would discover that it was time to seek Mr. Balliboy's van in the market-place; for one must be careful not to be left behind, and though there is yet half an hour to spare, anything might happen: the van might run away.

For a while Theo's mind might remain at rest. But there is an aroma of disquiet in the neighbourhood of pessimistic thought, and as the van passed Max Gate the shadow of

Hardy's conifers would sow a doubt. Suppose the bottle were to break? The elm-trees at Owermoigne would only nurture the doubt with their commiserating sighs, their heads shaken in grave disparagement. Bottles do break; and glancing out of the window Theo might even see a broken bottle lying at the roadside. *He that sees every Churchyard swell with the waves and billows of graves, can think it no extraordinary thing to dye*; and no experienced Christian can doubt but that in that First Curse there was made a provision for bottles. The van would reach its last stopping-place, and Theo would quit the other passengers with the sad civility of Charles the First taking leave of his household. As he walked up the lane he would wade through a dark flood of gum.

'Violet, my dear, I have bought a bottle of gum for Dicky. It has a little brush tied on to it. But perhaps I have not acted very wisely. The bottle might break. I do not like to think of poor Dicky finding everything sticky, and he might cut himself on the broken glass. I'm afraid that I have been foolish. I acted rather impetuously.'

'Why, Theo, the bottle won't break if it's packed properly.'

'Perhaps not, my dear. Still I can't help thinking that I should have done better to buy glue. And a little brazier to melt it over. Though you always pack very well.'

During the evening Theo would revert once or twice to the gum, and weigh the advisability of exchanging it for glue, and the chances of doing so. Yet later in the evening Violet would hear a soft voice in the dark.

'Violet. Are you asleep? I don't want to disturb you if you are, but I have been thinking things over. There might not be room in Dicky's luggage for that brazier. It doesn't

A BOTTLE OF GUM

do to have too many parcels on board ship. So don't you think that the best plan would be to send the brazier to Africa by registered post?'

I do not know what Violet would say then. But I shall never forget the triumphant moment when she broke into one of Theo's bouts of dilly-dallying with the exclamation: 'Oh, get along with you, you old tea-pot!'

EARLY ONE MORNING

Just beyond the church, with five great tufts of wormwood in the garden, was Rebecca's cottage. In the early hours of the day the shadow of the church tower rested upon it, and in that shadow the buzzing of the house-flies seemed to sound particularly loud and solemn, like voices in church. The tower was five hundred years old, the cottage was aged sixty-seven, as any one passing it who knew how to read and subtract could tell for himself, for the date 1861 was incised on a plaster tablet above the porch.

Rebecca, a mere chit as compared with the tower, was older than her cottage. In the village she was noted for having once sold a teapot to an American lady. She lived on an annuity, having been for nearly forty years a lady's maid to a celebrated beauty. Now she kept hens.

Though the church was so fine, the living was a very poor one, The parsonage was let to a retired bank manager, and the Reverend Arthur Clay lodged with Mrs. Gamble, a widow, who cleaned the church, and whose son gardened for the parsonage. Though Mrs. Gamble cleaned the church, she stopped at that, making no attempts to clean its incumbent. Throughout the year the priest was a picture of his name – muddy in winter, in summer, dusty. But then he was not a man for any woman to make a pet of; he was young, lean, and anxious, and bit his nails from loneliness; and when the revised prayer-book was thrown out by the House of Commons he went unshaven for three days and wept with rage and mortification; no bishop with a taste for meddling with better men's collects could have wept more bitterly than he.

From his upper window Mr. Clay would look across the churchyard to Rebecca's cottage, and wish that he lodged there. Twice a day she stood among her tufts of wormwood throwing grain to her hens. She had only to come to the door with the enamel dipper in her hand for them to hurry to her, scrambling, jostling, leaping with spread wings. Their cackle could be heard across the wide churchyard. And presently would come a silence, while they ate the scattered grain. If only his flock would come as willingly to his feeding-times, receive as devoutly to their souls' health the good grain he cast before them!

Early one morning, one May morning, Arthur Clay threw down the pen on his sermon, stretched himself, and looked out of the window. It was the hour before sunrise, sad and pure. The thought came to him that instead of going to bed he would go for a walk. He would go into the fields and smell the musky hawthorn blossom, and watch the rabbits scampering along the hedge. It would be an adventure. A sturdy yew-tree grew beside Mrs. Gamble's house, which abutted on to the churchyard, and rather to his surprise he found himself climbing out of the window and slithering along a bough until his feet touched the ground. This was certainly an unusual way of leaving the house – in fact, he had never employed it before; but at this hour of the morning one way seemed as good as another, and indeed to shin down a tree heightened his sense of adventure, so that for a moment he felt as blithe as a boy who has got up early to rob an orchard or a bird's-nest. But he was standing among graves and among tombstones. *Watch and Pray*, said William Blackbone. *Be Ye also Ready*, said Benjamin Dive, and as if with mumbling and toothless jaws Harriott Marley from her battered and tumbling stone mouthed out to him that she was born in 1802, and that the rest of her story had long ago sunk into the earth. The truant priest was quickly sobered. He walked uneasily among the graves, pretending to take an interest in the inscriptions; but in his heart he felt rebuffed, suspecting that his dead parishioners were no better disposed towards him than those living. 'I don't like them,' he whispered, 'and they hate me.'

Now he had forgotten his wish to walk in the fields. He turned his back upon the graves, and leaned over the wall which separated the churchyard from Rebecca's garden. It was an old woman's garden, overgrown, dishevelled, full of mysterious rubbish. He saw a scabby brown bath-can, a sheaf of bed-slats, a rag rug, a broken chair, a bird-cage. Near the ash-heap stood a rusty kitchener, its oven door wrenched off; and an elder-bush had grown up beside it, half-smothering it with green boughs. Immediately beneath him was the hen-house, with its door propped to with a frying-pan. He began once more to think of Rebecca's hens, those good quiet birds that spent such harmless days pecking in the long grass, that passed such peaceful nights restrained by a frying-pan, that came so willingly to feed upon the good grain. Ah, it was better to keep a cure of hens than a cure of souls!

Dreamily he leaned against the cold wall, dreamily he listened. At last he heard a voice, speaking close at hand, speaking within the hen-house.

'Philip is ageing, the white hairs grow out of his ears. I think I should like to be a widow - but then, do I want to lose him? One gets so accustomed to a husband.'

Arthur Clay recognised the voice of Mrs. Gillespie, whose husband rented the parsonage; and presently he heard Mr. Gillespie speak in his turn.

'What's that you say, my dear? Now if only you would get a cataract, like Milton, I could watch Lily making the bed as often as I pleased.'

'Doh, Mi, Sol, Doh! Last Sunday I touched high A. Grand Opera, I want to sing in Grand Opera. I want to be famous and break a rich man's heart, and drive through this dead-alive place in a Rolls-Royce, envied of all. And if I should run over one or two of those brats, I shouldn't be sorry'.

This was Sheila, who taught the Infants in the school, and walked out with Henry Price.

'Those pills haven't done it, and I've swallowed half-a-crown's worth,' lamented Mrs. Perrit. 'Whatever I'm to do, with another coming so soon, I'm sure I don't know. Unless it should die. I'd best insure it, on the chance. Damn Clarence!'

'The Rev-er-end Ar-thur Clay!' Mr. Sycomore, the

churchwarden, scanned the name sneeringly. 'He thinks himself a gentleman, does he? I've got three leaping bugs in a box that I'll loose in the pulpit, come Sunday. They'll learn him!'

'If I could get hold of that squealing Sheila, I'd give her something to squeal for.'

That was Mr. Spider, the other churchwarden.

'Death! Death! One day I must die.'

That was the voice of bland Mr. Comlock, who kept the shop.

'O Sheila, Sheila! Why are you so cruel to me, when I want to be cruel to you?' groaned Henry Price.

'God damn and blast Rebecca Hardy,' said the voice of Mrs. Gamble. 'Last winter her pullets laid six to mine's one. I wish a cancer would get her!'

The sun had risen, and Arthur Clay stood in the shadow of the church tower. Already the holy flies were buzzing over the garbage heap. He stopped his ears to shut out the voices that came from the hen-house. Even the power to condemn had left him; he felt one impulse only – to escape, to forget.

'I will go to bed. I will try to sleep,' he said; and turning, he saw where his lamp burned still. No, not there! – he would lie down under the yew-tree.

It was at that moment that he saw the greyhound. A bitch, milk-white, and young, she came leaping towards him over the graves. She fawned at his feet, jumped up on him, sidled her slim head against his waistcoat, and fled curvetting away again. He was nothing to her; it was only the young life in her which made her so affectionate; caressing him, she caressed herself. Yet he watched her, for she was beautiful. White and fleet, she bounded over the graves like blown spray. It was her own delight that she frolicked with, chasing it from grave to grave.

Now, from the furthest corner of the churchyard, she came prancing down on him, as though her joy were hidden in his trouser pocket and she had this instant scented it out. She rolled at his feet, she sprang in the air and licked his nose, she nuzzled him, she struck him with her fore paw and whined beseechingly.

'What do you want, doggie? What do you ask of me?'

At his words she danced round him, frisking with delight, telling him clearly how clever he was to understand her, how clever she was to make herself understood. She took hold of his coat and began to pull at him. He went with her. Loosing her hold she ran on a little way, then stopped, looking back at him, wagging her tail; and seeing that he still followed, she ran on again.

Thus she led him past yews and headstones to a grassy bank under a lime-tree; and here she began to dig. She dug busily, the earth flew out from under her fine scratching paws, her white muzzle became powdered with dust. Suddenly she sat back on her haunches, looking at him, and at the hole, and at him again, and whined. He stared into her dark diamond eyes. 'Rebecca!' he said.

She jumped up, pleased, and ran elegantly to him and thrust her cold wet nose into his hand. But she was not finished with him yet, for now she began to tug at his coat once more, and this time it was towards the church that she led him. He pulled out his keys, and unlocked the priest's door, and following at his heels she stepped in after him. Inside the church she seemed perfectly at home, and trotted round it, snuffing and ascertaining. At last she came to the space under the tower where the furry bell ropes hung. Of these she chose out one, and tried to take hold of it; but it was too bulky for her jaws, and so she stood waiting, standing on three legs with a rather anxious expression, her eyes fixed on him, the tip of her tail slightly stirring. He took the rope from her and began to pull.

At the first toll of the bell, as the grave sound sleeping above them unfurled its vast wings and floated abroad, she sprang up on to the church chest, and couched there. There she lay, watching him, motionless, with her crossed fore paws dangling over the edge of the chest, like an effigy. The vast wings overhead began to flap more slowly; they drooped, and were folded in silence. He tolled the bell again. Another bird flew out. The air of the May morning became its wings, it hovered over the countryside like a hawk, He tolled the bell a third time, Rebecca's cock woke up, and answered that other bird.

He had been tolling for nearly quarter of an hour when the noise of a door thrown violently open made him look round. Mrs. Gamble had entered the church. She carried a dustpan and brush, and wore a bonnet; but her face looked a little different. It was a pig's face, with small angry eyes, and a hairy snout. She advanced upon him, and he could see her nostrils working. As she passed a white marble tablet she turned a little, and cleaned it with a sweep of her large tongue.

'Now what's all this, Mr. Clay? Whatever's taken you, to rouse us out of our beds with that nasty bell?'

'Rebecca is dead,' he answered, and tolled the bell again. 'Our sister is delivered from the burden of the flesh, from the miseries of this sinful world.'

Though he spoke sternly, as befitted a priest, his mind was disquieted; for he foresaw Mrs. Gamble's rage at finding a dog in the church, and how she would drive it out with blows and curses. Devouring beast that she was, she would run after it on all fours, and tear its white flank with her teeth. No soul, nothing so newly-made, gay and confiding, should be treated so. But his uneasiness was of short duration, for glancing furtively over his shoulder he saw that the greyhound bitch was gone.

OVER THE HILL

Like a stone into water death drops a weight into the ground, and the ripples spread. A movement is set up, things are changed – sometimes a life, sometimes the position of an ornament on a chimney-piece. When one old gentleman died at Nice where his young wife had taken him for his health because she did not like the English winter, another old gentleman in Dorset was moved from the east side of a hill to the west. It seemed to him that he had been moved much as a chimney ornament might be – plucked up and set down elsewhere without a word of warning; but that was because he was deaf and did not hear his granddaughter telling her husband that now, with the estate being sold piecemeal, the time had come to buy the flint cottage, for live next door to Mrs. Loppet she would no longer.

The flint cottage stood a good half-mile out of the village, and was grand. It had a gentry-like staircase, ascending from the passage to the landing instead of leading from the front kitchen into a bedroom; it had a wall round it instead of a fence, the door opened with a little key instead of a large one, and the pump was said to embody several modern ingenuities. Besides being grand, it was damp; but damp in a grand manner, not just damp here and there where a wall needed repointing, but imperceptibly damp all over, an unalienable freehold damp.

From the moment of arrival old Jacob knew what he was reminded of. Once, many years ago, he had gone on a journey to Salisbury, and at Yeovil Pen Mill he had been put for some time in a waiting-room. The flint cottage was like the waiting-room. The fire smoked, and the new pictures all represented the kind of place to which one is invited to travel by train.

'Come and sit here, grandfather, and warm yourself while I settle things.' But he sat down by the window instead and looked out. The waggon which had brought him with the last load was going back to the village. It vanished, and he was looking at the hill.

Every indentation of its dull, serene slope was familiar to him, and every mutation of stars that the year hung above it, for while he still worked he had been a shepherd, and the flint cottage was on the way to the sheepwalk. When this aspect of the hill met his eye he knew that sight of the village lay beyond it, and quickened his steps. Now he sat still, and it hid the village from him.

So the hill, however familiar, was changed in his eyes. It had been a landmark; it was now a barrier. It had been a rise of ground over which he walked; now it was a bulk. And staring at it day after day he began to think of it in terms of weight, and those uncounted tons of chalk and loam seemed to lie heavy on him.

He had time to think, time to have queer fancies. For many years Jacob had not walked without a stick, and his stick had been mislaid in the move. With an old man's obstinacy he would not use any stick but his own, and though his granddaughter offered him her umbrella, and her husband cut an ash-plant, for it irked them to see him sit moping always in the same place, he was not to be shaken.

It was almost three weeks before the stick was found.

'I knew you'd be rare and pleased,' she said, when she brought it to him. He did not show much pleasure, eyeing it heavily as though it were another train to catch. But late that afternoon, when no one was observing him, he went out and walked over the hill. It was a brilliant autumn day; the smoke rose straight into the air. He knew every chimney, he told the mumbling outlines of the thatched cottages like a flock, and there, late with her washing as usual, hung on the line Mrs. Loppet's purple bloomers, and all the little Loppets' pinafores. Beyond the washing were his own apple-trees. The leaves had hung on late this year; the trees still looked bushy. Some believe in pruning, some do not.

And then he remembered that now he lived in the flint cottage, that the trees were his no longer.

But he would not turn back, though for the next fifty yards with every step he seemed to leave his bowels behind him. Once fairly into the village, things were easier. Neighbours were there, shouts of greeting reached his ear, he was asked after his health, and the common demeanour conveyed that by moving beyond the hill he had become something rather rare and lofty. So he was able to pass his cottage with a cold, safe heart, and going to the inn he became merry, and boasted about the new abode that could provoke so many free drinks. On the way back he was not even aware that his feet had stayed before the old entry; for Mrs. Faux, whom neither age nor liquor could abate, had him by the arm and was seeing him home.

'I'll see 'ee home-along, daddy, to thee's country estate. 'Tis town 'ouse and country 'ouse with 'ee now, I reckon.'

OVER THE HILL

Mrs. Faux's kingdom was not of this world. She could cure warts, bring back a lover, and overlook cattle, and so she could afford to praise the flint cottage on this evening visit, tweaking open all the cupboard doors, endangering the patent pump by frolicking with it, and giving to all she pried into its meed of admiration and belches, careless that her own cottage was wattle and daub and that her well ran dry. But even so she could not be immune from a twinge of envy, and on the morrow it was natural for her to say, 'Old Jacob do be turned a sloppy drinker.'

It was quite true. Jacob, who had once had a head like iron, now became maudlin and peevish on half a pint of cider. But the young people put no obstacle in his way when he went over the hill to the inn. The old fellow had few pleasures, he was failing, and they gave him the liberty given to an old dog, too old to chase the fowls or do anything but dodder from one interesting gate-post to another. They knew he would not come to any harm; he would not even get wet. For he retained his weather sense, and by looking at a March cloud could tell if he would have time to walk back before the hail came clattering, or no. People used him as a weather-glass; a woman seeing him turn back to the cart-shed for shelter would run to fetch in the dish-clouts from the line. But long and enforced exposure to the weather had been the price of his cunning, and rheumatism was in his bones. The flint cottage did not agree with him, his fingers grew too stiff to clasp the stick he leaned on - one day, just on the brow of the hill, he stumbled, fell, and could not get on his feet again. As he twisted himself about, complaining, he discovered that he had gained a new view of the village, for, having fallen on his back, he now saw it the wrong way up. At this discovery he ceased to struggle and lay in a tipsy content, pondering this novel aspect of creation, until a passer-by came and righted him, and led him home.

This seemed likely to be his last view of the village. Lying heated in the wind he had caught a chill, and when he was allowed out of bed again he had forgotten how to walk, and it was not worth while to teach the art to so old a baby. So he sat by the window and looked at the hill.

Although he had lived for a year at the flint cottage, walking home to it as duly as the sheep in the Green Park walk at nightfall to the summit of their hill, the fancy that it was a waiting-room had never quite left him, Now, with nothing to do but wait, this fancy became strong. Turning over in his mind the contradictory facts that this was a place to wait in only, and that his family were living, scrubbing, cooking, and eating in it as though it were a dwelling like any other, he reconciled these in the conclusion that they must all be living in the flint cottage until the time came when they would return to the old home. A waggon had brought them. A waggon, surely, would come to fetch them back. It was a long time in coming; but then he had waited a long time at Yeovil Pen Mill.

His deafness had so closed in on him that he had little to say to the outside world, and awaited the waggon for the most part in silence. But at last, hearing him for the ninth or tenth time complain of its delaying, his granddaughter listened more attentively, and understood what was in the old man's mind.

'What am I to say?' she asked her husband. 'He's so childish, I shan't ever make him understand we are here for good. Yet I don't like not to say anything, the poor soul does fret so.'

OVER THE HILL

'Tell him it's coming next week,' he replied. 'Weeks – years – he won't notice no odds. 'Tis this year, next year, some time, never, with he nowadays.'

The advice was good. Elsie was a quick-witted woman and could always find some excuse why the waggon should not come till next week.

'It's haysel, grandfather, and the farmers are working to carry it before the moon changes.'

After the hay harvest came the oats, the corn, the barley. Then the hurdles must be carried into the fields where the ewes were to be penned, or Mr. Lovel had loaned his waggons to the new clergyman, who had such a deal of furniture, or the horses were ploughing.

This policy kept the old man pretty quiet, but in other ways he was increasingly a trouble. He was now so stiff that he had to be shoved and supported up and down stairs, and little Daphne had to sit by him at meals to guide the spoon to his mouth. It would have been simpler to keep him in bed, but he insisted, with weeping and rage, that he must be where he could look out of the side window whence he could see the hill, and watch for the first sight of the waggon coming to fetch him from the waiting-room.

'Will it come next week, Elsie?'

'It's coming today, grandfather. You watch out for it, for today it's coming at last.'

He watched, but no waggon came. Nothing came over the hill but a car, a thing of no interest to him. But hearing the horn Elsie jumped up and cried, 'Here 'tis – here 'tis!'

The car stopped at the door.

'Silly cow thee be if thee don't know waggon from one of they motoring cars.'

'Yes, but this be come instead of the waggon. Now let

me straighten you, so's you can start tidy.'

She was very quick, and flurry had reddened her face as if with shame. Before he knew what had been done to him Jacob was in his hat and coat, and standing before the car. There was a passenger inside already, a woman wearing a cloak and veil. She was a strong woman. While Jacob was doddering on the step of the car she leaned forward and gave him such a haul as he in old days had given to a sheep stuck in a ditch.

The wind blew Elsie's bobbed hair across her eyes and he noticed that she was hatless. Through the open door he saw the furnished house.

'Where be furniture to bide then? 'Baint 'ee going to bring furniture?'

' 'Tis all right,' she shouted, leaning flushed into the car. 'You be going first, we will come after you.'

The door slammed between them, the car jolted back and forth; having turned, it went over the hill. There was the village, that he had last seen inverted. Now it was the right way up once more. But that was about all he had time to notice, for the car went swiftly, carrying him to the county town infirmary.

I AM COME INTO MY GARDEN

Mr. Thomas Filleul lived in the Old Rectory, just a quarter of a mile from the village of Bishop's Nancy. The Old Rectory was a small house with latticed and jessamined windows, a celestial and a terrestrial globe standing just inside the front door, one on either side where many other people place umbrella-stands, and handsome brick chimneys set on diamond-wise.

After passing the house the road runs for thirty yards or so under a high wall, a flint wall with courses and buttresses of small red bricks; and any sensitive and reasonably greedy passer-by would know that within this wall was the Old Rectory kitchen-garden.

Ever since the days of Solomon it has been known that the best gardens are gardens enclosed, gardens with four walls and a green gate; but there was never a better walled garden, not even in Scotland, where there are such hot hairy yellow gooseberries so unabashedly appreciated by ring-ousels, than Mr. Filleul's sister and spouse; a garden with no nonsense about it, nor pergolas nor peevish rarities, but four rich square beds, a row of frames, a potting-hut, a corner for the roller and a long south wall.

There hung a rusty thermometer and there, amiably crucified, their branches held in place with strips of blue cloth and large peggy nails, grew three pears, three plums, three peaches, one quince, and two greengages.

Everyone his own fancy. Some people might have chosen a different arrangement, substituting a nectarine for the third peach, apples and cherries for plum and pear, or discarding the quince altogether – a fruit that is not universally admired because of its slight suggestion of onions – and trying a fig instead, though in such a kind soil they would do well in planting their fig to chasten its deep roots with some slates or brick-bats: but the existing arrangement of the Old Rectory south wall entirely suited Mr. Filleul.

No bishop could have loved his Nancy better than he loved his fruit-wall. Every morning of the year from early February onwards he would stroll out of the breakfast-room, and having given a twirl to the celestial and terrestrial globes as though dallying with the idea of a visit to China, say, or Madagascar, or a flight to Aldebaran, he walked with decision through the shrubbery and through the green gate, and into the walled garden. There every week-day, and often on Sundays too, was old Mole the gardener, ponderingly engaged in something or other, potting, pottering, or what-not; all fine old crusty gardeners have the same grave and devious activities. After a few words on the conduct of Mole's God, the weather, Mr. Filleul would proceed to the gravel walk before the south wall, and there he would pace up and down, observing his fruit trees, the plums and the peaches, the quince, the pears and the greengages.

I AM COME INTO MY GARDEN

These were his loves, these were his darlings. Other men watch with passionate attention wives or children, the growth of a philosophical system, the behaviour of some bacilli, migratory birds or the Stock Exchange. Mr. Filleul watched his wall-fruit – the bud rounding and swelling like a drop of dew, and then the blossom: the calyx, too, rounding and swelling in its time, and then the fruit.

These were his loves, these were his darlings; endeared to him by louring anxieties, exquisite surprises of relief. On March midnights he would wake up and hear the wind rumbling in the black chimney, trees cracking in the frost or the dense especial silence which tells of a heavy snowfall. 'My poor fruit-trees,' he would sigh into the blankets; and perhaps in less than a week's time he would walk into his garden and behold the first blossoms alighted here and there on the bare twigs like stars. When he said farewell to them at twilight the few stars had become many and on the morrow there were as many again. The snow-white of pear-blossom, the milk-white of plum – he could foretell from practised love exactly the tint of each tree, as astronomers know the hue of the stars, and he knew, too, how the colour of the blossoms would vary with the colour of the weather, the snow-white and milk-white on an overcast day deepening and solidifying, as it were, into muslin white and ivory; while on the contrary the pink of the peach-blossom rarefied under a grey sky. But though he knew their way so well his wall-fruit never dulled to him, and each blossom was a virginity. It made his heart stand still to see their innocent audacity, such pinks and whites at the hazard of black storm-clouds, biting winds, hail-stones like bullets, shrivelling frosts, an April sun 'too rash, too unadvised, too sudden,' and to think how helpless they were, they and their fruit, in the interplay of elements as helpless as themselves.

Herrick deplored to see the blossoms fade away so fast, a lyric that perhaps was inspired by somebody else's fruit-trees, for surely in his own orchard at Dean Prior the petals fluttering to the ground would suggest other and more cheering expectations than a grave. Mr. Filleul, at any rate, beheld the blossoms falling with an equal mind. He looked forward to the harvest of these disappearing virginities which had been fertilised by brown bees and soft winds, or in bad seasons by a camel's-hair paint-brush. March like a lion, the Blackthorn Winter, the Feast of the Ice Saints – these perils being past there came the summer months, May, June, July, the comfortable seasons of Sundays after Trinity, with day after day, week after week, the small green fruit rounding, colouring, ripening, hidden at first, modestly, behind a screen of young leaves, then growing rounder, growing bolder, seeking the sun, seeking the approving glance of Mr. Filleul pacing up and down the gravel path in a Panama hat.

No fingering, no pinching, for him; he was too wise for that. He walked up and down, walked and waited, how much happier and wiser than Solomon among his brides and concubines! How much safer, too! – for though he could hear the little Whittys, the naughtiest children in the village, morning and evening running to and fro from school, the wall was high and coped with glittering glass, they could not climb over to pill and raven. And old Mole would never steal the fruit, he did not like the fruit except as something to grow beyond the achievement of other gardeners. With his pruning-knife, his squirt, and his tarred brown netting he was like a comfortable eunuch tending and guarding Mr. Filluel's Seraglio.

The bees hummed along the borders, and every seventh day the sound of bells, the voice of a holy swarming came floating over the flint and brick wall from the village of Bishop's Nancy, telling of yet another Sunday after Trinity. Rhubarb and green gooseberry and morello cherry with a dash of brandy in it, raspberry and redcurrant and blackcurrant – such were tarts that Mrs. Looby cooked for her master's Sunday luncheon as spring warmed into summer and summer waxed into harvest. And all the time the fruits of Mr. Filleul's loves along the south wall grew rounder and riper, becoming at last the virgin brides themselves, supplanting their virgin April mothers.

Throughout the year, from early February onward, time walks beside anyone who walks and waits in a garden, step for step pacing up and down a gravel path; but towards the close of July time begins to take longer strides, he outsteps his companion, he goes before him and trampling boldly over the border goes up to the wall-fruit and gives the boughs a shake, saying: 'See, it is ripe, it is ready to pull!'

However tenderly and reverently, however much like a Bishop cherishing his Nancy (for after all she may have been his god-child, why should we always think evil?), a country gentleman may admire the ripening fruit along his south wall, these long loves must come at last to consummation, and there arrives a Sunday after Trinity when it is proper that he should pick and eat. Indeed, if it be a good season, he must eat quite industriously, or the wasps will get at the greengages before him and the pears, neglected, will, like any other ripened lady left an hour or so too long, begin to grow sleepy.

Mr. Filleul was, in his quiet way, as greedy as you could wish. He had the knack of taking pleasures with that ceremonious piety which increases any pleasure an hundred-fold, he kept, for instance, a little silver-bladed pocket-knife for this express pleasure only; and yet as year followed year he recognised with distress that there was something which made him feel rather sad when the time came to eat his fruits which he had loved so long. Two or three bites, a sweetness in the mouth, a cool sufficiency slipping down the gullet, a core or a stone to throw away - that is what it is to eat fruit. The consumption did not satisfy him; he did not really enjoy his enjoyment as much as he meant to. And worst of all, he felt, was it to know that it was not the fruit's fault. No, it was he who failed his brides when the moment came to eat them.

'Taking them one with another, pears with peaches, plums with 'gages,' said Mole, standing beside him in his Sunday waistcoat and in the ex cathedra manner he allowed himself on a non-working day 'Taking them one with another (for as for quince, I don't make no account of he, be year what it may, corn or roots, wet or fine, quince don't falter) this be the best show I reckon to have seen on south wall.'

Mr. Filleul made no answer. A feeling such as saddened Augustine among the courtesans welled up in him, and as he looked at his fruit-trees the tears were not far from his

I AM COME INTO MY GARDEN

eyes. The sun which had ripened his brides and would soon undo them flashed among the glass which topped the flint wall. From behind the wall came the sound of small sturdy boots, of scuffling and graceless frolic: it was the little Whittys on their way to Sunday School.

The noise grew fainter as they trailed past.

A light came into Mr. Filleul's eyes. He dashed like a madman to the green gate, he ran violently through the shrubbery, denting the smooth turf with his long strides and startling three woodpigeons, two blackbirds and the tortoiseshell cat, he whisked past the kitchen window and cleared the begonia bed. The Whittys were just passing the house.

'Come in,' he cried, pulling open the front gate: 'come in, all of you, and eat my fruit!'

A VILLAGE DEATH

When Mr. Kidd the shepherd began to draw his old age pension the farmer who employed him, speaking as a taxpayer, proposed to deduct the amount of the pension from Mr. Kidd's wages. Mr. Kidd knew himself as a good worker; he had served the farmer for many years, and the lambs he drove to market always fetched top prices there. With the indignation of self-respect he refused the proposal. The farmer said no more and two months later dismissed him.

Mr. Kidd sold his dogs and now lived without even their company; for he was a bachelor. He had his savings and his pension, and he made some odd shillings by jobbing gardening and shaving his neighbours for Sunday. Twice a day he visited the inn, much as some people go to church, as a sober social habit. He was a quiet man. Since no one could breathe a word of scandal against him little attention was paid to him; and he had been looking ill for some months before any one troubled to remark that Mr. Kidd was looking poorly, and had a swelled face.

The swelling increased, and gathered to a sore, and broke. Mr. Kidd walked two miles to the panel doctor and

A VILLAGE DEATH

came back with a bottle of liniment. The swelling came again, and again broke and discharged, and Mr. Kidd began to wear a white handkerchief round his jaws. His expression had always been one of extraordinary simplicity and goodness; his swelled face gave him a curious resemblance to those puff-checked cherubs which are carved on tombstones. But though he looked like a cherub he looked ill also, his flesh fell away, and his clothes, which had seemed so closely part of him, now hung on him indifferently, as though they might shortly leave him and find a new wearer.

Spring came, but Mr. Kidd dug no gardens, for he was on the club. As the weather grew warmer it began to be noticed that Mr. Kidd's sore smelled unpleasantly. Blood and matter stained the handkerchief. He visited the doctor again, and brought back another bottle of liniment. He would go no more, he said; two miles there and two miles back was farther than he could walk. The doctor, speaking privately and as man to man, said that he had known for months that Mr. Kidd had a cancer. It was now inoperable, and as time went on its growth would prevent Mr. Kidd from swallowing anything but liquids. There would, of course, he said, be considerable pain, but nothing could be done for it, since the hospital did not take inoperable cases. The infirmary? Kidd was no pauper, he had his pension and his savings; besides, Kidd would never consent to the infirmary, these old fogeys were all like that, calling it The Poor-house. Meanwhile, he would send out some more liniment, and look him up later in the summer.

Mr. Kidd still kept about, and still visited the inn,

though now he drank but rarely. It seemed rather that he went there craving obscurely for the company of his kind. So handy with his sheep, he had not the knack of looking after himself. There was no district nurse, but daily the inn-keeper's wife washed his sore and changed its wrappings. This act was an honour to her, body and soul; but Mr. Kidd was a good man and a good customer, she said, and she would stand by him. She continued to stand by him even when the trade of the inn began to suffer. It was unpleasant to drink in Mr. Kidd's company now; to eye and nose he was too sensibly a *memento mori*, and customers suggested that Mr. Kidd might be given a hint to keep away. When he walked through the village people turned aside and mothers called their children into the house. Presently it was said that Mr. Kidd's bucket would infect the common well, and that if he did not die soon something really should be done about him.

He must have known that he was shunned. But with obstinate patience he went on as though unconscious of the mingled fear and pity which he evoked, still dragging himself slowly to the inn to have his sore dressed, to sit in the bar parlour alone with the buzzing flies. Sometimes, pausing in the strong sun, he would look at the sheep on the hill – his old flock. He had been a good shepherd; if one of his sheep grew scabby he dressed it; if it were taken with an incurable sickness he put it out of its pain. But Mr. Kidd had been brought up a Christian, it would not have occurred to him that the same merciful dealing might be applied to a man, nor would he have approved of such an idea.

He remained in the village until the autumn. The inn-keeper's wife was losing her health through worry and nausea, and custom had become so bad that her husband and she were forced to give up the inn and move elsewhere. This, and his weakness, and the force of public opinion, at last brought him to the infirmary, where, just before Christmas, he died. People in the village, busy with their Christmas, spared a moment to say that he was a good man who never harmed anybody, and that it was a mercy he was out of his misery.

FOLK COOKERY

We had done our best with whist drives, socials, sixpenny hops, and a flower show to raise the money for a village nurse. Now the Ladies' Committee was planning how to make up our deficiencies.

'I feel strongly,' said Mrs. Beggerley Blatchford, 'that we should make a little book of Old English cookery - local lore, you know. And sell it at the post office and the railway station.'

We had rather expected her to feel like this. The B. B.s have a great deal of local and regional piety. Morris-dancers trample their lawn, their halls resound with sackbuts and fipple pipes, their cushions have hand-woven covers, rugged as granite.

'Elwin could print it for us,' she continued. 'And then we could charge much more for it. Hand-printed books always sell so nicely.' (Elwin is Mr. Beggerley Blatchford and owns a hand press.)

She was well away now. 'And the dear old people who contribute the recipes will feel they have done their share. That would be so nice, too. Suppose we each comb half a dozen?'

Most of our dear old people had been allotted to us when

FOLK COOKERY

we remembered Mary Granby, absent from this meeting because her 'Eton Crop' haircut could be attended to only on Wednesdays, when that godlike Mr. Harry visited the county-town hairdresser.

'Well, now, who's left over to give Mrs. Granby?' said Mrs. Beggerley Blatchford. 'There's Mrs. Bugler, and Mrs. Trim, and Mrs. What's-Her-Name; you know, the good old thing with that dreadful husband. You know. He drinks, and was rather tiresome on election day.'

'Mrs. Sturmey?'

'Mrs. Sturmey. I think three would be quite enough for Mary Granby.'

On my way home I met the grocer's van, which nourishes us three times a week. The vanman likes conversation. He understood that it was with no bad intent that I asked him what staples he sold the most of.

'Bread and soap,' he replied unhesitatingly.

'And groceries?'

'Well, tinned salmon. We sell quite a lot of that. Then there's cereals. Here it's all Grape-Nuts, but over at Canon's Caudle it's Rolled Oats. Then there's cheese. And vinegar. And in summer it would surprise you how well these new lemonade crystals go.' He came running after me to say he had forgotten jam.

Different people demand different approaches. Jane Pitman, who was next on my list, is one of those who like a direct approach.

'Mrs. Beggerley Blatchford wants to know what your mother ate,' I said to her.

'Bread and scrape, Miss. Same as we.'

'Suppose your father happened to bring back a hare?'

'Sell it. Hare meat ain't wholesome for the likes of us,

not while smells come out of chimney pots and tongues do wag in folkses' headses.'

I went next to Mrs. Goshawk, who, it developed, looked more sympathetically on the folklore of cookery. Old-fashioned ways had more to them, she said, and she had never had a tin-opener equal to the one she started married life with. Mrs. Rump, who happened to be borrowing a large-eyed needle from Mrs. Goshawk, agreed as to the virtues of times past. Look at the doctor's stuff we get now, she said. Old Dr. Faux had a pill that went through you like a ferret.

Miss Owles told me that if you rub a wart with a piece of raw beef, the beef will wither and so will the wart. But you couldn't do it with imported beef, she said. Mrs. Tizard, after long thinking, gave me a recipe for furniture polish, and a warning never to eat mushrooms after the first of October. Mrs. Cockaday gave me some medical advice of a kind which Elwin Beggerley Blatchford could never be asked to print; a recommendation to keep to dark teapots, for they made the tea stronger; and a large bunch of flowers.

When we came to pool our results with Mrs. Beggerley Blatchford, the total was disappointing: dark teapots make the strongest tea; chewing a clove will ease toothache; tough meat can be softened by burying it for a night and a day; sheep pastured in a churchyard don't make wholesome eating; a pint of warm beer stirred with a red-hot poker will cure the backache. And we had Miss Owles' cure for warts, and the recipes for Mrs. Tizard's furniture polish and Mrs. Tucker's grandmother's Kettle Broth, which was made by pouring boiling water on a sliced onion and some stale crusts. All the investigators had been told that mushrooms are poisonous after the first of October. 'There is the same belief in Yugoslavia. Isn't that fascinating?' said Mrs. Beggerley Blatchford. 'We must put in a little footnote about that. Folklore is so wonderfully universal.'

Mrs. Beggerley Blatchford's own discoveries were of a more Arcadian nature. They included bramble-tip cordial, cowslip pie, and candied hemlock. I, for one, did not believe in them. Mary Granby was the only one still to report.

'Now, Mrs. Granby,' said Mrs. Beggerley Blatchford, 'you are our last hope.'

'Well, I could do nothing with Mrs. Bugler, and Mrs. Trim was in bed with rheumatism, so I left her. But I've got these.' She opened a notebook. There was a great deal of pencil writing, in a singularly careful and childish hand. She read to us '"Turnip Tantivy. Take three turnips, five pounds of raisins, a pound of the best butter, half a bottle of whisky, pepper and salt, mix and fry in a large iron frying pan that has a flavour of bloaters. When the turnips have taken up all the whisky, turn out into a pie dish."

'"Cottage Stew. Take some partridges, three or four; a pheasant, a fowl, a good hare, two pounds of the best beef-steak, green bacon in thick slices, vegetables, and herbs. Season richly and stew in a pot for three hours, Then pour in about a teapotful of port wine, and simmer for another hour."

'"Flummery. Cover the bottom of a deep basin with sliced quinces, strewed with nutmeg. Lay on them slices of Double Gloucester cheese. Then more quinces. Then more cheese. Go on doing this till the basin is two-thirds full. Pour in enough rich cream and old rum in equal quantities to cover them handsomely, and eat with cake."

'Mrs. Sturmey was out at work.' Mary Granby explained. 'But her husband was at home, and he dictated these recipes to me. He said this was how his old mother used to cook.'

'How very interesting.' answered Mrs. Beggerly Blatchford. 'Quite in the traditional spirit of English cook lore! But I wonder if we ought to include these recipes in our book. You see, Mrs. Granby, we hope our little book will be used by our dear villagers themselves. Perhaps these recipes would be a little ambitious - not quite in keeping with their simple tastes, dear souls!'

The meeting broke up soon after this, and Mrs. Beggerley Blatchford has not called the Ladies' Committee together since. Elwin is now hand-printing a booklet on Our Neolithic Remains.

THE JENNY CAT

'And beauty draws us with a single hair.' Whoever made that assertion must have lived in a city. In our Dorsteshire village we pay very little attention to beauty. Some startling form of ill-health, reprobate manners, or a tandem bicycle would have much stronger drawing powers than beauty. But for all that, and against our better judgment, we cannot help giving a great deal of our attention to Lucy Cutlet.

Lucy's beauty is of a kind we had never seen before; in fact, we did not recognize it as beauty at all until it dawned on us that she bears a great resemblance to Anna May Wong. This likeness enskied Lucy. In the village we have just the ordinary human faces. None of us are in the least degree like the superior beings who appear in picture papers, except possibly Mrs. Troy, who is the image of Socrates. But Socrates does not figure often enough in the papers for this to make a beauty of Mrs. Troy.

Lucy Cutlet has straight black hair, cut in a smooth bang over her smooth forehead. Her face is shaped like a heart on a playing card; between her serene eyebrows and her high cheek-bones, her sliding eyes glitter like black cherries dangling from a forbidden tree. She has a long, slender neck and long, slender legs.

It was Lucy's long legs that first demonstrated her as someone to be reckoned with. Till the day of the Sports we had known her only as one of those two Cutlet girls who had newly come to be servants at the Manor. Lucy entered for the Young Women's Race and won it, leaping through the tape while the other young women were still halfway down the course. The next race was for Married Women. It had not occurred to us that Lucy would enter for that, too, but she ranged up, explaining that she was deputizing for Mrs. Bugler. Quellingly handicapped, Lucy won the Married Women's Race too, won it for the enthusiastic Mrs. Bugler. Major Cumfrey, who was managing the Sports (he manages everything, explaining that such things are nothing to him after having lived for so long in the Argentine, where one sees life in the raw), was enthusiastic also. Mopping his face with a red cotton handkerchief, he strutted up and down exclaiming 'Well run, Longlegs! Haven't I got a fine parlour-maid?'

Then came the Young Men's Race. They were off, thundering over the dry turf with their arms flying and their mouths open, when Lucy Cutlet, not to be restrained, leaped into their midst, tore past them, and won that race, too.

It was at the Sixpenny Hop that evening that we acknowledged the likeness to Anna May Wong. Lucy's white organdie (theretofore we had looked on white organdie as suitable only for young children that require constant laundering) floated like thistledown among a variety of Sunday trousers. As she danced, her smooth bang swayed over her smooth brow, her face remained pale with powder. Only her impetuous ears became a

THE JENNY CAT

brilliant rose colour.

*

We began to collect information about Lucy. We learned that she was engaged to a sailor, but this did not prevent her walking out with the two sons of a farmer who is one of our neighbours. The elder young Mullen is considered to be a young man of great ability and likely to rise in the world; he resembles his mother, and has never been known to stand a drink to anyone. The younger young Mullen is a softer character. Lucy walked out with them quite impartially; she even walked out with them both at once. We were expecting something in the Romeo-and-Juliet line, for it was known that the parent Mullens looked higher for their sons than a servant-maid, even a servant-maid who could run like a gazelle and look like a film star. What happened was that Major Cumfrey hastened into the post office one morning and telephoned the doctor to come at once for a case of wounding. Lucy, while preparing breakfast, had fallen out with her sister and thrown a knife at her. The knife went some inches into Hilda Cutlet's thigh, the Manor kitchen was painted with blood, the Manor breakfast indefinitely postponed.

Major Cumfrey, however, was more gratified than not. He had seen a lot of knifing in the Argentine - a lot of hot-blooded passion, too. As he said, an English parlour-maid who can jerk a knife into her sister's thigh through all those petticoats is a rarity. All he wished was that Lucy would sharpen the dinning-room knives to the same edge.

Hilda did not seem to bear any malice. When Lucy, as she later re-counted to Mrs. Bugler, set fire to the Manor roof by leaving a flaring lamp under a wooden beam, Hilda made everything all right by hiding the lamp in a cupboard and explaining that a rat's tail got into the bedroom candle. Lucy, looking out from under the blankets, added that the rat was as large as a Pekinese, and Major Cumfrey, after a few reassuring anecdotes about raccoons and county families, went downstairs with the fire-extinguisher.

Meanwhile the Montagues, that is to say the Mullens, were in a terrible way, declaring that they would rather see their sons lying dead before them than married to a servant-maid – for it was as yet unknown which young Mullen would get Lucy. It had leaked out that when the young Mullens took the family car and drove to the Lenten Lantern Lectures on Tuesday evenings their religious impetus took them no further than the lane behind the Manor. Here they halted the car, turned out the headlights, and were joined by the Cutlets. The day that the policeman walked up the Manor drive we thought it pretty certain that Mrs. Mullen had carried out her threat of issuing a summons for seduction.

It was not the summons but a subpoena, summoning Lucy Cutlet to bear witness before the magistrate in a case of car-stealing. Two profligate young men, it seemed, had caused a car not their own to crash into one of the nation's telegraph poles, and when Police Constable Ardle investigated the matter he happened to recognise a moonlit ivory-and-ebony Lucy Cutlet sliding out of the car and moving smoothly toward a ditch.

As far as appearances go, Lucy made a perfect witness, wearing a neat black tailor-made and an eye veil. But when the magistrate, with a natural confidence, asked her if she knew the two young men in the dock, she disconcertingly replied that she didn't. Nor could she be induced to recollect any of the other things she was invited to bear

THE JENNY CAT

witness to. Her mind was a blank as to the car, the route, the time, the telegraph pole. As question followed question, she began to look grieved - sorry, no doubt, to be such a disappointment to a grey-haired gentleman. And, as though some word of explanation were due, she volunteered, 'I had a drink at the dance. I can't remember what I drank, or who gave it me. But I expect it was too much for me.' There was a world of regret in her voice, regret chastened by philosophy; she seemed to be setting the whole court an object lesson in decent fatalism.

It seemed to us that Lucy had done very creditably. One would not expect a young woman with so much humanity to incriminate two young men who had gone to the trouble of stealing a car in order to take her for a moonlight ride. Shortly after this Lucy demonstrated her humanity further by going singlehanded to the defence of Mr. Mullen's sow when the sow was attacked by Miss Thomson's Alsatians. If anything could have softened Mr. Mullen's heart, this attention to his sow should have done it. But Mr. Mullen continued to frown on Lucy, and Mrs. Mullen now talked of feeling herself in conscience and honour bound to ascertain the name and address of Lucy's sailor in order to let him know how Lucy was going on.

*

Day by day Lucy looked more beautiful and more like Anna May Wong; day by day the elder young Mullen looked more morose and the young young Mullen more ardent. Over Major Cumfrey's brow came lines of care. He hires his shooting from the Mullens, and though it is only rabbits, he would be loath to lose it. Every sheep's eye that the young Mullens cast on his parlour-maid endangered Major Cumfrey's excursions over the bosom of wild nature, where a man can be a man and not a mere domestic drudge, chased from room to room with the butcher's book and inquiries as to when the sweep can get into the library. 'Never be a bachelor!' he exclaimed to me. 'Miserable Samson that I am, women dog me. Look at those worthless animals there! Bitches, every one of them. Look at my house! Women spring-cleaning in every room. Every one of my seven sisters is alive, and all my cats are Jenny-cats!'

There was a Sixpenny Hop last Wednesday, and for some reason we had all made up our minds that this Hop would settle it, one or other of the young Mullens placing an engagement ring on Lucy Cutlet's finger, or one or other of the old Mullens living up to the threat of confronting Lucy with her sailor. Everyone in the village attended - everyone, that is to say, but Lucy. Lucy, Hilda said, had twisted her ankle and was staying in to poultice it. We were badly disappointed in Lucy. The dance without her was mud, and for the next twelve hours we thought meanly of her.

Next morning the news went round that Lucy had been away all night, and was away still. About midday she came back in a taxi. She would say nothing, save that she had influenza and must go to bed at once. Those who had seen her in the taxi said she didn't look like influenza to them, but to Major Cumfrey's eyes it looked like influenza, for he went back from the inn with a bottle of rum for poor Lucy.

All that day we hung around, waiting for bulletins on Lucy's influenza. The child who carried up the Manor's afternoon milk was mobbed as she came away. Lucy was no better, she reported. She was asleep. Many were the heartfelt vows and prayers we offered up that night for Lucy's speedy recovery. Young Mrs. Turbot sat up till two in the morning, watching from her window in case Lucy should walk in her sleep. And in the morning 'Lucy' was the first word on our lips.

Lucy was a little better, we heard. Lucy was cured. The rum, as Major Cumfrey had foreseen, had done the trick. That afternoon the welcome, the beautiful news went around. Faithful at the last, Lucy had spent Wednesday night with her sailor.

TWO MINUTES' SILENCE

In the country, we British don't do much about Armistice Day. On the preceding Sunday, the parson tells us it's due round once more, and maybe; if the eleventh of November is fine, a charity collector will come to the village with a tray of poppies to sell. Otherwise, we content ourselves with reading in the papers about the doings in Whitehall. These don't vary much from year to year. The maroons go off, the last stroke of Big Ben dies away, the pigeons fly out, nothing is heard but the whir of their wings and the quiet sob of a woman. Sometimes the sun shines, sometimes it doesn't – we think a lot of the weather in England – but the maroons, Big Ben, the pigeons, and the woman can be relied on.

As for the Two Minutes' Silence, we never attempted it. It is not possible for twenty men scattered over eight hundred acres to be organised into a simultaneous silence. And in November the country is pretty silent anyhow.

This year it was different. A gentleman called Major Cumfrey has rented the Old Manor House He is energetic and affable, and immediately fell out with the parson. Major Cumfrey said the church belonged to the people, by the Lord Harry it did, at any rate on a weekday, and as

TWO MINUTES SILENCE

Armistice Day fell this year on a Wednesday, the people should have a service of their own, a sensible service, with no prayers and no nonsense about peace. It was all this nonsense about peace that spoiled Armistice Days. So it was arranged that the women of the village who had lost anyone in the war should assemble in the church, hang up a wreath on the war memorial, observe the Two Minutes' Silence, and come away again. That was our official programme, arranged by Major Cumfrey. Unofficially it was understood that the proceedings would end with Mrs. Rump playing 'Oh, Rest in the Lord,' by Mendelssohn, on the organ. She likes playing it, she plays it a lot, and this touch of music would remove any suspicion of bleakness that might otherwise hang about Major Cumfrey's arrangements.

The wreath was magnificent, made of Haig Fund poppies with gold trimmings. Everyone subscribed for it, and when we saw Mrs. Turbot carrying it up the lane we felt properly gratified. We haven't any pigeons, and the church clock has not struck for years, but the sun was shining, quite as well as it could in Whitehall, we reckoned.

We went into the church at ten-fifty-five - about a dozen of us, all women - and knelt down in our places. Mrs. Turbot kept on consulting her watch, and sobbing. At eleven a.m. precisely she stood up on the pew and hooked the wreath on a nail above the memorial brass tablet. Then she went down on her knees once more looking relieved.

*

It is always difficult to judge time, especially in a church, where one is accustomed to things seeming to drag. When I looked at my watch, it was nearly ten minutes past eleven. Other people were looking at their watches, too, shifting the hands that supported their bowed heads and opening one eye to glance down at the watch face. Time went on; presently it was eleven-fifteen. We knelt on, preserving the Two Minutes' Silence. No one wanted to be the first to disturb it; it would have seemed heartless at such a solemn moment to do anything abrupt. Besides, no one could think what to do. But the strain was considerable. Then the silence was broken by a rather unpleasant noise. Actually, it was Mrs. Rump, try-ing over the pedal part of 'Oh, Rest in the Lord' on the windless organ. Being deaf, Mrs. Rump was unaware that the organ pedals clatter. But they do, and in that silent, stony little church the noise of the organ pedals was exactly like the rattling of bones.

At eleven-twenty-three there was a loud report, which we knew to be Major Cumfrey's shotgun. He was close to the church - we could hear him distinctly - hallooing on his dogs after a rabbit.

'Bess! Bess! Seek him out, seek him out, good dog! Confound you, Rosy! Come here, damn you! Come here, you worthless, mudlarking trollop, you!'

Young Mrs. Turbot, who was sitting in the front pew, jumped up, turned round to face the kneeling congregation.

'Hymn 246,' she said, in a tone of wrathful decision.

DIEU ET MON DROIT

We had been perfectly satisfied with our Jubilee celebrations in the spring of '35. Every child under fourteen in our Dorset village had worn a golden paper crown. There had been a great deal to eat and drink, a bonfire, three accordion players and a cornet, and dancing till four in the morning.

However, some adverse comments broke out later on, especially among those whom most of us in the village call our betters. Miss Woden, who plays the organ in church, regretted that Mr. Truebone, whose function it was to call for three cheers for King George after the largest rocket had gone up should have seen fit to follow this by calling for three cheers for 'wold King Edward,' a sentiment greeted with equal enthusiasm. Rear Admiral Pinne (Retired) pointed out that the hired flags believed by us to be flags of friendly foreign nations, were in reality quarantine flags, and must have indicated to any competent eye that our village, instead of rejoicing in a sovereign's Silver Jubilee, was announcing simultaneous outbreaks of cholera, plague, and yellow fever. And Miss Pinne, who is trying to make us Scout-conscious, discovered by inquiry that seventy per cent of the children were under the impression that the Jubilee was in honour of our postmistress, who is also our oldest inhabitant, and who was the person selected to hand out to the children the Jubilee souvenir mugs.

Our betters decided that any future celebrations must be of a more guided nature, and they undertook to do the guiding. There was scarcely time for them to do much about the Royal Funeral, but they got to work good and early on the Coronation. Everything was planned: the speakers, the decorations, every item of our behaviour, from the opening fanfare by Scouts and Brownies to the hour of 11:30 p.m., when we were to leave off dancing. The arrangements were sealed and concluded at a village meeting early in November.

Then came the news of the Abdication. It reached us by Mr. Pigeon, the mail-carrier. 'King has abdicated,' he said, 'and all the trains are late.'

We were standing in front of the post office. It was a foggy day, and we felt pretty melancholy. We felt for the Pinnes, too. 'The poor Pinnes won't be able to hold up their heads,' mused Mr. Pigeon, 'after all the trouble they've took over Coronation.'

I said there might still be a Coronation.

'Twont be the same to them,' asserted Mr. Pigeon. Admiral loved that young man like a son.'

'Doesn't seem like Christmas now,' mourned Mrs. Pigeon.

While we were discussing whether the handsome young man on the grocer's presentation calendar was meant for King Edward or King George, a notice appeared in the post-office window:

DIEU ET MON DROIT

VILLAGE MEETING

> A meeting will be held to discuss the revision of the arrangements for the Coronation on Jan. 27th at 7:30. It is hoped all possible will attend. Brenda Pinne, Hon. Sec.

We hold our village meetings in the school. It is a melancholy building with Gothic windows looking out on to the churchyard. Mr. Pretty, our esteemed blacksmith, was in the chair. He looked careworn. Miss Pinne, the Admiral's daughter, was beside him.

In the front row of chairs was Mrs. Pretty, looking steadfastly at Miss Pinne. They had fallen out pretty sharply over the question of whether Stanley Pretty should become a Scout or no. Mrs. Pretty had won, but she had not been as magnanimous as a victor should be.

It was a comment on the sad vicissitudes of life that the minutes of the previous meeting should record the obsolete arrangements for the Coronation. When Mr. Pretty came to the words 'It was agreed that Admiral Pinne should undertake to order fifty-three souvenir mugs,' a sigh and a shaking of heads went through the audience. After the minutes, Mr. Pretty said a few words. A man of just mind and a compassionate nature, he conveyed to us that in his opinion both the abdicated and the succeeding monarch had personal merits and much to bear. When he had referred once or twice to 'the late King Edward,' Miss Pinne leaned forward and whispered sharply. 'The Duke of Windsor.' Mr. Pretty went on to give a few kind words to Queen Elizabeth and then, his eye resting on Mrs. Pretty, expressed a hope that the late Duke Edward might also in time know the comfort of a domesticated fireside.

The Admiral, the Vicar, and Miss Woden drew down their upper lips. Miss Pinne ejaculated, 'Heaven forbid!'

'I beg your pardon?' said Mrs. Pretty.

'And so, ladies and gentlemen,' concluded the chairman, 'we are met here tonight - and I think we may congratulate ourselves on a very full attendance, though I do observe a few absent faces - to thrash out, so to say, this little business of revising the Coronation.'

The Admiral had now released his upper lip, and spoke. 'Some of our previous arrangements, of course, can stand. Others will need certain modifications. We must not lose sight of the fact that in this Coronation we shall be rejoicing in the thought that beside our gracious King we shall have our gracious Queen.'

We listened to the sad noise of the rain falling on the tombstones.

'Such a welcome thought!' said Mrs. Pinne to Miss Woden, in a stage undertone.

'I suppose,' said Mr. Truebone, 'that will mean modifying the mugs.'

'The previous mugs,' said the Admiral, 'must, of course, be jettisoned. But that need not trouble us. I have heard from the makers, and I understand that they will be prepared to take them back again, free of charge, provided we buy the new mugs from the same firm.'

A considerable whispering and shuffling now arose among the backward chairs. Ignoring it, Miss Pinne said, 'And here is a specimen of the *new* mug. I feel sure we shall all like to look at it.'

'Here!' exclaimed Mrs. Pretty. 'I want that Edward mug, if you please! I don't want to disappoint *my* child. He's a patriotic child, whatever some people may say.' And she glared at Miss Pinne.

Meanwhile the whispering had swelled to a tumult, and

DIEU ET MON DROIT

one could hear such phrases as 'Worth five times the money already,' 'Not for love or money,' 'Why, it will be historical by the time the child's grown up.'

Then, out of the tumult, voices aimed themselves at Miss Pinne.

'Please, Miss, will you put down my Eddie and my Doris and my Sheila and my Alice for Edward mugs? They've set their hearts on them.'

'And my Doris and my Jimmy too, Miss, if it's all the same to you.'

'My Billy and my Alice and my George, Miss Pinne.'

'Mrs. Lockett, two George mugs?' said Miss Pinne hopefully.

'No, Miss. Two Edwards, Please.'

'My Harry and my Hazel, Miss.'

'My Ruby.'

'My Ronald and my Bobby and my Alan and my Suzy.' Miss Pinne's pencil was twitching like summer lightning.

'I think we must have a show of hands,' said Mr. Pretty. 'Will those mothers who wish for Edward mugs for their children please put up their hands?'

Hands went up all over the room.

'Now those in favour of the George mugs.'

Three hands went up, two of them gloved.

Once again there was silence, and we listened to the noise of the rain falling on the tombstones. Mr. Truebone got up and slouched to the door.

'Perhaps. said Mr. Pretty, 'the best expedient would be for the children to have both mugs.'

'My Cuthbert don't want no George mug,' said Mrs. Lockett.

'Come to that,' said Mr. Lockett, 'why should they have

mugs at all? Can't a child drink out of a cup?'

Mrs. Pigeon recalled that at an earlier meeting some had been in favour of medals rather than mugs. Would it be a good plan to go back to medals? Mrs. Nokes said that you might as well give poison to a baby as a medal, for it would be sure to swallow it. Mrs. Lockett added that even if you put the medal away till the child was old enough to appreciate it, ten to one you'd mislay it.

Meanwhile a strategic notion was enlightening the Admiral. We saw him conferring with Mrs. Pinne and Miss Woden, with much nodding of heads. The notion was unfolded to the Vicar, who then nodded also.

'The thought has just struck me,' said the Admiral, 'that we might find the way out of our difficulties by quite a fresh alternative. How about a book?'

There was a dumbfounded silence among the Edward faction, but Miss Woden exclaimed. 'What a good idea! So much better than a mug. One never comes to the end of a book.'

'And the babies could not hurt themselves on it,' added Miss Pinne. 'The tots would enjoy the pictures.'

'Of our King and our Queen, and of the Empire. I often think we do not think enough about our Empire,' said Mrs. Pinne.

'Admiral,' said the Vicar, 'you have hit on the very thing! The Admiral proposes that since mugs are not universally acceptable, each child shall receive a book. I second that proposal.'

Mr. Pretty was just about to put it to a vote (and though no one wanted books, the unanimity of our betters was so compelling that probably books would have been carried) when Mr. Truebone slouched dreamily back again.

'About they mugs,' he began.

'We are now discussing books,' said the Vicar suavely.

'About paying for them, I mean,' continued Mr. Truebone. 'They Edwards, they won't be taken back unless we have they Georges. And 'tisn't all of us, seemingly, as wants a George.'

'Looks as though we should have paid for mugs and not have them,' mused Mr. Pigeon.

'It's an awkward consideration,' said the chairman. While we considered, Mrs. Nokes was heard saying to Mrs. Wally that it was a pity the mugs had been bought so previous. Mrs. Wally replied that it was a pity, too, that they had changed the kings. It made such a lot of awkwardness.

Mr. Nokes asked how much the books would cost. The Admiral said, 'We need not trouble about that, my friends. Mrs. Pinne and I will be delighted to pay for the books.'

'And so,' said Miss Woden, 'thanks to Admiral Pinne, we are wafted out of the little difficulty.'

'No, us aren't!' shouted Mr. Nokes. 'For what about the money that's gone on the Edwards we're not to have?'

'Mugs is what we wanted, and mugs is what we should have,' said Mrs. Pretty, raising her voice.

'Mugs is what we'll be if we pay for them and don't get them,' added Mr. Lockett.

Everyone began to clamour for mugs.

'Them as wants mugs put up their hands!' cried Mrs. Pretty. A forest of hands appeared. 'There! That's carried. We want mugs.'

'Very well,' said the Admiral. 'But let me make one thing clear. We cannot celebrate the Coronation of King George with mugs bearing a portrait of the Duke of Windsor. If you want mugs, you must have the correct mugs.'

'It's Edward mugs we want!'

'Edward mugs, they Edward mugs!'

The unhappy Mr. Pretty, sweating heavily, was thumping for silence with an ink bottle.

'Ladies and gentlemen, ladies and gentlemen, *please*! May I suggest a kind of a compromise? Since this Coronation is taking place under, so to speak, rather invidious circumstances, can't we give a certain measure of appreciation to both parties?'

'Hear, hear,' said Mrs Truebone.

'I propose we give each child a George mug –'

'But my Eddie and my Doris and my Sheila –'

'And an Edward mug also.'

Mr. Truebone seconded. The proposal was carried. Mrs. Pinne rose to her feet. 'Oh, very well!' she said. 'But I tell you this. *You can pay for your Edward's yourselves.*'

Mr. Pretty asked if there was any other business. But our betters were already gathering themselves up to go. Mr. Pretty and Mr. Truebone and I stayed behind to put back the chairs and extinguish the oil lamps. Mr. Truebone had given Mr. Pretty a cigarette, and they were talking about seed potatoes. Outside was the rain, and the shuffle of feet, and the noise of the Admiral's car and the Vicar's car being started up. As I went by, I heard Mrs. Pinne's voice, louder than the growls of a reluctant self-starter, saying the word 'Bolsheviks'.

IF THESE DELIGHTS

'Of course,' said Mrs. Gumfreston, the new tenant of the only grand house in our poor neighbourhood, 'I can't myself imagine having a dull moment here. There is so much going on in the English countryside. Flowers! Birds! Henry and I have been putting up nesting boxes all the morning.'

'My father got a great deal of pleasure from a rain gauge,' said I.

'Did he? How original! How practical! I love rain.'

A pleasant morning had turned to a solid downpour. At the end of the Gumfreston's vista of lime trees I could see the slope of a field and a sullen wet man working there.

I took another teacake. They were homemade and very good, though small.

'But I feel,' continued the lady, 'and Henry feels too, a lack of joy in this place. The village life seems so flat and dreary. I suppose it's been neglected for a long time. Every village needs a centre.'

'Perhaps we *are* rather quiet,' I said.

'They are all charming creatures, and so friendly. I feel at home with them already. But nothing seems to happen.

Does anything happen?'

'Mrs. Cowey's daughter, Rosy, was married last week,' said I. 'But as she is expecting a baby at any moment she was married quietly, so I suppose that hardly counts. Last Sunday there was a strange lady in church, and the offertory became much larger than usual. And yesterday the shepherd came home from the infirmary. But they tell him he will never be fit to work again, so this morning he hanged his dog.'

'How ghastly! Henry, do you hear? A dog hanged.'

'Poor brute!' said Mr. Gumfreston. 'What sort of dog?'

I said it was an Old English sheepdog, and they looked as though they had heard of the death of Lord Baldwin.

'But I don't mean this sort of thing, these gloomy things,' she cried. 'Does nothing ever happen by way of gaieties, nothing to lift people out of themselves?'

'Oh yes,' said I, glad to be able to please. 'During the winter we have a whist drive once a fortnight.'

'No dancing? No music?'

'People like whist drives best.'

'My mind is made up.' Mrs. Gumfreston spoke with decision. 'This village must have a proper party, and Henry and I will help with it. And it shall be a nice, friendly party, with lots of old-fashioned games to make it go, and old-fashioned dances. And we will encourage people to sing, and nobody will be stiff or stuck-up, and perhaps I might do a little performance on my accordion. That would be nice and proletarian, wouldn't it?'

'If you want a party,' said I, 'Mr. Chilmaid is the man to consult.'

'Mr. Chilmaid?'

'The undertaker. He always helps with the whist drives.'

Mrs. Gumfreston did not seem to relish the thought of co-operating with Mr. Chilmaid. But Henry was strongly in favour of it, and there was that in his manner which made me think there might be some truth in the rumour that he intended to succeed Sir Decimus Tottenham, our venerable Conservative M.P.

Mr. Chilmaid had no doubt at all on this point. A man in office himself, he could smell out, I suppose, intentions of office in others. Mr. Chilmaid is Chairman of our Parish Council; he is also People's Churchwarden and Treasurer of the Restoration Fund. Funeral pomps, of course, are his natural domain, and when we had an inquest in the village he acted as Master of Ceremonies and everyone admitted he did it in a masterly way.

Secure in office, and experienced in office, Mr. Chilmaid spoke with a certain condescension of Henry Gumfreston. 'I understand, Miss, I am given to intimate, as it were, that our newcomers are contemplating a little jollity. Well, I don't see why not.'

I said, duly and truly, that the success of the jollity would depend on Mr. Chilmaid's co-operation.

'I don't see why not,' repeated Mr. Chilmaid, kindly.

'Not that I fancy that me and Mr. Gumfreston would stand eye to eye politically. He won't prevent me from knowing my own mind and voting as I think fit. But that's no reason why we should cast cold water on any harmless scheme of theirs. I read my Bible, Miss. And while I am quite in agreement with rendering unto Caesar the things which are Caesar's, I am also bearing in mind a text about taking the fatted things of the Philistines.'

I said it was a very comfortable text. 'Let them do their part,' pronounced Mr. Chilmark. 'Variety is the salt of the earth; it would do us no harm to see their notion of suitable refreshments for man and beast. I suppose they'll do the refreshments?'

'Surely,' said I.

*

Mr Chilmaid went down the road asking some crows in a rhetorical manner why we should not let ourselves be livened up a bit. And when I next met Henry Gumfreston I remembered to mention to him that Mr. Chilmaid was a very influential man locally. 'An undertaker can do a great deal in a country district.' Henry nodded and gave me a grateful Conservative glance. As I had intended, he thought I might be a good influence with the influential Mr. Chilmaid, and as I had also intended, I was invited to be there when Mr. Chilmaid and the Gumfrestons consulted together.

I went early. There were whisky and sandwiches and a box of cigars, and we sat not in the drawing room but in Henry's study, a room less insistent upon class distinctions.

Presently Mr. Chilmaid was shown in. He had rendered unto Caesar to the extent of a very neat suit, preternaturally clean boots, and hair smoothed with a clamp brush. In one hand he held a tightly rolled piece of paper, with the other he accepted a pretty stiff glass of whisky.

While Mr. Chilmaid drank and glanced around at the furniture, the Gumfrestons explained their hopes. 'We want to feel that we are among friends. We want to be neighbourly.'

'I'm sure you feel as we do, Mr. Chilmaid, how essential it is to foregather,' said Mrs. Gumfreston.

'All work and no play, you know, Mr. Chilmaid,' said Henry.

'Yes, yes, exactly! Don't let us forget how to play.'

'The Rector very kindly suggested the Church Room. For our part, we would like to undertake the buffet.'

'Cakes and ale,' interposed Mrs. Gumfreston gleefully. Henry explained that this was a figure of speech. Actually, so he understood, the use of the Church Room precluded the – er – stronger liquors.

For ten minutes by the clock on the mantelpiece they explained to Mr. Chilmaid, becoming with every sentence more neighhourly, more overflowing, with good will and syllabubs. And Mr. Chilmaid drank his whisky and said 'Quite so' and 'Just so.'

'But you, Mr Chilmaid, are the person to advise us. We put ourselves in your hands.'

'I've been thinking.' Mr. Chilmaid set down his glass. 'This sort of festive occasion, if I'm rightly understanding you, is something that we in Thistleby-sub-Ham might call a novelty. A very pleasant novelty, I'm sure.' The Gumfrestons bowed in a dispensing sort of way. 'But one,' continued Mr. Chilmaid, 'that is new to us. Not that we have not had our social gatherings in the past. But they have not been mooted in this carefree al-fresco spirit; they have always had a purpose. At our whist drives, we play whist. At the children's Christmas party, we rally round for to watch the children. At the

Coronation festivities, there was the Coronation.'

'Mr Chilmaid,' said I, 'was marvellous at the Coronation.'

'I did my part, I hope,' said Mr. Chilmaid. 'But this here gathering,' he continued, 'is a problem. And at the very commencement and initiation we must launch it as such. We must begin by striking a decisive note.'

'Just what I feel myself,' declared Mrs. Gumfreston. 'Let us be without any formality, let us be spontaneously ourselves from the very start.'

Mr. Chilmaid raised the hand that held the judgment scroll. 'And I flatter myself I have here the very article. Something that will put us all at our ease.'

He unrolled a small catalogue and began to read aloud. '"Musical Seats."'

'Perfect!' said Mrs. Gumfreston. 'That dear old game! What could be better?'

'"Plain, Squeak, Cat, Canary, Donkey,"' continued Mr. Chilmaid. '"Unobserved place one of these little instruments upon a chair. When your friend takes a seat, watch him jump."'

'Ha-ha!' said Henry.

'Or this, now. "Jumping Sore Finger Joke. One of these bandages on your finger is sure to elicit many sympathising inquiries until, at a given moment, a spring is released, causing the bandage to fly a considerable distance, much to the consternation of those present." Then there's the Educated Mouse,' continued Mr. Chilmaid, shuffling the judgment scroll. 'Mice always amuse when there's ladies present. "Performs tricks you could hardly believe possible. You could call it your tame mouse and create a lot of merriment." Or there's the Picnic Spider. "One of these spiders, dropped into a glass of beer" – 'or lemonade,' said Mr. Chilmaid, mindful of the Church Room, '"will cause a lot of fun. When dry it will float, or it can be made to sink to the bottom, and there the drinker finds it, to the joy of the onlookers. The insects are made of black celluloid, perfectly clean and quite unobjectionable, except in appearance." Six for a shilling they are,' said Mr Chilmaid pensively, 'but that's not much to create the right festive feeling.'

'I think it's wonderfully cheap,' said Mrs. Gumfreston, 'but –'

'Then there's several sorts of Mirth-making Squirts – Cigarettes, and Buttonholes, and the Squirting Mirror. "Press the rim gently and Niagara Falls is let loose." Then there's Matchbox with Mouse. Mice again, always popular. "When a friend asks you for a loan of a match, hand him this trick box and when he opens it a hidden spring is released and it immediately gives forth a most alarming wailing cry. The stand slowly rises, and so will the hair on your visitor's head, in a concertina manner."' He beamed at us. '"Just press back into position,"' he concluded.

This was more or less what Henry, mindful of a constituency, was doing to Mrs. Gumfreston.

'A few items of this sort will make the world of difference to your Social. They'll lift it up,' said Mr. Chilmaid, 'onto a plane where all can meet, high and low alike.'

'Excellent, admirable,' said Henry. 'Well. Mr. Chilmaid, you've solved our difficulties. And I'm sure we can't do better than to leave the final choice to you.'

Mr. Chilmaid rose and extended the scroll.

'I'll leave the catalogue with you, Mr. Gumfreston, if you don't mind. I daresay you'd like to run through it yourself. It's a mine of unexpected surprises. Of course, they're not all so refined as those I've picked out. But they're all surprising.'

And with firm alacrity he picked up his cap and went away. I went away, too, soon after. It seemed to me that the Gumfrestons would like to be left alone with their dead.

MAIDEN NEWTON STORIES

THE FAMILY REVISTED

'Speaking for myself,' said Mrs. Bogle, 'I believe that this fuel-rationing scheme has been *planned*.'

The Canadian pilot who was spending his leave with the Killdews (Sir Ludovick and Lady Killdew had relatives in Canada) looked up, startled. He was a polite young man, so polite that he was now attending Mrs. Bogle's Sunday Salvage Afternoon and slicing metal butts off old cartridge cases with the rest of us in our Dorsetshire cottage, but stirring behind his politeness, as a deer stirs in a thicket, was a regretful conviction that the English are given over to cynicism and levity, and here was further proof of it. The rest of us, who know Mrs. Bogle better, understood that she was not speaking of Sir William Peveridge and the Secretary for Mines but of that somewhat jesuitical agency which she refers to as A Power for Good or Something Behind It All.

'Because of family life,' she continued. 'For think how it will draw us together! The whole family sitting round the fire, just like the old days, you know, when roasted crabs hiss in the bowl.'

'Sounds like cruelty to animals to me,' remarked Miss

Webb, the land girl, in an undertone.

In an undertone, Mrs. Bogle replied, 'No, Shakespeare.'

'Considered in that light,' said Mrs. Larpent, 'I call it belated. Of course, all plans are, except possibly layettes, and one's usually behindhand with them. How can fuel rationing revive family life when none of us has any family left? I can't believe that the hissing of a roasted crab, or the drowning of a parson's saw, either, come to that –'

'More Shakespeare,' Mrs. Bogle said, patting Miss Webb's knee soothingly.

'– is likely to lure Bill back from Iceland,' Mrs. Larpent continued, 'and Susan from Dover, and Isabel from Delhi, and the cook and housemaid from their factory. On the evenings when George isn't on A.R.P. and I'm not washing up in the canteen, I suppose we shall sit by the fire in total silence. But we do that anyway.' She whetted her knife on the carborundum and took up another cartridge case.

'I've never been able to understand why one talks of sitting *round* a fire,' observed Miss Pilgrim. 'At the best, one can only sit hemispherically.'

Speaking together, the Canadian said, 'Campfires,' and George Larpent said 'A survival from the great hall of the Middle Ages, when the fire was in the middle of the room and the smoke went out by the roof.'

'Really?' Mrs. Bogle tossed a handful of metal butts into the tray for waste cardboard. 'How interesting! And it does quite as well for an oil heater, doesn't it?'

Delighted with this further revelation of Something Behind It All, she continued with vigour, 'Besides, why need it be only one family? It might be two or three. Because, of course, what Mrs. Larpent says is perfectly true. None of us can call our families our own just now. But if we took turns spending the evening together – those of us that have evenings – we'd be keeping up the tradition of family life, wouldn't we? And think of the saving! Why don't we plan out our fireside rota here and now?'

There was an evasive pause, broken by Miss Pilgrim saying, 'People in the East burn cow dung, don't they?'

'We did ourselves last winter,' said Lady Killdew. 'It gives a splendid glow once it's kindled.'

'The glow,' said her husband, 'doesn't last.'

'Personally,' said Mrs. Larpent, 'I have been thinking deeply about the Venetian custom of wearing a farthingale and having a little charcoal brazier underneath it and a devoted follower to puff the brazier.'

'Oh, my dear, ' said Mrs. Bogle, 'I'm afraid you will be disappointed. It's almost impossible to get charcoal.'

'In the last war,' said Miss Webb, 'my mother one day was in a train, going from Ely to Scarborough, and it was winter, and the train wasn't heated. And then a man got in, and after he'd settled down he produced two lengths of rubber gas piping. And he put the top ends into his mouth, and tucked the bottom ends into his boots, and began to breathe. After a bit he noticed my mother noticing him, and he took out the two bits of piping and explained that he suffered terribly from cold feet, but by breathing into his boots he kept them quite cosy. He was a commercial traveller.'

'Well, that was practical,' said the Canadian.

'Not in this war!' cried Mrs. Bogle. 'Rubber, you know. Really, my plan is much the best. We must share our firesides. And I'm going to suggest that you all come to us every Monday and Thursday. We shall have our work, you know, and the wireless going, and perhaps Sir Ludovick would read aloud – one never seems to get much reading done in wartime. And we could talk over our various problems. There is always so much to talk about. Or would Tuesdays be better than Mondays? We could eat roast chestnuts, and –' Here she caught sight of Mr. Bogle approaching the table. 'Oh, Hereward! You're just in time to hear what we are planning for next winter, such a delightful scheme for saving fuel. We're all going to ...'

Meanwhile, Mr. Bogle, a large man moving with extraordnary stealthiness and speed, had attained his objective and was saying to the Canadian, 'You're the fellow I need. Just walk round the garden with me, will you? I want some advice about felling a few trees.'

'I don't know much about trees,' said the Canadian. 'My family lived in an apartment house.' But he rose obediently, for he was a very polite young man.

'Trees, Hereward?' Mrs. Bogle said. 'Surely you're not going to cut down any of my dear trees? Not the old crab apple - so mossy! *Not* the Spanish chestnut, for we are just planning how we shall roast chestnuts when we are all sitting together reviving the family!'

'Must grow more food,' said Mr. Bogle. 'Besides, logs may come in handy.'

'But, Hereward, both the kitchen stove and the sitting-room grate are too small for logs. We discovered that last winter, and you know how tired you got of carving them smaller.'

'The study grate isn't,' said he, and speedily, stealthily retired, taking the Canadian with him.

Mrs. Bogle flushed, and the sudden colour and the round-eyed, wondering-stare that watched the fading-away of another illusion made her look momentarily young again. And each one of us, I suppose, condemned the churlish Bogle and hoped that nice young Canadian, the soul of chivalry, might be kicking him outside in the shrubbery. There was a hush, but necessarily it had to be brief, and before Mrs. Bogle's predatory good intentions could revive, Lady Killdew said to Mrs. Larpent, 'Lucy, dear, there's one thing we *must* talk over before we go home. When are we having our Drive for Bones?'

ENGLAND; HOME AND BEAUTY

Above the mantelshelf was a portrait of an English poet of the nineteenth century, a minor poet but sufficiently immortal for visitors to the Sillery household to feel a slight shock on learning that John Sillery had also been mortal enough to be Mr. Sillery's grandfather. On the mantelshelf, which was long and wide, were most of the objects one expects to find on an English mantelshelf: some photographs, a stoneware jug holding pheasant tail feathers and another holding spills, a clock, a tobacco jar, a pair of Georgian silver candlesticks, a tortoiseshell box, and a bottle of dog medicine. In the grate, for it was summer, was an arrangement of fir cones, rather dusty. Before the hearth was an elderly Persian rug, and standing in the centre of the rug was a machine gun, mounted on its tripod and looking like a pet alligator.

In through the French windows came Mr. Sillery and Major Puncheon, both of the village Home Guard, and a dozen women. The women were of various ages and various degrees, but all of them were flushed and most of them were out of breath. For few women are accustomed to throwing overhand, and the Ladies' Shooting Class, having mastered the theory and practice of shooting with a rifle, had this afternoon gone on to a study of the hand grenade. Now twelve pairs of eyes were fixed beadily on the pet alligator.

'This,' said Mr. Sillery, 'is a machine gun. It is set up ready for action.'

Mrs. Dowling, whose neuritis was chronic, ceased to rub her fore-arm. She folded her arms and waited.

'And a very useful weapon, too,' added Major Puncheon.

'Which bit do you pull first?' inquired Mercy Hazard. She was flushed but not out of breath. The flush was partly pride. War had taken her three brothers, but not before they had seen to her education. Mercy's hand grenade had repeatedly gone over the bough of the walnut tree and, as a result, Mercy's hair was now hanging over her eyes. She pulled out a pocket comb and settled it, still gazing at the machine gun.

'We will begin with how to load it,' said. Mr. Sillery. 'This is the belt.' It passed from hand to hand, and Mrs. Dowling commented to Mrs. Damon that it looked rather like those old-fashioned papers of pins, and Mrs. Damon replied that she could do with one of them nowadays.

'The cartridges are dummies, of course. You all know a dummy by now.' The Ladies' Shooting Class assented. They stood in a half-circle round the hearthrug while Mr. Sillery and Major Puncheon explained and demonstrated.

'Do you all understand, ladies?'

'No. I don't.' Mrs. Goose spoke shamelessly and seriously. When Mr. Sillery renewed his explanation she listened with a critical expression, as a cat listens at a mousehole.

'Thank you. I've got it now.' She stood back a little, digesting her invisible mouse.

'Suppose the enemy don't bob up where you think they will,' said Mrs. Johnson. 'Do we have to lug the whole thing round to fire it in the other direction?' A faint tinge of scorn for male impracticality was in her voice. As Major Puncheon showed how the gun could be slewed around and raised or lowered on its stand, she smiled forgivingly. 'Very nice,' she said. 'Handy, isn't it, Mrs. Cullen?'

'I seem to have heard,' said Mrs. Canty, 'that machine guns get very hot. This one's water-cooled, you say. Suppose all the water gets used up, what then?'

'It would jam,' answered Major Puncheon. 'But that's been thought of. You've asked a very. sensible question, Mrs. Canty, but there's an answer ready for it.' He explained the cooling system.

'All the same, wouldn't it be a good plan to take a can of water along? We don't want any more trouble about running short of water, like we had last month with the fire practice.'

Mr. Sillery flushed. Mrs. Canty, having loosed her arrow, listened to Major Puncheon's further assurances and declared herself satisfied, for at heart, like most termagants, she was a magnanimous creature.

'I suppose it takes more strength than a rifle,' insinuated Mercy Hazard.

'Try for yourselves, ladies,' said Sillery.

One by one, the twelve ladies knelt down behind the

alligator, gravely, as at a shrine. Mrs. Cullen, the first to experiment, pulled the bolt with such determined vehemence that she fell over backward. No one smiled, and the others, calculating their pull as carefully as though it were some flavour going into a pudding, managed very adequately.

'Well' said Mrs. Johnson, the last to rise. 'Well, thank you very much, I'm sure. I daresay we could all manage that, at a pinch.' Which was one of the comforts, Mrs. Goose was murmuring to Miss Cutler, about being a woman. One had to turn one's hand to anything almost. One thing more or less didn't make much difference. Miss Cutler replied that, speaking for herself, she'd always had quite a liking for machinery. Once you got the hang of it, you must admit it was very reasonable. 'Though I'd be scared stiff if I had to drive a car,' she said. 'Think how you'd feel if you hurt someone accidentally.'

All this while, Mrs. Ben Hazard, Mercy's sister-in-law, had not said a word. She was a long, quiet young woman, moving with a kind of uncompleted elegance, as though she were really a nymph but imperfectly educated as such. Her silence would have surprised no one, but now that it was clear that she meant to say something, the others listened, waiting for her to speak.

'Go on, Phyllis,' whispered Mercy.

'Yes, I will. Mr. Sillery, Major Puncheon, there's talk going round that you ought to be told about, and I'm going to tell you. Mr. de Lacy Smith has been talking about our class. And he's been saying that we'd be more use learning to milk than learning to shoot. That's what he's been saying. And you ought to know about it, I reckon.'

'Actually, I do know about it,' said Henry Sillery mildly. 'And I think we can just leave it at that.'

The class did not feel quite that way.

'*Milk!*' exclaimed Mrs. Canty. 'All I can say is, I could milk Mr. de Lacy Smith off his legs. And so could you, Mrs. Damon, and Mrs. Goose, and Mrs. Cullen, and Mrs. Johnson. Milk, indeed! I'd like to see him finish off our old Crumple.'

'S'pose he'll want us to learn knitting next.'

'Crochet more likely! No one's ever got hurt with a crochet hook, I believe.'

'What I say is, why not learn milking too?' said Mrs. Cullen. 'Them of us as don't know already. You come round one afternoon, Mrs. Hazard, my dear. I'll soon teach you. There's a bit more knack to it than shooting, naturally cows being what they are. But you'll soon pick it up. And that'll spike his guns – if he's got any.'

Standing by the hearth with an expression gravely demure, Mr. Sillery looked uncommonly like his grandfather. Major Puncheon began dumping some wooden boxes on the table. 'Now, ladies, you must learn how to fill,' he said. 'Here are some empty belts, here is some live ammunition. The first thing to notice is …'

They moved toward the table, their fingers crisped, their faces mettled with emulation. Mrs. Damon glanced inside an empty box.

'The picture shows you the way to put the belt back,' explained Major Puncheon.

'Very sensible, too,' approved Mrs. Damon.

'This filling the belts is a job in which you ladies can be very helpful,' said Mr. Sillery. 'I'm afraid it's dull. But I

ENGLAND; HOME AND BEAUTY

do assure you it's useful.'

'And when the time comes,' said Mrs. Dowling, inserting cartridges with dexterity and thinking how like pills they were, 'shall we sit beside our men, doing it while they shoot them off?'

'Well, no. I'd prefer you to be doing it in a cellar. One doesn't want to waste lives.' Mrs. Dowling worked as neatly as before, but her face fell.

'Or ammunition,' added Miss Cutler. 'Suppose something came along and hit the box. It would all go off before it could be used.' Mrs. Dowling, reconciled to the cellar, agreed.

Undirected, they had settled themselves at the table before the boxes of cartridges as for a sewing party. Major Puncheon glanced at Mr. Sillery, who nodded. There had been no accidents to the Ladies' Shooting Class, but at times a certain possessiveness had shown itself, Mrs. Goose in particular becoming so attached to a rifle that she had developed a long-standing insomnia (first brought on, she said, by Goose's snores, which many a time had woken her up all of a tremble, thinking them bombs) and a conviction that a rifle handy beside the bed would be the only certain cure for it. Who knows what passions might not be aroused by an unchaperoned alligator? So the two men unshipped the machine gun and carried it away. The women worked on without comment, but a certain feeling of tension as he was leaving the room compelled Mr. Sillery to remark that he hoped they would find their job more interesting now that they had seen what a machine gun looked like. There was an absence of sentiment in their farewell glances which suggested that they did not assume they had seen the last of it.

After that he had to put away the goats. Returning, he paused on the lawn and cocked his ear. Though upholding his ladies, he still could not quite believe in them, and he wanted to know what they were like when left to themselves. They were womanly enough to be talking their heads off. Presently, Mrs. Cullen's voice emerged.

'When I was down in Devon helping my sister with her first baby,' she was saying, 'Bert – that's my brother-in-law – came back on compassionate leave. And he was telling us all about the Sten gun. Now, *that's* what I want to get ahold of. On the whole, it's more like a rifle, because you load it with a magazine. And in the handle there's a button marked 'A,' just like a telephone. When you press it one way . . .'

IT'S WHAT WE'RE HERE FOR

Mrs. Leopard slid her arms cautiously down the sleeves and wrapped the twenty-guinea coat (discarded by Lady Killdew) round her alley-cat pregnancy. Lucy Bogle and Kate Larpent, Women's Voluntary Services, Crockleford, Dorsetshire, gazed at the transformation they had wrought. A minute before, Mrs. Leopard's pinched face had been streaky with tears and she had sat twisting her hands in her lap. Now her face was merely pale, and her hands relaxed and fell asleep like kittens inside the fur cuffs.

Lucy Bogle turned to Kate Larpent and said warmly, 'It fits her beautifully, doesn't it?'

'It needs shortening,' said Kate Larpent. 'Are you good at sewing, Mrs. Leopard?'

Mrs. Leopard replied that she could do anything with a needle.

'A good wrap-over too,' added Lucy Bogle. 'Now forget all your troubles and go off and have a nice lunch at the British Restaurant. We've got a wonderful British Restaurant. And remember, there's nothing more for you to worry about. Lodgings, milk clinic – we'll get everything fixed for you. That's what we're here for.' Mrs. Leopard crossed the office, past empty jam pots and heaps of clothing and mounds of soldiers' socks. Kate Larpent looked after her.

'One moment,' she called. 'What about shoes? You mustn't go about with your heels all worn down. You might trip.'

Mrs. Leopard obediently sat down and removed a battered pump. 'Threes,' she said.

Murmuring something about those land-girl shoes, so nice and solid, Lucy Bogle buried herself in a closet. Mrs. Leopard took off a white cotton sock, rolled down a silk stocking, exposed an ankle. Kate Larpent turned slightly green and said in a controlled voice, 'That's bad.'

'Awful!' Mrs. Leopard agreed. 'Oh, they're awful. Sometimes I don't hardly know how to walk. That's why I gave up that job at the hospital. Those stone floors. I couldn't stand it, really.'

Emerging from the closet, Lucy Bogle dropped a pair of shoes with a crash which proclaimed their solidity.

'Good heavens!' she exclaimed.

'Your *poor* veins! You must go to the clinic this very afternoon.'

Mrs. Leopard pulled up her stocking, put on the sock, glanced briefly at the land-girl shoes, and replaced her pump.

'I'll ring up the doctor right away,' Lucy Bogle said. 'We've got a wonderful clinic.' Mrs. Leopard began to cry again. 'I was going to see the children this afternoon,' she said. 'I'd got a woolly for David and a little dress for Jean, and some chocolates off my ration.'

'But there's no bus to Long Twizzel today. And you can't possibly walk,' Lucy Bogle said.

Mrs. Leopard wept more bitterly. 'I worry about them so.'

IT'S WHAT WE'RE HERE FOR

'Of *course* you do,' said Lucy Bogle. 'But you needn't. You said yourself how well they looked when you saw them last week, and how much they'd grown since they've been there.'

'They're well enough,' Mrs. Leopard said, 'but their clothes are awful. And so dirty, too. They look like country children.' Her voice faded in despair.

'I daresay they're a little grubby,' Lucy Bogle said. 'But think how happy they are with Mrs. Welland. Even if she is rather a slattern, she's got a heart of gold.'

'Ever since they was evacuated,' said Mrs. Leopard, 'Mrs. Welland has been writing to say they needed this and that. Every week I've sent her money. Twenty-five shillings, and thirty shillings. Sent registered. I've stinted myself to send money to her. And she's had all my coupons, too. And when I went there, they were in rags.'

'We'll soon put that right,' said Lucy Bogle. 'That's what we're here for. This afternoon Mrs. Larpent will try to find some nice, warm clothes, for them – let me see, David's five and Jean's seven – and then you can take them out by the Saturday bus. The clinic will have given you your first injection by then, and you'll be feeling so much stronger.'

'I don't want to say anything against Mrs. Welland. I daresay she's kind at heart,' Mrs. Leopard continued. 'But I couldn't help speaking a bit sharp to her when I saw the state they were in. She didn't like it. I could see that. And now I'm afraid she's taking it out on the children.'

'Oh no!' Lucy Bogle cried. 'She's the kindest, most motherly woman!'

'They aren't her children,' said Mrs. Leopard. Her grief had communicated itself to the coat. It looked a second-hand coat now, shabby and down trodden.

After Mrs. Leopard had gone reluctantly off to the clinic, Lucy Bogle said to the silently tidying Kate Larpent, 'Say what you will, Kate, it's the child that matters.'

Together they re-read the investigator's note containing Mrs. Leopard's brief and lamentable history:

Confidential. Mrs. Leopard, Londoner, mother of two evacuated children at Mrs. Welland, Long Twizzel. Husband in the army, serving in Middle East. Pregnant. Baby due in December. Husband left England in February. Now lodging at 3 Vine Terrace, but landlady will not keep her after Sept. 19th. Receives army allowance but bad manager. Not wholly desirable character.

'How many children has Mrs. Welland – children of her own,' asked Kate Larpent.

'Six, I think, or seven. Why? That wouldn't make any difference. She's a born mother.'

'I daresay Mrs. Leopard's coupons would make a considerable difference,' said Kate Larpent, and tore up the note.

'Oh, Kate, what a wonderful *rock* you are! You always look at things in such an unprejudiced way!' Lucy Bogle exclaimed gratefully.

*

For two ladies looking at things in an unprejudiced way, Lucy Bogle and Kate Larpent got a good deal of emotional release out of managing everything for Mrs. Leopard. A pair of shoes, size three and practically new, was obtained from Lady Killdew, the only member of the local W.V.S. whose feet were not sensibly broad and untrammelled. Old Miss Ensor, so kind and so clean, was persuaded to make

IT'S WHAT WE'RE HERE FOR

over her parlour as a bed-sitting room, and the billeting authorities were persuaded to pay part of the rent. On the plea that flannelette was impossible for a winter baby, the standard layette was considerably embellished. On the hypothesis that morality is entirely a matter of self-respect, the storeroom was combed for undergarments which would help Mrs. Leopard to think well of herself. Lucy Bogle, replying to the torn-up note, assured the investigator that W.V.S. would gladly cope with Mrs. Leopard. It was what they were there for, rather than to judge anyone's private life. Kate Larpent, in the course of a telephone conversation with Mrs. Dimple, W.V.S. representative at Long Twizzel, lured Mrs. Dimple into some parochial reflections on painted London mothers coming down and unsettling evacuees and then bit her head off with the reply that painted London mothers were more hygienic than dirty country ones. And the report of the clinic doctor that Mrs. Leopard weighed ninety-four pounds, had five bad teeth, and needed special care was hailed by Lucy Bogle and Kate Larpent as a personal triumph.

*

Miss Ensor's bed-sitting room, Lady Killdew's shoes, and the morally stimulating underclothes, however, had to wait for more than a week before Mrs. Leopard reappeared. She had been to London, she explained, to see her mother. She looked more ill - and more dramatically fragile - than ever. It was distressing that on the heels of this quite plausible explanation Mrs. Dimple should visit the office to report that for the last week Mrs. Leopard had been frequenting the Rose and Crown at Long Twizzel and drinking sherry all day with a young civilian who had a dark complexion, wore pointed shoes, and left without paying the bill.

'I can only hope he is the father of the child,' she said.

Kate Larpent replied in her most unprejudiced tones, 'I have always understood that the father of a child born in wedlock is the child's father.'

Mrs. Leopard, returned from London, as she explained, was pleased with the shoes and glad to hear of Miss Ensor's bed-sitting room. But the under-clothes brought tears to her eyes. 'They're lovely, I'm sure. I bought a rayon dress for my Jean, just this colour, and sent it down for her birthday. But when I asked Mrs. Welland where it was, she said it never got there. You're so kind, you W.V.S. ladies, I don't suppose you'd think evil of anyone. But why are my David and my Jean in rags and the little Wellands all dressed up to the nines? If I could have a little place of my own, and all of us be together, I wouldn't worry so. But all my things, except a few forks, went in the blitz.'

'You mustn't worry now,' Lucy Bogle said to her. 'David and Jean have all the clothes they need. We made up a specially good parcel and Mrs. Dimple took it to Mrs. Welland herself.'

'I didn't see any new clothes,' Mrs. Leopard said. 'I went up every day but one last week, but that Mrs. Welland, she never said a word about new clothes, and both the children looked like something the cat brought in.' Persuaded to accept Miss Ensor's bed-sitting room in lieu of a little place all her own, Mrs. Leopard departed, clutching a hot-water bottle.

'Poor thing, how very incompetently she lies,' said Kate Larpent. 'One can't help feeling sorry for her.'

Lucy Bogle agreed. It was so hard on the baby that was coming, she added. And it was the baby, wasn't it, that they were concentrating on?

*

During the next week the life that was coming called for no attentions, but on the morning of October 6th Kate Larpent looked up from a sea of socks and observed that they might expect Mrs. Leopard at any moment.

'Oh! Oh, dear! Poor creature. Do you really expect her?' Lucy Bogle asked.

'On a cycle.'

'But, good heavens, Kate, she mustn't bicycle. It would be –'

Just then Lady Killdew came in with several recipies for green-tomato chutney collected in India. Most of the spices, as she observed, would have to be cut out, and one couldn't expect to find tamarinds, mangosteens, and okra in Dorset. But she didn't suppose anybody would know the difference if the W.V.S. fell back on apples. 'And by the way,' she added, 'talking of apples and the fall, do you think your poor little Mrs. What's-Her-Name could be persuaded to use a rather quieter pub? It distresses my husband to see me so constantly vanishing into the snug of the Pure Drop, especially as he paid for that coat.'

Lady Killdew was followed by Miss Ensor, who was very sorry, but would Mrs. Bogle find other lodgings for Mrs. Leopard, please? She would rather not say more, since every one of those Commandos was some mother's son and ready to die at any moment, God bless them.

When Mrs. Leopard came in, the subject of lodgings was troubling her also. The idea of a little place of her own, where she could have the children, and the forks, and a few little extras to make out with, had quite taken hold of her, she said. Sorry as she was to disappoint that dear old Miss

Ensor, she didn't feel she could settle anywhere but in a little place of her own. 'Speaking for myself, I'd put up with anything,' she said. 'You know what I'm like, you know I'm not one to ask for things. But it's my David and my Jean. I can't leave them there to be trampled on day and night. Their father worships those children, and if he knew the way that Mrs. Welland –'

The telephone rang and Kate Larpent answered it. It was Mrs. Dimple, who wished to report that she had taken those clothes up to the little Leopards and did the W.V.S. know that the police had come to Mrs. Welland's cottage about some woollen vests which Mrs. Leopard had sent? . . . No? Well, they had. Mrs. Welland had put the vests on the children only that morning, and when the police saw them, they said they were the ones the store had reported stolen and had taken them away there and then. Wasn't it dreadful?

'I'll inquire into it at once,' said Kate Larpent briskly. 'Of course it's atrocious. And quite unlawful. I suppose it was your local policeman? Thank you so much for reporting it.' She replaced the receiver as though she were putting a sword back into the scabbard. Inside the warm coat Mrs. Leopard was trembling convulsively. Her mouth hung open and her black eyes rolled like fruit that the wind will in a moment smite off the bough.

'I think I'll go off now and have a look for a little place.' She rose, and then uttered a cry of anguish and sat down again, clasping her belly.

Tea, a hot-water bottle, smelling salts from Lucy Bogle, a cigarette from Kate Larpent, sal volatile from the chemist's, and the gas fire turned on regardless of fuel restrictions presently turned Mrs. Leopard to a delicate

IT'S WHAT WE'RE HERE FOR

pink and got her mouth shut. Lucy Bogle rang up her doctor, who gave it as his opinion that Mrs. Leopard was clearly a case for the infirmary. But of course they must get her consent to it.

Both ladies were remarkably eloquent and persuasive about the beauties of the infirmary.

'It's nothing to be ashamed of, you know,' Kate Larpent said. 'All you'll want is a nice dressing gown, and we'll see to that. We've got such a specially nice infirmary here, not like an infirmary at all. And you'll have company, you know. No more lonely nights, no more trudging from shop to shop on those poor feet of yours.'

'They'll let you smoke, you know,' said Lucy Bogle.

'You'll be *so* happy there,' Kate Larpent continued. 'You'll be so comfortable you'll never want to come out.'

'Of course you can come out when you like,' Mrs. Bogle assured her.

'*We* shall look after the children,' Kate Larpent said. 'I shall go over to Long Twizzel tomorrow. Myself.'

Mrs. Leopard sat up, blazing. 'Don't you believe a word she says! I swear to you by the living God, Mrs. Bogle, that there Mrs. Welland is the awfullest liar that ever went about behind an apron.'

She finished off a cup of cold tea and promised to come back after lunch, when the W.V.S. would have arranged everything and the Relieving Officer would be there to meet her. Everything was arranged with guilty alacrity. Kate Larpent observed once or twice how admirable the Public Services were. Lucy Bogle said how it would have delighted Charles Dickens.

'By the way, Kate,' she asked, 'who was it that rang up while she was here. Wasn't there something about a policeman?'

'Policeman?' Kate Larpent appeared to be searching her memory. The telephone rang. She snatched off the reciever and handed it to Lucy Bogle. Lady Killdew became audible.

'Is that you, Lucy? I've got a message for you from your Mrs. What You-Call-Her. I recognized her – at least I recognized my coat – and I asked how she was. She asked me to tell you that she had found lodgings after all. She had met a friend and was going back with her by bus. To stay indefinitely.'

'Yes' said Lucy Bogle. 'How – how nice. How excellent. Did she say who the friend was?'

'Oh yes. She introduced me. A hearty, round-about sort of person. But of course you know her. She's the foster mother to Mrs. Panther's evacuee children. Why are you laughing, Lucy? Isn't she Panther?'

'No, dear – Leopard. Did she say anything else?'

'No, nothing in particular. Just the usual things. How she wouldn't know where she was without the W.V.S. And so on.'

TABBISH

It was always a shock to Flora Crutwell's friends when they learned that her unique and invaluable MacTavish was a widow that at some time or other the devoted Tabbish, as she had been known to the Crutwells since Flora was a baby, had gone off and got married, and that actually her surname was not MacTavish but Jones. Filling out the story, Miss Crutwell would explain that the marriage had been brief and comically disastrous and that poor old Tabbish had been overjoyed to return – after what was really no more than a night out – to the tranquillity of the Crutwell establishment. 'They fought like tigers. And Tabbish used to chase him round the house, making the sign of the cross over him with a red-hot poker.' Then the hearer would exclaim at this unexpected streak of ferocity in Tabbish and Flora would say that Tabbish was a Fiend when roused.

Unroused, Tabbish was a small, dusky, sad-faced old woman. Her pale, wide-set eyes, staring from dark circles, gave her a mad, kittenish expression, and like some bewitched kitten she darted about the house in endless pursuit of duties.

'Tabbish,' said Miss Crutwell, 'never sits down till midnight. Then she puts a shawl over her head, takes off her shoes and stockings, sits down with her feet in a bucket, and says the Rosary. My earliest memory is waking up in my cot and seeing Tabbish with her feet in a bucket.'

The English never tire of stories about eccentrics, which is odd, since all the English are eccentrics. Stories about Tabbish contributed substantially to Flora Crutwell's success as a diner-out, and the war embellished the repertory. There was, for instance, Tabbish's determination to recognize as a second cousin every kilted soldier she set eyes on, her stratagems to procure a baby's gas helmet to save the poor cat creature, her descent to the air-raid shelter in London carrying the cat creature, the plate basket, her umbrella, five jars of real marmalade, and two personal whisky bottles, one containing whisky and the other holy water. Air raids, said Miss Crutwell, were the breath of life to Tabbish, and it had really been quite a shame to drag her away from the city when the blitz at last made it necessary.

But country life, too, had its challenge for Tabbish. The Crutwells were a Civil Service family and Jones had been a boilermaker; not since her distant girlhood had Tabbish set foot off a pavement. But on the day of arrival in Twizzel Bishops, Tabbish had scarcely brewed a pot of tea for the furniture removers before she was out in the neglected garden, snatching at groundsel, saying that the potatoes must be got in before the new moon, and choosing a place for the henhouse. And when, after a decent interval, neighbours began to call on that new Miss Crutwell, the door would be opened by a breathless Tabbish wearing a gardener's apron, carpet slippers plastered with mud, and as often as not clasping a hen to her bosom.

*

What with Tabbish, anecdotes of Tabbish, and a great deal of natural bonhomie, Flora Crutwell was soon established

TABBISH

as a godsend to her new neighbours. It was so providential, too, that Tabbish was a septuagenarian. No call-up but Death was likely to affect her, and as house after house became servantless, Tabbish was loaned out to minister to the sick, to clean up after Red Cross whist drives, to polish silver, cut sandwiches, wash baby clothes, lend a hand with spring cleanings, tend incubators, and cook gala luncheons for visiting generals or husbands on leave. Very soon the whole *beau monde* of Twizzel Bishops was relying on Tabbish and partaking of Tabbish's clothing coupons.

'What way would I be needing the things?' inquired Tabbish. 'Haven't I the run of all Miss Flossie's old gear, and the creature as fickle with her coats and skirts as a film body?'

'It's really a kindness to Tabbish,' said Miss Crutwell to Caroline Edgeworth, who needed some of Tabbish's coupons for her daughter, who was getting married. 'She prefers to go about like a ragbag, and the only use she has for a stocking is to hide money in. Heaven knows how much she's got put away. But I do know she's much better off than I am, and when my brother Cedric had to go off at a moment's notice to Syria she forked out fifty pound notes without batting an eyelid, let alone her National Savings and what the missionaries get out of her. All I ask is that you leave a coupon or two for me, unless you want me to dance at Bibby's wedding in a pair of galoshes.'

*

Bibby Edgeworth's wedding was followed, in the early summer of 1943, by the wedding of Bibby's younger sister, Sackie.

'Mother says she positively can't face it without your angel Tabbish,' remarked the bride-to-be. 'But after this she vows and swears she won't borrow her again till Dad's funeral.'

'That's all right, my child. You shall have her. For a week, if you like, and I will live on canteen buns meanwhile. I'll tell her.'

'Well as a matter of fact, I was thinking of asking her myself, gracefully concealed in the form of an invitation, you know.'

'Aha! And touch her for a coupon or two at the same time. Well, go with my blessing. But don't you dare to take them all! Tabbish's coupons are dearer to me than my life.'

A few minutes later Miss Edgeworth reappeared, looking sullen.

'She says she hasn't got any left.'

'The old squanderbug!' exclaimed Miss Crutwell blithely. 'Still, it's your own fault, Sackie, for marrying into the Navy. If you'd married something in a kilt, Tabbish would have given you enough for a trousseau.'

*

That evening, when Tabbish brought in the bedtime cup of tea and said that the hot-water bottle was in Miss Flossie's bed and would there be anything more just now, Flora looked up and remarked, 'I'm thankful you saved our last coupons from that raiding little Sackie Edgeworth. As it is, I don't know how we shall make out till the next lot.'

'I was thinking,' said Tabbish, and paused.

After a while Flora said, 'What about? Don't say it's towels. I'm sure we've got enough towels.'

'I was thinking, Miss Flossie, that maybe you'd be sparing me to go up to London for a day. Or two, maybe.'

'Oh, Lord! Well, heaven knows you deserve it. What for, Tabbish?'

'The United Nations, Miss Flossie.'

'The what? Oh, yes, that do! Tabbish, you're nothing

more or less than an old pleasure-seeker.'

'Whiles, I weary for a procession,' said Tabbish.

'I know, I know! A procession with bagpipes, and the pipe major no other one than your Auntie Bell's third boy's daughter's stepbrother-in-law. And you'll faint your way into the front row, and wave, and cry your eyes out. Isn't that it?'

'And I was thinking, too, that maybe I'd go up the day earlier and buy myself a decent-like pair of shoes. I've got the five wee coupons left.'

'Nonsense, nonsense ! I'll lend you a pair of mine. I'll lend you my new ones.'

'If I should be meeting any of my own folk, I'd prefer to be standing on shoes of my own,' said Tabbish.

Civil Service families have their fighting traditions, and once roused to a sense of her danger, Flora Crutwell put up a brisk defence. Tabbish's feeling about shoes was quite natural, of course, she said, but it was also ridiculous, pig-headed, and impracticable, for the shoes one bought nowadays were just not worth buying; they wore out immediately. It was unpatriotic, too. All the leather in the country was needed for Army boots. Tabbish might as well snatch the boots from one of her kilted cousins as buy herself a pair of shoes that she would wear for one day and never again. It was also unpatriotic, come to that, to make the trip to London. Didn't Tabbish remember the poster in the railway booking office saying 'Is Your Journey Really Necessary?' How would she feel when that stared her in the face? Travelling was frightful anyway. Tabbish would have to stand the whole way there and the whole way back, she would be worn out, far too tired to enjoy herself. It would be bound to rain, too — it always rained for processions – and getting wet through would mean bronchitis, and at Tabbish's age bronchitis was no joke. She, Flora Crutwell, would never be able to forgive herself if Tabbish got bronchitis. And all this for five minutes – it certainly wouldn't be more – of pipe music and white-spatted marching.

'Honestly, Tabbish, I've a good mind to forbid you going.'

'You'll not do that,' said Tabbish. 'You'll not dare affront me while I'm getting more coupons in the autumn.' There was no anger in the words; only a profound, melancholy disapproval sighed through them, like a wind sighing through fir trees.

Defeated and left to herself, Flora Crutwell drank up her cold tea and walked about the room, straightening books and tweaking cushions. It was a distinguished room – the shelves were full of contemporary books, some of them even inscribed by their authors, and reproductions of modern paintings hung on the walls – but for all that she felt herself back in the nursery stamping to and fro between the battered rocking horse and the tall fender, eyed hatefully by the good little girls and trusty terriers of the *Pear's Annual* pictures on the nursery walls. Tabbish was cross with her – horrible, crosspatch old Tabbish! She was angry and might even go away. Life without Tabbish, Miss Crutwell without her unique and invaluable MacTavish . . . She was beaten, and knew it.

AN UNIMPORTANT CASE

It was a January afternoon, still and sunless. The sky was covered with a web of grey cloud, the fields showed either the whity-brown of the chalk soil where the plough had bared it or the grizzled tint of winter grass. One had only to look at the telegraph poles along the high-road to know that one was in an unimportant part of England, and that the road was of no great importance either.

Along this road a man and a girl were walking. The man was bareheaded, he carried a suitcase. The suitcase was battered, and his raincoat was shabby, though he had belted it in round the waist, and this gave it a certain air of swagger. He walked with a slow upspringing stride, the gait of someone who walks as a matter of course and without any interest in the act of walking. He was small and lightly built, but he carried the suitcase easily enough. He was young, but the crown of his bare head was already going a little bald.

The girl was plump. Her coat had cuffs and collar made of rabbit imitating some more expensive fur. She seemed to be walking with much more energy than the man, taking rapid decisive steps and swinging her arms. But it was obvious that her town-bred gait would flag long before his.

It was a silent day, and they walked in silence. When a car

went by the girl fell behind, drawing close to the roadside, and then hurried forward to walk by the man's side again. Now, at a turn of the road, she spoke.

'Look at those trees, Alan. Whatever are they?

'Some sort of willow.'

Where the road dipped down to a small stream a group of sallows rose out of the pinched grey landscape. The leafless boughs were a brilliant astonishing tint of flame-colour.

'Don't they look like a fire?'

'They go that colour at this time of year,' he answered.

'They *do* look lovely. Just like a beautiful big fire that someone's lit up out of doors.'

Presently he asked her if she was feeling cold. She shook her head, staring at the trees.

A car approached, and again she hurried to the side of the road. But this time she remained behind, loitering, staring at the trees as though she would fill her eyes with them.

'Alan! Stop a minute, do! I *do* believe . . . Yes, there is! Look, there's a house there, in among them. And it's empty!'

It was a bungalow, small and new. But the windows were broken and the track leading off from the road was overgrown with brambles.

'It's empty,' she repeated. 'Alan, let's have a look.'

Already she had turned down the disused track, her heels twisting in the ruts. He glanced this way and that along the road. There was no one in sight, and he followed her.

All round the house were the willows, screening it from the road. He lifted the broken gate, and they passed into the little enclosure, that must have been meant for a garden though now only the sagging wire-net fence distinguished the grass within from the grass without. He took her arm and kissed her.

AN UNIMPORTANT CASE

'Shall we live here, Ivy?'

'Oh, Alan!'

Her voice expressed such profound feeling that he dropped her arm, and stood holding the suitcase and looking at her with an expression almost of enmity. But in a moment she was gay once more, and exclaiming;

'What a love of a little green water-butt!'

She went up to the broken window and looked in.

'What's it like inside?'

There was no answer. Only when he was beside her, staring in at the dusky room, did she whisper;

'It smells as though they'd had a fire in here.'

'Just what they have had. It's been burned out.'

Still pungent, the smell of burning dwelt in the empty room, and the gay paper on the walls was blackened with smoke.

They walked round to the back of the house. Here the stale smell of burning was stronger, and the charred woodwork and broken roof showed where the fire had burned its worst. A plank had been wedged against the door to secure it, but he knocked it aside and together they entered. Neither spoke, and it was as though they had walked into a church, for their demeanour was awed and constrained, and their feet knocked loudly on the echoing floors. Only one room was tolerably intact, with a ceiling, and the colour of the paint and the pattern of the wall-paper still discernible.

'Hadn't they done it up pretty, too?' said Ivy compassionately.

They stood looking out of the broken window at the willows burning under the grey sky.

'Do you know what I'd like to do? Light a fire, and have a cup of tea.'

With a grave face he opened the door, and called into the desolation of the back of the house,

'Parker! Bring in the afternoon tea. And don't forget to polish the silver tea-pot.'

'No, but I mean it, Alan. I *would* like a cup of tea. Here, give me that suitcase.'

She rummaged in it, and presently fetched out a little spirit lamp and a kettle, a tea-infuser, tea screwed up in one piece of paper and sugar in another, and a bakelite mug.

'There! All we want's a drop of water from the water butt. You can drink rain-water if you boil it.'

'Good Lord, Ivy, fancy you bringing all that along.'

She blushed.

'I thought it might come in useful, us being on the road. I thought we might want a picnic, sometime. And anyhow, I had to bring along my spirit lamp because of curling my hair.'

'Gipsy Ivy,' he said. 'You'd look pretty with gold earrings and one of those gipsy hats with ostrich feathers. You look pretty anyhow, my darling.'

'Get busy with that kettle,' she replied.

Left to herself, she dusted a piece of the floor and arranged the lamp and the mug and the infuser, her eyes darkened with brooding pleasure. This was romance, this was what she had foreseen when she ran away to go with Alan. She sat back on her heels, and sighed with contentment. A soft rustle from the corner of the room answered her sigh. It came from a heap of willow-leaves, which had blown in at the broken window and lay drifted in a corner of the room. The rising wind that wagged the bare stems outside stirred them where they lay. They were thick, they were heaped up like a bed.

'Pardon the absence of milk,' she said grandly. They sat

down on the suitcase and shared the strong sweet tea from the bakelite mug.

'Alan. I've got another idea now. Suppose we stay the night here? We could get some sticks, and light a proper fire to warm ourselves.'

He shook his head.

'Someone might see the smoke, and then we'd be copped for trespassing.'

'Never mind. We'll just go to bed early, then.'

'Bed?'

'Look at that lovely great heap of leaves. Soft as a featherbed.'

'You wouldn't like it, Ivy darling. You've never slept on a floor, you don't know how hard it is, and how cold. Better push on.'

'I *would* like it, I would. I'd like it better than sleeping in places where they look at us so paltry and suspicious. And if we slept here, there'd be nothing to pay.'

'There wasn't much to pay last night.'

She was silent. That morning they had gone from their lodging without paying the bill. It was her first taste of dishonesty, and though she laughed at the time, and told Alan about the time when she went to the cinema in her mistress's stockings, she was uneasy at heart. He saw her face cloud, and knew why.

'She was a horrible woman, anyway,' he said.

It was seven years since he had been regularly employed. Looking for work had turned imperceptibly into tramping the roads; mates had been friendly and girls kind, and after a shallow fashion he had been contented with his lot. Then, amid the dreariness of a holiday resort in winter, Ivy had come to the door holding out a clumsy sandwich, and suddenly her round bright eyes had filled with tears of pity and she had slammed the door in his face to stand weeping behind it – he had heard her through the door, and her steadfast fibbing replies to her employer's cross-questionings about young men and cold meat. Since that day the road had no purpose except as leading to a job; and now he had Ivy with him, and the job was still to seek. But to her the road was romance, and to be footsore with walking through a winter's day a proud adventure after being footsore with trudging all day up and down the stairs of a provincial villa. Let her have her thrill while it lasted, he thought, his gipsy Ivy.

After dusk he went out and collected fallen willow-leaves in his raincoat. Each time that he came in with a fresh load it was as though he brought a sighing summer with him. They had half a loaf and a couple of saveloys, these made their supper; and with his raincoat beneath them and her coat above them they fell asleep in the rustling willow-leaf bed.

In the morning she began to pack the suitcase.

'Even when we have a little place of our own, Alan, I will always remember this house and how happy we were.'

'Would you like to stop on for a bit?'

She looked up, astonished. The willow leaves drifted around her, for now a strong wind was blowing, and they swirled about the room in the eddying draught.

'Stop on?'

'I'm thinking we might as well. The wind's gone round to the north, we shall have snow if I'm not much mistaken. Might as well stay where we are for a bit.'

'And be snowed up?' Her voice was delighted 'Oh, Alan! Would you really like to?'

'As a matter of fact, I shouldn't be sorry. I'm not feeling

too grand, this morning.'

He had heartburn, and felt dizzy, he said. She brewed him some more tea. After a while he asked her to walk back to the village to buy a loaf, and some cold meat, and some more tea.

'Go now, before the wind gets worse, there's a good girl.' As she was leaving the house he called after her,' Remember that tea.'

When she returned he was lying under the willows at the back of the house with his face to the ground, writhing, and clutching at the grasses.

'Is that you, Ivy girl? Go along in. I'll come in a minute. But I've got to be sick.'

She fell on her knees beside him, spilling the parcels. He raised up a face livid with agony, and said in a loud inattentive voice,

'Don't you hear what I say? Get along in, I'll come presently.'

She went indoors and began to arrange her provisions along the window-sill, staring at the bright twisting flames of the willows outside. After a while she saw that something was volleying through the broken panes, and spotting the loaf and the parcel of cold meat. It was snow. The food would be ruined if she left it there. As though the pound loaf and the four ounces of ham were leaden weights she moved them out of the way. The willow leaves whirled about the floor. She tried to heap them up into a bed again, for Alan would want to lie down when he came back.

Alan was lying in the snow, being sick. With a sob of panic she fled out of the house.

At first, amid the whirling snowflakes, she could not find him. He had crawled farther under the trees; he lay quite still, his face was pinched and grey.

'O Lord, I've had such a doing.'

'A cup of tea will do you good. Are you better now, Alan?'

'Such cramps!'

'A cup of tea's what you want. Come in, my darling.' He got up, groaning, and was immediately bent double with pain. Somehow she hauled him into the house and he lay on the leaves, sipping tea and shuddering.

'Don't you suppose you're going to cover me with that coat of yours,' he said after a while. 'No, I won't have it. O Ivy, I don't like to play you up like this.'

'Try to get off to sleep now,' she said.

She sat watching him. Cars went by along the road, going so fast that no one in them would guess there was a house among the willows. She wondered what time it was. The whirling snow seemed to obliterate time. At intervals Alan got up, groaning, and went out to be sick, and came back shaking and shivering. After the fourth bout he did not protest when she spread her coat over him as well as his own. Sometimes she made him tea. There was a moment when she realised that she herself was famishingly hungry, and she ate the loaf, almost without knowing it. Fewer cars went by now. She looked out of the window and saw one pass with its headlights on, sallow in the haggard dusk of snow. Night was coming.

'Alan! Alan!'

He stirred, but did not open his eyes.

'I am going to the shop. I shall be back in half an hour.'

He nodded drowsily. He doesn't understand, she thought. Out of the far world where he was lying he murmured:

'Be careful with those cars.'

The snow clogged her steps, it was difficult to run. She

met a woman who said that the doctor lived at Enley.

'Where's Enley?'

'About two miles along the road.'

She ran on. The woman hurried after her.

'You're going the wrong way for Enley, my girl. Enley's back-along.'

She turned about, and the wind met her. Enley, and the doctor, must be beyond the bungalow, then. She began to wonder if she should stop and have a look at Alan before she went on. Better not, it might torment him to see her, and then to see her go out again. But she would look through the window, there was still daylight enough for that.

Where the track turned off there was still daylight enough for her to see deep footmarks in the snow, large and new beside the scuffling print of her own tread. A man's track. Suppose some tramp, some awful tramp, had gone into the bungalow for shelter. Suppose he had attacked Alan, killed him? . . .

After the glimmering white dusk the darkness of the house was like a blow. The blow of darkness was followed by a stab of light. The beam from an electric torch turned from Alan to her, and a voice said:

'Is this your young man?'

Though he spoke kindly, he was a policeman. So instantly she began to lie, explaining that Alan had been taken ill on the road, that they had come into the bungalow for shelter that they had only been there for a few hours. The beam of light from his torch dwelt for a moment on her, then flicked onward to the suitcase, to the loaf, to the kettle, to Alan lying huddled under the coats with his feet sticking out. He was lying so still that if it had not been for his heavy snoring breaths she would have thought he was dead.

'He can't stay here, you know. I'll get on my bike and telephone. It'll have to be the ambulance.'

'Oh God, is he as bad as that?'

He was going. She called out;

'You'll come back, won't you?'

For now it seemed to her that she could not bear to be left alone in this desolate house that was so icy cold and smelled of stale burning, hearing the willow-leaves drifting about the floor and the wind rumbling in the chimney. She knelt down by Alan, rearranging the coats, patting him, and trying to read his face in the bleak dusk that echoed the pallid snow-covered landscape outside. He is asleep, she thought. I must not wake him. And a moment after her anxiety became too strong for her, and she tried to rouse him. He did not answer. She touched his cheek. And at the contact with her cold hand he flinched, and burrowed his face into the leaves with a complaining moan. Appalled at having hurt him she started back. But presently her body's need mastered her, and whimpering and suppliant with cold she squirmed herself under the coverings and lay beside him. He did not stir.

The policeman came back. So substantial and well clothed, he seemed to warm the room by entering it. Ivy had never supposed that she could be glad to see a policeman, but now in her relief she began to chatter, to apologise that there was nothing for him to sit on, to offer a cigarette.

'Thank you, but I don't smoke,' he said. His voice sounded gloomy and constrained. Presently he said:

'You'd better start packing your traps.'

While she packed he stood by the window fidgeting with a notebook, and every now and then he drew a slow considering breath, and held it, as though he were about to speak, and then puffed it out again.

AN UNIMPORTANT CASE

'Your name, please?'

'Ivy Carter.'

'And is this man called Alan Young?'

'Yes, sir.'

'And did you both spend Tuesday night at Mrs. Hamble's, 7, Pond Street, Gillinghurst?

'Yes. We're together,' she answered defiantly.

'Well, I'm sorry to tell you that your young man's wanted on a charge of fraud. And you will be wanted as a witness. And it's my duty to take you both in charge.'

She was mute, and his first sensation was one of relief that she should take it so quietly. But after a while he began to wish for any lamentation that might break the silence, for it was as though he had spoken among shadows.

It had been a neat piece of work on his part, or rather, since he was not thinking of them, for it seemed likely that by now the pair would be a day's journey hence, it had been a good piece of observation. No. To be quite honest, it had been an accident. It had been the colour of those trees, burning sombrely amid the snow, that had caught his eye. He had looked at them, thinking of the bright fire that awaited him at home, and of how glad he would be to get into slippers, and light a pipe, and exchange the wide bleak landscape for the curtained room, small and bright as a jewel. And then he had noticed the footprints along the track, and would have supposed them to be the track of some village child, for they were small, if it had not been for the separate indentation that betokened a woman's shoes with high heels. That's what it is to have quick eyes, and training.

The man called out in a high frightened voice:

'Ivy, Ivy Where are you?'

'It's all right, darling, it's all right. I'm here.'

'Oh, Ivy, I think it's coming on again. Ivy, don't go.'

'Of course I won't go.'

He tossed among the rustling leaves, and under cover of the sound the policeman moved gently into a dark corner. Training. That was it, training. He began to rehearse the evidence he would speak. 'On Thursday the 27th of January, shortly after 5 p.m. I was proceeding' ... A voice from the Bench struck into his imagined words. 'Speak up, can't you?' A difficult gentleman, Mr. Courthope, and likely to be none too merciful with this pair, for of all things he resented most the unemployed, and for the last ten years his wrath against them had been growing. He must remember to speak up, to speak as one is trained to do. Training. That was it. Duty.

'Ivy, I thought you'd gone. You won't go, will you?'

'Never, my darling. Nothing shan't part us.'

Headlights reared up above the hill. They neared, they slowed to a standstill. The willow boughs stood out, black as charcoal, they cast the pattern of a net on the snow. With a sigh, with a feeling of profound embarrassment, the policeman stepped forward.

THE MOTHERS

The children of England get their primary schooling either in national schools or church schools. Only a blind man could remain unaware that the school at Long Twizzel was a church school – and he, if he got inside it, would have known by the smell, which was vaulted, mouldy, and gothic. It was a very small building with an inordinately high-pitched roof. Over the peaked porch was engraved in curly figures, 1859. Inside, high above the chimney-piece and the rusty stove-chimney, was a faded watercolour portrait of a young man in Hussar's uniform, and under the portrait was painted in letters equally curly: D. C. H. 1833-1855. *Christi in pauperibus suis.*

For years the watercolour Hussar had been no more than a variant of the school walls, like the lancet windows, and the map of the world with British possessions coloured pink. The windows were cobwebbed, the map was flyblown, the young man was faded. They were all educational, all of a piece. But in September 1939 Mrs. Pitcher began to tell the class how the young man, full of virtue and gallantry, had died for his country fighting the Russians, that he was young Mr. Dewhurst Charles Bunter, and that the sorrowing Hunter family had built the school in his memory. This revived his colours. Every child in the village knew Sir Charles and Lady Hunter, who came to Long Twizzel every autumn and shot partridges – though with no perceptible sorrow for a soldier son.

Mrs. Pitcher herself was another demonstration that the school was a church school. She was a middle-aged woman with an anxious contentious face and a bilious complexion. Every line of her body, every note in her voice, registered superiority and how painfully superiority is attained and preserved. She had a crippled husband, who cleaned the church. It was also rumoured that he cleaned for Mrs. Pitcher, and cooked their midday dinner – a fact, if true, equally disgraceful to himself and to his wife.

To be so superior, to have so many sick headaches and a husband who cooked for her, added to Mrs. Pitcher's statutory unpopularity as village school-mistress. Mrs. Mutley, Mrs. Bing, Mrs. Alsop, and Mrs. Bert Hawkins – whose maternity provided a steady quota of the Long Twizzel school attendance – were always on the look-out for further reasons to dislike Mrs. Pitcher. Now, to her affectedly small consumption of beef sausages, her stuck-up airs at Holy Communion, her nonsense about birds-nesting, and her old rain-proof, the war added a series of rousing new grievances. War was no sooner declared than Mrs. Pitcher started putting ideas into the children's heads. She told them about the bombing of Warsaw, and the shooting of Polish civilians. She told them of hospitals burning and children starving. She told them about submarines and food supplies, and made them wear their gas-masks for half an hour every Monday. When she

THE MOTHERS

started to tell them about German concentration camps and the persecution of the Jews it was felt that these outrages had gone far enough. A deputation of mothers, sullenly mumbling, called upon Canon Dimple, and Canon Dimple called upon Mrs. Pitcher.

'One must remember, Mrs. Pitcher, that these are simple country children. They are not likely to come in contact with these horrors.'

'That is why I thought they ought to hear about them. If we are in the war, they should know it.'

'Surely, surely! Of course we must all take our part in the struggle. For instance, there are the special prayers. You use them, do you not?'

'Every morning.'

'Excellent, excellent! Then I have been thinking that it would be good to set up a School National Savings effort. *That* is a campaign in which we can all share.'

'Several of the children are buying savings stamps already. But do you think that's enough?'

'Well, every little helps. And later on, no doubt, there will be other openings for service. The farmers, for instance, will certainly need occasional labour. And for the rest I venture to suggest that it will be wisest to concentrate on the British effort. After all, Mrs. Pitcher, we are British first and foremost. Well, I suppose we must soon be thinking about Christmas decorations. *Good* afternoon, Mrs. Pitcher.'

Concentrating on the British effort, Mrs. Pitcher soon afforded the village mothers another reason for dislike. She had two sons in the army, and both were non commissioned officers.

'My son here and my son there, and sticking up bits from picture papers all over the place,' said Mrs. Mutley. 'I suppose she thinks she owns the war.'

Pictures of Libya, pictures of India. In the autumn of 1941 the pictures of India were supplemented by pictures of Singapore. In January 1942 the pictures of Singapore had to be removed and their place filled by pictures of the United States – for, as Canon Dimple remarked, we are English-speaking first and foremost. The shadow of death is always a reconciler, and for some weeks after the fall of Singapore every mother in Long Twizzel, overlooking the past, was sedulous to enquire of Mrs. Pitcher if she had heard anything about Sergeant Pitcher yet, if she expected to hear soon, if the strain was not terrible, and if it was not too awful to think of anyone being taken prisoner by those torturing little Japs; and in return Mrs. Pitcher, more than ever ghastly with superiority and sick headaches, would speak with a rigid elegance about patriotism, sacrifice, and a willing endurance.

By the spring, of course, she was as briskly loathed as ever. Indeed, Mrs. Pitcher was always particularly unpopular in spring because of Nature Study.

In spring it is the duty of every village school-mistress to foster a love of nature and kindness to animals. While encouraging the children to gather wild flowers for the Easter church decorations she must remind them not to uproot primroses and violets, or tear up bluebells, or break off boughs from fruit trees, or trespass into the Manor woods after daffodils. In spring too she must avail herself of young lambs and birds' nests as the ideal means of approach to a reverent understanding of biological processes, and also prevent the children from stealing birds' eggs, cutting the wings off fledglings, and throwing stones at valuable pedigree calves. For years Mrs. Pitcher had hated spring. In spring her headaches were at their worst. In spring her chilblains broke. In spring the cuckoo came, and sang on and on, shouting her down as she led the school prayers and the recitations of the multiplication tables and 'The Lake Isle of Innisfree.' In spring the children were nothing but little nuisances; and the lambs and the birds were nothing but nuisances either – always provoking to sin, and not able to look after themselves.

In the spring of 1942 Mrs. Pitcher realised with horror that a pair of swallows had chosen to build in the peaked porch.

'Shoo, shoo !' she exclaimed, waving her umbrella. 'Don't you build here, you silly creature!'

The mother swallow flashed past her, no more to be turned aside than a bullet.

There was nothing for it. On the morrow Mrs. Pitcher gave the children a lesson on the swallow. The swallow, she said, is a migrant. Every spring swallows come to England in order to have their little ones, flying all the way from Africa, led by the most wonderful instinct (*and more fools they*). All through the summer we can see them catching flies, horrid little stinging flies, in order to feed their babies. And in autumn, warned by an instinct equally wonderful that there would be no more flies, they gather their young ones and fly back to Africa (*if they have survived to do it*).

'Africa's where the fighting is,' said Mona Mutley. 'I expects lots of swallows get killed there now, don't they, teacher?'

The swallow, with young ones to feed, catches more than twice its own weight of flies in a day, continued Mrs. Pitcher. Every one loves the swallow, so clever, so harmless, and so useful, catching the flies that would otherwise become such a nuisance. Such wonderful little birds have had many beautiful poems written about them.

'Your other son's in Africa, isn't he, teacher?' said Ruby Bing.

On no account was the swallows' nest in the porch to be touched. Any child climbing up to finger it, or daring to steal one of the eggs, would get the cane. For they must all be proud that a mother swallow had chosen to build on the school, actually inside the porch. Next year the swallows, if not molested, would come again. And perhaps by then, said Mrs. Pitcher, they will have seen a great British victory in Libya, and we shall be at peace.

The swallows' nest became an obsession with Mrs. Pitcher. If the birds had been building in her stomach she could not have been more painfully aware of them. Above the yawns and the giggles and the scuffling feet and the droning voices of the class she heard the whirr of the swallows' flight and their twittered conversations. Steadfastly glaring at Bobbie Mutley or Irene Alsop she still saw their shadows flash past the window, momentarily flicking aside the steady beat of the sun. The plastered nest, the beam splashed with their droppings, the fragments of down that stuck to it – she knew it as well as her own parlour. And hearing the first squawks of the fledglings she began to sweat and tremble. Still the nest was untouched. She could not make out why. She had not noticed that the children realised - better than she, maybe - how jealously she watched over the nest in the porch, and so found it more convenient to go birds' nesting along the hedges.

One wet Saturday she said to her husband that she reckoned the young swallows would be flying by midsummer. He looked up from his own preoccupation, and said:

'Looks like Tobruk will have fallen before midsummer, too. Why don't you think about your own flesh and blood for a change, instead of those bloody birds?'

His expression was so haggard and furious that she turned away and began to busy herself with the window geraniums. Suddenly, with a sort of bark she rushed out of the room.

In the school-porch was Kenneth Fearon. Why him? she thought; he had always seemed a negligible creature, pale and dull and born to be bullied. He had thrown a rope over the beam and noosed it, and now was swarming up the rope. She caught him by the collar and swung him down.

'Now what are you up to? Are you after those swallows?'

He was silent, staring at the ground.

'Are you after those swallows, I say?'

He drooped before her. With the tip of a pale tongue he moistened his pale lips.

'Why can't you leave them alone? Don't you know it's wrong to take birds from the nest? Why, it's cruel! Think of the poor mother!'

Still he was silent.

'Do you hear what I say?'

He wriggled, and wrenched himself free. Scrabbling up

handfuls of pebbles he began to stone the nest.

'I hate them! I hate them! I wish I had a gun, I'd shoot the lot. No, I wouldn't! I'd catch them and wring their heads off.'

The porch was full of his screams, his stampings, the noise of pebbles spattering against the beam. Suddenly the swallow flew in. Straight as a bullet she aimed herself at the nest, folded her wings, disappeared. A moment later the doorway was darkened by the shape of Mrs. Fearon, panting violently.

'What are you doing to my Ken? I could hear him half across the village?'

'I shall have more to do to Kenneth,' replied Mrs. Pitcher. 'He is a very naughty boy.'

'If you dare lay a finger on him. . . . Look at his clean collar, all pulled about. Never you mind *her*, Ken. Come along with me, and shut up, do!'

'I hate you all!' he exclaimed, and escaping between them ran down the street.

The swallow flew out again, to hunt more food. The two women, their anger dashed by embarrassment and a kind of dismay, stood watching its flight, each glad to have an excuse not to look at each other. Smoothing back her wet red hair Mrs. Fearon mumbled:

'Upsetting a child like that. . . . Now he'll be sick, like as not.'

'You had better put him to bed,' said the schoolmistress coldly. She began to walk across to her house. Mrs. Fearon unnoosed the rope, and followed her, looking like a frustrated hangman.

'Good-afternoon, Mrs. Pitcher. Good-afternoon, Mrs.

THE MOTHERS

Fearon. *What* a dreadful day!'

Composing themselves they turned and greeted Mrs. Dimple.

'Still, I dare say the gardens need it. The Canon was saying that if it weren't for the hay he'd really have to pray for rain! I've just seen Kenneth, Mrs. Fearon. So wet, poor child.'

'Oh!'

'Any more airgraph letters from your boy in Libya, Mrs. Pitcher?'

'No.'

'Ah, well! Of course he's busy just now, isn't he? How lucky I am to meet you both! I'm just going round to explain to the members that our next Mothers' Union meeting will be on the twenty-first. The Canon is going to talk to us on Motherhood. Of course, you'll both come, won't you?'

RAINBOW VILLA

'So I have decided to come back.'

Her face was flushed, for she had spoken at length, and with vehemence. Now, realising that it was not usual to pour out such confidences, and so energetically, to the house-agent, she added with sharper decision and a grander manner:

'Quite decided. I am positive it is what my dear brother would have wished. And I have ordered the furniture to come from the repository next week.'

At the mention of the dead the house-agent's face took on an easier posture. The expression with which one acknowledges a dead client is formalised, familiar, calling for no difficult adjustments.

'Ah! One does not see many people like Mr. Ensor nowadays.'

'I dare say not.'

The flush had died away, leaving her face pale with the dirty pallor of age. The vehemence had died away too. She was thinking that Francis would not have approved this promiscuous washing of family dirty linen. There had been no need to tell Mr. Genge that living with Florence had turned out badly, and certainly no need to describe how silly Florence had been about bacon and air-raids. It should have been sufficient to say that she had decided to come back to Rainbow Villa, where she had lived for so long with Francis, where now she would live alone. On the desk between them a ledger lay open. The house-agent looked again at the clean page, so elegantly written, so singularly free from erasures and additions that it resembled a tombstone.

But he looked at it as though it were so importantly full as to be almost undecipherable.

'November 1938. Nine-teen-thir-ty-eight. Practically three years ago.'

'Two years and eight months.'

'The war,' said Mr. Genge. 'The war. It seems to emphasise the lapse of time, does it not?'

'Do you find it so? I can't say that I notice much difference. Time seems to go about as fast as usual. Of course, I can remember several wars,' said the old lady.

'Seeing so many changes,' said the house-agent, 'being, so to speak, on the spot, and seeing them personally, makes pre-war days seem quite distant days. War brings changes. 'That is inevitable. We must bow to it.'

He looked so bowed, all of a sudden, that Miss Ensor said:

'I hope you have not had any bereavements.'

'No. No, not actually. Actually not. But one sees so many changes. Especially, perhaps, in my profession. Changes of ownership. Changes of tenancy. Changes . . .'

His tone indicated that the changes were mostly for the worse.

'No doubt,' said she. 'However, I don't expect to find Rainbow Villa much changed. It is really providential that you couldn't find me a tenant for it.'

No failure on his part, but the exorbitant rent she insisted on demanding for that small and unattractive house was the reason. But the representative of Messrs. Angel, Genge and Chilmaid replied, sadly and meekly:

'No, we failed over the tenant. But of course one must bear in mind that the house has not been wholly unoccupied.'

'Oh, that billeting business. Poor fellows, I was very glad to think of them there, with a sound roof over their heads.'

Mr. Genge gazed into his book.

'December thirty-nine to March forty. Twelve weeks, Thirty-five men.'

'Shocking!' said Miss Ensor. 'Such overcrowding. But better than tents.'

'Oh, undoubtedly. The only possible, the only patriotic view to take. Better than tents. Yes. Particularly as the season was so severe. Yes, indeed! Which reminds me, I fear you may find a few little dilapidations. A little damage to the interior woodwork. Some of the palings missing.'

'Why?'

'The weather, you know. Such unusually low temperatures. In fact, I think they may have helped themselves to a little firewood. Very natural. A way they have in the army you know.'

'H'm'

'Of course,' Mr. Genge continued, 'we submitted our claim to the War Office. The forms went through some time ago. To the appropriate department,'

'Well, haven't they paid yet?

'I think not. No. Actually, not quite yet. But, of course they will. It is merely a question of a little patience.'

'They should have done it long ago,' she said. 'What else was damaged?'

'Oh, very little, considering. A pane or two of glass. Various small fixtures. I think the schedule is downstairs. I could have it brought up to you if you wish.'

His hand hovered over the desk telephone.

'Don't trouble. I can see for myself, for I'm going there now. I am catching the midday bus.'

'No, no!' exclaimed Mr. Genge. 'That we cannot permit. Our junior partner, Mr. Brown, will drive you in his car.'

His tone of voice had become suddenly warm, free, bestowing.

'Oh, very well. That will be very kind of him.'

There was no answering warmth and reception. With the flippancy of old age she seemed to regard Mr. Brown and the bus as pretty well equivalent. And while Mr. Genge was implying down his telephone that Miss Ensor was the most precious, the most highly valued, of all the firm's clients – as Mr. Brown would, of course, be aware – she was unconcernedly reading the notices of fat stock and farm implements for sale by auction.

To Mr. Brown, who had not seen her before, Miss Ensor seemed unbelievably old: so old that if she had fallen to pieces under the strong midday sun of July, beating down on the street, it would have been a quite natural confirmation of words he had heard once or twice from Mr. Genge on the subject of Rainbow Villa . . . *She'll* never need the house again!

But instead of falling to pieces Miss Ensor climbed into the car as nimbly as a spider.

A jolt, he thought, might finish her yet. But though his agitated misery made him drive abominably, jolts did nothing to Miss Ensor beyond swinging her hat a little farther over one eye.

For Mr. Brown was a compassionate young man, and so much disliked the thought of any unpleasantness, any sight of suffering, that he had prepared himself to be a conscientious objector, not knowing that the state of his aorta would reserve him for civilian sufferings only. Miss Ensor however turned to him briskly and said:

'Why aren't you in the army, young man?'

'My heart,' murmured Mr. Brown; and thinking that she was probably a rather nasty old lady, rude and overbearing, became even more afflicted: for it is doubly painful to be sorry for people you can't like.

'H'm'

They drove in silence for some miles. He thought of mentioning the country, the prospects of a good harvest, the changes . . . no, no, good God! Not changes! Not with that wrecked building awaiting them, the mammocked billet of thirty-five freezing soldiers, that Aunt Sally of evacuee children, that doss-house of tramps, that habitation of stray cats and foxes. Suppose that at the moment they arrived a tramp . . . ?

Before he knew what the words would be he had asked:

'Why Rainbow? Why was it called Rainbow Villa?'

'My brother named it.'

They took the right-hand fork. The road swung between fat hedges, everything in sight looked arrogantly green, arrogantly thriving. If only the house had creepers on it, ivy, ampelopsis, anything to muffle the first impact, make the truth less raw . . . ! But it hadn't. And again his thoughts returned to the question, Why Rainbow ? – of all names the silliest for a bare square box of drab roughcast, standing like a sentry-box at the side of the road staring at the landscape with blank rectangular eyes, three above and two below.

RAINBOW VILLA

'I'm afraid it may be rather a shock . . .'

But the words had been got out too late, for already the car had rounded the bend and the shock had been received. He drew up. After a minute she began to scrabble at the window-lever, saying:

'How does this thing work? I want to get out.'

In his hand the keys of the house flashed. At Genge, Angel, and Chilmaid all keys were polished regularly, such small details make a good impression. But there was no need of them, for the door was off its hinges. Instead, he lifted aside the porch of flimsy wire trellis, which had collapsed across the threshold,

A stab of light fell on the sitting-room floor, coming through the hole in the roof and the great gap in the flooring of the room above. It shone on a piece of crumpled paper, on which was printed: *To Let. Apply Messrs. Angel, Genge, and Chilmaid, House Agents, Estate Agents, and Auctioneers, Marketplace, Durnford.* It shone, too, on splinters of broken glass and on excrements. They crossed the passage to the corresponding room. Here, too, was broken glass; but it had been swept into a corner, and the centre of the room was occupied by a bed of withering bracken-fronds. On the hearth were some toe-rags, and the scattered ashes of a fire, and a rusty kettle and two beer bottles stood near by.

Looking upward, Mr. Brown said in a voice of dreamy misery:

'The ceiling of this one seems pretty sound.'

Silent, she walked out. He followed her to the foot of the stairs. Steps and banisters had been hacked away.

'I don't know if it's worth while going up. I will, if you like.'

Still silent, she turned and went into the kitchen, and on from there to the scullery. There was a scuffling noise, and a cat leaped out of the copper.

'Poor thing! Poor pussy!'

Her voice reminded him of a doll his sister had had, a doll which when you pulled its strings said *Papa! Mamma!*

Standing behind her, ravaged with embarrassment and incompetent pity, he actually began to wring his hands. After a while she moved over to the copper, and looked inside.

'No kittens.'

Had she gone mad, an octogenarian Ophelia, or was she revenging herself by playing on his feelings? When he heard a car approach and halt outside, he was so desperate that he really believed that Mr. Genge, repenting, had followed in order to take on himself the burden of this ghastly situation. But the car door did not open; and presently two voices, ladylikely loud, were heard.

'Isn't it frightful? A direct hit. We've had quite a lot of them round here, you know.'

'Looks more like blast to me.'

'Oh, do you think so? I wonder where the crater is. Did I tell you about Penelope's land-mine? Of all the amazing strokes of luck . . . !'

Fortunately the old lady was rather deaf. But the visiting voices were loud, and their diction was clear, and agonised by the thought that Miss Ensor might at any moment hear her property (suffering, so Mr. Genge said, from the inevitable dilapidations of a house left empty in war-time) mistaken for a bombed house, Mr. Brown raised his own voice.

'It's chiefly the woodwork, you know. It was so fearfully cold that winter, and some little delay, I understand, about coal. We have sent in a claim for that and for the windows.

RAINBOW VILLA

Though to do the men justice, some of the windows have gone since. There are so many children about now . . . rather wild children. I often wonder if it's seeing all the wreckage in blitzed towns, that makes them so destructive when they are sent down here. Psychological, you know. Of course, the roof . . . But both winters were very severe, and probably the frost cracked the cement, and slates are so easily dislodged. It's not so bad in here. That's the advantage of a bricked floor. I'm afraid Mr. Genge did not quite prepare you for it. The truth is, he has been so extremely busy, and labour and materials are so hard to get just now, and . . .'

Perfectly inattentive, Miss Ensor burst into tears, uttering the loud crowing sobs of second childhood. Snorting and sobbing, she swept past Mr. Brown and his clean handkerchief and his red compassionate face, and went weeping through her ruined house, and out into the glaring sunlight.

'Look! Oh, the *poor* old thing!'

Both ladies leaped from the car and hurried to Miss Ensor. No wonder you're upset. It's the shock, isn't it? So frightful, seeing one's home devastated, everything gone in a minute. I do feel for you so frightfully. We both do. I suppose you've lived here quite a long time? That makes it worse, doesn't it?'

Now, while the first lady was patting Miss Ensor, the second lady looked up into the blue sky and exclaimed:

'Brutes! Inhuman brutes!'

'My God, yes! Still, I suppose it's some comfort to think we are doing it to them now. But that won't put your poor house back, will it? We are so sorry for you, you know. It's ghastly, just ghastly ! But I'm sure you mustn't cry like this. Can't we take you somewhere and give you a nice cup of tea?

That's what you want. Something to pull you together. You'll feel better then. Really, you will. Do come with us, we can all get introduced on the way to tea. After all, there's no room for all that nonsense in war-time, is there? That's one comfort, it has brought us all together in such a rational way.'

'Another comfort,' said the second lady, 'is that it only got the house, not you. That sort of comfort grows on one, I assure you. I *do* know, because my own poor little flat was torn to ribbons; and if I'd been able to get a taxi I'd have been back in it, and in ribbons, too. After all, life means a lot, doesn't it?'

'Oh, it certainly does,' rejoined the first lady. 'And everyone's being so marvellously brave. Think of all those poor souls in the East End, how splendid they all were. And I'm sure you're going to be just like them after you've had that cup of tea. And then you can tell us all about it. Was it a night raid or a daylight?'

This time they paused, and Miss Ensor could speak.

'It wasn't either. It was thirty-five billeted soldiers. And two hard winters. And some evacuated children. So I understand. And a vilely incompetent and dishonest house-agent. There he is. You'd better ask him.'

The two ladies looked incuriously at Mr. Brown, and looked away again.

'Oh, I say. What rotten luck ! Really, it looks just as if a bomb had got it.'

After her furious speech Miss Ensor was again in tears.

'Poor old soul!'

'Of course, billeting can be the very devil. Did I tell you about Badger's billiard-room?'

'He did. Still, one gets compensation, doesn't one?'

'Oh, yes. All that's seen to. A bit slow, of course, but

wizard when it comes.'

'Well, you can't expect the poor old War Office to turn themselves into walruses and carpenters, can you? After all, they've got to win the war. But they always pay up in the end.'

'Oh, yes, they pay all right. Ultimately. There's nothing to worry about.'

Raising her voice, she repeated the words, and added:

'You're sure you won't come and have some tea? But I dare say you want to have a heart-to-heart with your house-agent, so we won't take up any more of your time. But do cheer up, won't you? I'm sure everything will turn out much better than you think. It's only a question of time.'

The second lady added her plea that Miss Ensor should cheer up and remember that it might have been a bomb. And acknowledging Mr. Brown's rigid glare with rigid inattention both ladies stepped into the car and drove away.

After a while Miss Ensor began to weep less violently, and presently to sob only, and then only to hiccough. In a rather hen-like way she began to tweak up groundsel from a vaguely-distinguishable circular flower-bed. Mr. Brown, sighing heavily, began to pull up groundsel too. But seeing her pause, and look at him with fury, he said:

'I'm afraid we ought to be getting back. That is, if you have been here long enough, and don't mind.'

BOW TO THE RISING SUN

'Some girls,' said Miss Doris Butt, assistant to Mr. Caldecott, of the Fuel Control Office, 'would get married right away and start a baby. Not that I should find it so difficult, but I'm not the sort of girl that would. I shouldn't feel it right, somehow. Would you, Mrs Stanley?'

The older woman murmured that she wouldn't, and went on searching through the file labelled *Memos from Ministry*.

'Though, of course, it wouldn't apply to you, would it?' Miss Butt said.

Again the older woman murmured her agreement. At 9 a.m. she had become a clerk. It was now noon, and it seemed to her that during the last three hours she had gained considerable insight into Miss Butt's private life but regrettably little into running of the Fuel Control Office.

'No, of course not,' Miss Butt said. 'For one thing, you're married already, and for another, you're over the age. Can't you find it?'

'It doesn't seem to be here,' Mrs. Stanley said.

'Never mind. Maybe it isn't. Maybe I put it into *Pending*. Dear, dear, I'm afraid you'll be rather lost without me! But you won't be the only one. Poor Mr. Caldecott, he'll be quite a lost soul, really. You see, he depends so much. Of course, it isn't as though I were going into the A.T.S. When Mr. Caldecott called me in and told me that, try as he would, he really couldn't get me deferred again, he said to me, "Now, on no account, Miss Butt, are you to worry. I'll see you don't get sent into the A.T.S." And I said to him, "No, indeed, Mr. Caldecott. I'm sure you couldn't bear to think of my legs in khaki stockings." Of course, you see, having worked for him so long, I can say that sort of thing to him. It cheers him up, I daresay. A smile for everything and everyone. Besides, I understand him. Still, it's got to be. My King and Country want me. That's what they said in the last war, isn't it?'

'Yes,' said Mrs. Stanley.

'Those last-war songs are having quite a comeback, aren't they? They're a bit hymny, but swinging them puts more life into them, doesn't it? I can't abide anything without life in it. I suppose you can remember the last war quite well? And I wasn't even born then. Somehow, it seems funny, doesn't it?'

'Is this it?' Mrs. Stanley asked, handing her a mimeographed sheet.

'Yes, that's it. That's what you've got to go by now. So you'd better cast your eye over it.'

Mrs. Stanley began to read. Miss Butt began to sing. Her voice had an appealing youthful roughness. Like the fubsy down on young bracken shoots, thought Mrs. Stanley, trying to concentrate on Kitchen Nuts and Bath and Bristol Coke.

'Then, there's anthracite,' Miss Butt said. 'Anthracite's tricky.'

'Why?' Mrs. Stanley asked.

'Well, you see, it's mostly the better people who want it,

people with furnaces, and they generally leave it to the last moment and then come in about it. I've got a list of them somewhere, but I expect I've mislaid it. You see, I know them so well. There's Miss Stebbins and the Reverend Cash and Miss Rylands – oh, she's a nuisance, that Miss Rylands! Comes in covered with shopping and says, "Where's the Fuel Controller? I want to see him personally." And poor Mr. Caldecott, he absolutely dreads the sight of her, and I have to invent no end of excuses. Mrs. Grandison – she's nice, she is; old Colonel Prowse, Viscount Abington, Mr. Hume-Pinney. Oh dear, what a shock it will be to them when they come in expecting to see me and find you! Lots of them bring me flowers. They know I'm so passionately devoted to flowers. But Mrs. Grandison generally brings eggs. Well, I suppose you've read all that by now. Now you might as well enter these up. It'll all help to give you an idea of the hang of things.' Miss Butt leaned back and began to polish her nails.

'Knowing how to manage them,' she said presently, 'that's the important thing. It just makes all the difference. The day I was called for my interview I heard Mr. Caldecott ringing up the Labour Exchange. "You ought to send Miss Butt into the Diplomatic Service," he said. "She's got the human touch." Of course, I do think he exaggerates. I'm not so marvellous as he makes out. I just don't bite their heads off the way he does. Still, you've got to have the human touch, though personally I've always found people perfectly sweet, especially the better sort of people, you understand. They come in raging, but somehow I soothe them down and they go away all smiles. There's Mr. Hume-Pinney, for instance. Well, last month he came in and he said to me, "Button" – lots of them call me Button; sort of short for Butt, and me being so tiny, it's natural – "Button," he said, "why have you sent me coke? I thought you loved me." "Why, yes," I said. "Wasn't there a message pinned to that coke – *With Love from Doris?*" And believe it or not, he went off perfectly happy, and it never even came out that Mrs. Grandison really had got his coal. Actually, you see, I'd got their applications mixed up. I suppose that's what Mr. Caldecott means by the human touch. And that's what you'll have to concentrate on, Mrs. Stanley, if you want any peace in this job. Otherwise it's squabble, squabble, squabble the whole time. Of course, I do admit it's a bit of a strain, always being a little ray of sunshine, but – You can take that call.'

A moment later Miss Butt snatched the receiver out of Mrs. Stanley's hand. 'Good *morning*, Colonel Prowse ... Yes, it's me. It's Miss Butt speaking . . . What? . . . Oh dear! Your greenhouses again? You know, what you need is a coal mine all of your own, really it is. Of course, we can't promise anything absolutely, but . . . Yes! That would be best. You come in and explain it all.'

Putting back the receiver, Miss Butt flew to the window sill, removed some rather exhausted daffodils to the wastepaper basket, and emptied their vase out of the window. Then she straightened her table a little and flicked some dust off the filing cabinet. Glancing at Mrs. Stanley, she seemed for a moment to contemplate freshening up the older woman's appearance too. Instead she sat down and began to renovate her makeup, busy as a kitten cleaning itself, and for five minutes was perfectly silent.

Then, with newly reddened lips, she began talking once more. 'Now, Colonel Prowse, who'll be coming in presently, is just what I've been saying. In fact, Mr. Caldecott says straight out he's one of my conquests.

Personally, I think he's rather an old dear. But you've got to take him the right way, you know, and be sympathetic about his old greenhouses and not mind his jokes, which are a bit Anglo-Indian, I admit.'

Mrs. Stanley put a sheet in her typewriter and began to type. Miss Butt raised her voice. 'Copying that memo now? You are taking hold, aren't you? Of course, I daresay when you're here it will all get more official. Everyone thinks I look such a baby, and I expect that's one reason why people like Colonel Prowse tend to make rather a pet of me and think me so marvellously efficient. Not that I'm anything out of the way, I'm sure. I'm just nice to them, and of course I never forget a face, and I've got a sense of humour. That's my little secret, really. How to win friends and influence people. Do you know, there was a book in America called *How to Win* –'

The door opened. Miss Butt sprang up, radiant and condescending. 'Good Morning, Colonel Prowse.'

'Good morning, Miss Butt.'

Looking up from her typing, Mrs. Stanley wondered why he had been referred to as old Colonel Prowse. Erect and trim, he had an appearance of indomitable middle age, and he carried a large bunch of pink carnations with almost completely successful assurance.

Miss Butt's glance slanted over the bouquet. Still holding it, he said: 'It's about my greenhouses, Miss Butt. I've just made over another of them for tomatoes and I must have extra heat. I've got a Land Girl, I've got some fertiliser, and now all I need is a little heat. Eh? Do you see my point, Miss Butt? Of course you do. You see everything, clever little girl that you are. So now, what about it?'

'Well, Colonel Prowse, I'll certainly mention it to Mr.

Caldecott when he comes in this afternoon. After all these preparations you do deserve a little encouragement, don't you?'

'I'll say I do.' Colonel Prowse nodded. His glance flickered over towards Mrs. Stanley, an examining, questioning, disparaging glance.

'Colonel Prowse, I've got something to break to you,' Miss Butt said. 'Something terrible!'

'Eh, What's that?'

'You're losing me, Colonel Prowse. You're going to lose your Button. I've been called up.'

'Good Lord!'

'Yes, they can't do without me any longer. Things must be pretty desperate, mustn't they, if they can't do without poor little me?'

'Rotten,' Colonel Prowse said. He was now studying Mrs. Stanley more attentively.

'Never mind, Colonel Prowse,' Miss Butt said. 'You're going to have Mrs Stanley instead. And I've just been telling her she must be specially kind to you.'

Still holding his flowers, Colonel Prowse moved across the room. 'How do you do, Mrs. Stanley? I hope Miss Butt hasn't been prejudicing you against me. I try not to be more of a nuisance than I can help.'

'Yes, I've been putting her wise about you. The gypsy's warning, you know.'

Now he was standing by the typewriter. 'Well, Mrs. Stanley,' he said, 'I hope you won't find it too bad here. You know, I think it's pretty marvellous the way people like you take on these awful jobs. I can see you know all about typing, though. That's a lovely bit of work you've got in there. It's a pity you shouldn't have a nicer office. It ought to be done up.'

'Well, Colonel Prowse, and what about beginning with my poor empty flower vase?' Miss Butt said.

'Eh? Oh yes! Flowers,' Colonel Prowse said. 'Yes, I generally try to bring a few flowers along to sort of brighten things up. These are nothing much, I'm afraid. But I've got some tulips coming on, and then there'll be roses. I'm rather proud of my roses.'

He laid down his bouquet by the typewriter and said: 'Well, I mustn't keep you ladies from your lunch. So it's good-bye, is it, Miss Butt? Best of luck, and thanks for all you've done for me. You'll remember about my little business, won't you, and put it through with Caldecott? Or perhaps I should ask Mrs. Stanley to see about it?'

After the door had closed and the brisk footsteps died away, Miss Butt said: 'Don't you think he's rather sweet? So touching, the way he brings his flowers along and then gets all shy about them and dumps them down anywhere. Well, thank God it's lunchtime! We'll go to the Old World, shall we? Want to wash your hands? You go first.'

In the washroom Mrs. Stanley found herself crying, weeping unavailing tears for the desperate idiot valour of the young.

THE PROPER CIRCUMSTANCES

My grandfather, a most amiable clergyman of the Church of England, had a terrible record with horses. He never bought a horse till he was sure it was the horse he needed, but no sooner was the beast in the rectory stable than it developed glanders or bit my grandmother or trampled on a churchwarden or couldn't walk uphill. In a month or so my grandfather, sanguine as ever, would be buying another horse. My grandmother said it was destiny.

I have never had to buy a horse. Why I have my grandfather so much in mind just now is because of Mrs Moor and Evie, our evacuees. Mrs Moor, when I first saw her, was sitting on a piano in a Rest Centre, holding a mug of tea. Three things about her made me notice her among the rest: she was so very large, she looked so very mournful, and she was the only person in the room who wasn't talking. I paused in front of her, much as one might pause before some oversized basalt deity in the Egyptian gallery of the British Museum, and just because she was silent and I can never let well enough alone, I asked her what part of London she came from. She replied that she came from Herne Hill.

Actually, the words she sighed out were 'Urn Ill.' And if

I had listened to the sound instead of the sense . . . But instead I began to think of Grace, my nurse when I was a little girl, who lived at Herne Hill after she married, and of the tea set I chose for her wedding present, with poppies and ears of corn rambling all over it, and of how much I had admired it, and also of how much dear Grace, if she were still alive and living at Herne Hill, would have disliked flying bombs. Meanwhile, I was asking Mrs. Moor how she felt after such a long journey in an open bus.

'*I'm* all right,' she said. 'It's Evie that preys on my mind. Because of her valve.'

Following the direction of her gaze, I saw Evie, a tremendous blonde girl with a heavy jaw.

'Bronichal, too,' continued Mrs. Moor. 'She's got a doctor's sirstifficket to say so, and he said to me, "Mrs. Moor, you must get her out of London or I can't be answerable." So we packed up and come. Not that I know where we are, for I don't.'

To see so large a woman not knowing where she was seemed to me peculiarly sad, considerably sadder than if she had been a small woman in the same predicament. Though I saw many women as pitiable as Mrs. Moor and many more prepossessing, during the remainder of an afternoon that I spent going from one Rest Centre to another with a disillusioned relieving officer, the thought of Mrs. Moor weighing so heavily upon the soil of Dorset without knowing where she weighed obsessed me, and by evening I knew we must have her. Evie, too, of course.

It was at this point that my grandfather cropped up. My friend Valentine, who lives with me, having listened to my reasons for thinking the Moors just the sort of evacuees she and I needed, changed the subject by asking me if I had inherited my eyebrows or my eloquence from my grandfather, to which I replied that as far as I knew I did not resemble him in any way. But I could only give him a passing thought, for we had to reorganize the house in order to give the Moors two bedrooms and a sitting room and that 'access to water and cooking facilities' insisted on by billeting regulations – access to water and cooking facilities consisting in our case of removing the 'Memoirs of Casanova' from the bathroom window sill and some cobwebs from the kitchen. We were still breathless with the task of finding suitable landscapes to cover the damp patches on the walls of the room that was to be the Moors' sitting room, and enough chairs with strong legs, when the Moors arrived. They were both much larger than I remembered. Even in the vasty halls of the Rest Centre, they were notably tall and big, but inside our house they seemed at least eight feet high. As majestic as a state funeral, they followed me round their new home. At intervals, Mrs. Moor said, 'That'll please Evie,' and Evie said nothing whatever unless Mrs. Moor refered to Evie's sirstifficket. Then Evie said coldly, 'Certificate.'

At last, bowing their heads, they vanished into their sitting room, where tea was ready for them. Tea is supposed to make English people feel happier, and Mrs. Moor had remarked that Evie felt hungry, not having fancied the dinner at the Rest Centre. But when I looked in half an hour later, Mrs. Moor and Evie were sitting mute and impassive, contemplating two boiled eggs that seemed by comparison to them to be the eggs of humming-birds.

'Now, she can't fancy eggs,' explained Mrs. Moor. 'Rather strange, isn't it?'

Duty called me away from analysing this fascinating

problem. When Valentine and I saw Mrs. Moor again, she was alone and in much better spirits. Evie, she told us, had taken a hot bath and had been so revived by it that she had put her hair in curlers and gone to bed, where she was waiting for her mother to make her a cup of hot cocoa. Stirring briskly, Mrs. Moor began to tell us something of her own sufferings through aerial warfare, matrimony, childbirth, nervous debility, and her best shoes. 'Seven and a half is what I take, with a wide fitting, but these having rubber soles, they should have been eights. And when they got me out I was insensible, and remained so for hours on end. You never saw such a ruin – the chimney vases from my own bedroom on the kitchen mat, and the pillows the girl was sleeping on two gardens off, and the lino, all inlaid it was . . . Never been able to scrub since,' said Mrs. Moor, looking at us firmly.

Hastily I explained that if any scrubbing got done in our house, it was done by us.

'. . . on account of my rheumatism,' continued Mrs. Moor, 'rising into my knees from my feet. Dr. Wilson, he begged me to stay at the hospital after I come to, but naturally my first thought was Evie's valve and the shock it would be to her to hear of her mum being buried, and her nervous from a child, and no wonder – never having had a home of our own till the bomb blew us out of it. Eighteen long years we lived with my husband's mother, bombs raining down all around us. Night after night I'd go down on my hands and knees and pray out loud, "O Lord, will I never be left in peace?" But that was after we'd moved to Herne Hill. Then it got quiet again and we really began to enjoy ourselves a bit, being on our own at last. I often say to my husband, joking-like, "Funny thing, it took us eighteen years to get a home of our own." Have to be tactful about it, for he fair worshipped his mother, being a widow.'

'Was she in the house when it was bombed?' Valentine inquired. Mrs. Moor nodded emphatically.

'Was she killed?' I asked.

'Not as much as scratched,' said Mrs. Moor. 'But she died of it. Six weeks later she died. From the shock. Evie was called after her, poor child. Ah, I shall never forget that night with the incendiaries. Might have been burned in her bed but for sliding downstairs as white as a sheet and spraining her ankle. All the top of the house burned out before we as much as noticed it being so taken up with Evie. Two baskets and a cannister they dropped in all, and I so heartbroken I never even went upstairs to look at it but slept for weeks on the bare boards without as much as a blanket under me and losing my flesh daily till my own relations didn't know me. "Lil," my sister-in-law said, "whatever's become of you?" And I couldn't speak a word, but I took her out into the garden and showed her all those lovely young cabbages I was counting on, burned as black as a crisp. Not that I ever eat greens myself.'

*

When, in my W.V.S. capacity, I have to cheer reluctant hostesses about receiving evacuees, I lay stress on the importance of arranging some sort of programme for their first few days. Day 1, a trip to the country town to register at the Food Office and choose a butcher. Day 2, a stroll round the village: 'This is our church. This is our ironmonger. Good morning, Mrs. Doe. This is Mrs. Rowley from London.' Day 3, a visit to the doctor. Day 4, with any luck, is Sunday. If not: 'Perhaps you would like to do a little washing.' Under this treatment, talents and proclivities unfold and confidence is established. Naturally I applied it to the Moors. Mrs. Moor responded most flatteringly. Before the end of the week she had rearranged her furniture, launched into making jam, and found herself a part-time job at the paper mills. But with Evie the method was a total flop. Even the Day 3 visit to the doctor, on which I had pinned my best hopes, miscarried. Though he renewed her sirstifficket and gave her a tonic, it was clear that he did so merely in deference to that Hippocratic oath which forbids one doctor to overthrow immediately the verdict of another doctor, for he refused an application for extra milk and extra eggs, and said that what her valve needed was more exercise. All this I learned from Mrs. Moor, when she had left off crying. Evie, with a brow like thunder and a jaw like murder, had dragged herself upstairs, panting, and gone to bed. 'Evie feels things so,' said Mrs. Moor. 'Though she doesn't say much.'

I agreed that Evie was taciturn. I had heard her say 'No' several times, 'Don't mind if I do' twice, and 'Hullo' once. Otherwise I had only heard her say 'Certificate'. Remarks addressed to Evie were answered by Mr. Moor, if Mrs. Moor was present, otherwise not at all. Having agreed that Evie was taciturn, I went on to say that she probably felt bored in the country but that we might reasonably hope she'd be happier when she'd made some friends of her own age. Mopping her eyes, Mrs. Moor said that Evie didn't like Americans. I said that we had some Royal Artillery, too, in the neighbourhood. Mrs. Moor replied that Evie really thought of no one but a boy friend in India, and that might be why her appetite was so uncertain. One moment she'd want a thing and the next

THE PROPER CIRCUMSTANCES

she wouldn't look at it. She'd been like that ever since she was a wee thing. Stung into speculation, I asked Mrs. Moor if she had any pictures of Evie as a wee thing, and she produced a snapshot of a very small Mr. Moor, peeping out from behind a monster in satin.

During the rest of the day, Evie was a veiled presence to us – a sense of something resentful in a bedroom. At intervals we heard Mrs. Moor carrying things upstairs on trays, at intervals we heard the bathroom toilet being savagely flushed, but even without this we should have been aware of Evie overhead, for she diffused a kind of atmospheric pressure which led me to trap the barometer whenever I passed it, though in vain. At evening there was a glimmer of hope. Evie's bedroom window opens, most romantically, above our small river, and Evie was observed leaning from the window, lost in girlish dreams, with one hand pillowing her cheek and the other gracefully dangling a tear-sopped handkerchief, while on the further bank stood an R.A. corporal, similarly lost in manly meditation – meditation about our chimney pot, apparently, though a moment's thought, as Valentine pointed out, must have shown that his mind was far from architecture or he would have been running for his life, since it was obvious that if Evie leaned out much further her specific gravity would tilt the house on top of him.

On the morrow, Mrs. Moor greeted us with the glad news that the post had brought no less than six letters for Evie, all from abroad, and that this would cheer Evie up when she saw them on her breakfast tray. She also mentioned that during the night one leg of her bed had gone through the floor. It was providential, really, for it might have been a leg of Evie's bed. Evie was such a light sleeper and if anything *did* wake her, it took a hot meal to get her off again.

Musing on Evie's insomnia, and on the worldwide nature of war, and on what a cheered-up Evie would look like, I went off to my work. Throughout that day I heard myself saying – I hope persuasively – that one cannot expect evacuees to be angels from head to foot, that faults can be found on both sides, and that above all one must not drift into becoming prejudiced. I may have persuaded others, though I doubt it. Myself I could not persuade. It was clear to me that I had drifted into being prejudiced against Evie; otherwise, why should I feel such distaste at the prospect of seeing her cheered up and why the curmudgeonly conviction that a cheered-up Evie would croon?

But the only crooning about the house when I returned that evening was being done by a great quantity of wasps. I followed the wasps to the kitchen, where Mrs. Moor was tying on jam covers and looking mournful. Evie, it seemed, was still upstairs in her bedroom (with appropriate trays), answering her letters. And tomorrow she'd have one of her headaches.

'Does Evie have bad headaches?' I asked.

'Awful,' said Mrs. Moor, and though there was pride in her voice, there was also apprehension.

Tactfully I turned the conversation to air raids, and Mrs. Moor was well away on an account of the flying bomb that wrecked the fish shop and how she could never forget the kindness of the Indian doctor who understood her sinking sensations and what she said to the lady in the Rest Centre who threw up all night – what else could you expect if you brought cold sausages all that way by open bus and never as much as offered to share them around? – and how the noise was for all the world like a giant that wasn't there riding a motor bike right over your head, not to say through it, when I became aware that there was a noise over our heads, too – a noise like a giantess who was weeping convulsively. Since Evie was above us, it was natural to connect this noise with her, but Mrs. Moor went on talking and hospitality constrained me to go on listening until the convulsive weeping turned to a steady cascading and Mrs. Moor broke off to exclaim, 'Don't say that girl's left the tap on!'

It was the house cistern pouring its contents through the overflow pipe onto the back porch. I turned off the water at the main and rang up Mr. Bobbin, who is not really a plumber but does his best. Mr. Bobbin came and borrowed a flashlamp and disappeared into the attic. Presently he reappeared with cobwebs in his hair, saying that he couldn't positively account for it but that he had found some string in the cistern, which might have been the trouble. He had removed the string and, unless it was grit or something perished, he hoped we'd be all right now. Just as he was leaving on his bicycle, I said, we'd turn on the water and see. The cistern filled and overflowed, so again I turned the water off, and again Mr. Bobbin borrowed the flashlamp and a hammer and some wire and disappeared into the attic. After a while he came down and wandered about the house, peering wistfully into cupboards for stopcocks that might be at the bottom of the mischief, and turning taps on and off. Then he named one or two plumbers in the county town who might have come out if it weren't wartime, said he would consult old Mr. Bacon, who'd be as good as any of them if he weren't past work and getting a bit rusty, and promised to come again when he had time.

DORSET STORIES

*

When Mr. Bobbin, a busy man, has time and comes again, there will be some more things for him to look into. The door of the cupboard under the stairs has stuck immovably, plaster is dribbling from above the kitchen sink, the lintel of the back door has shifted several inches out of plumb and looks as though Samson had been at work on it, and something undiagnosable has happened to the larder screen, so the larder is now quite unbelievably full of bluebottles. Though we assure ourselves that all this may be caused by Mrs. Moor going up and down stairs so often with trays for Evie, the theory – since Evie never sleeps on the roof – cannot account for the fall of soot in my bedroom or the flashes that come from the electric switch in the bathroom. Even if Mr. Bobbin can deal with these ailments, we shall still have the magpies that are eating all the green peas and the swarms of clothes moths that have suddenly infested every room in the house.

Many years ago I read a book called *Wild Talents*, a book about vampires, werewolves, and poltergeists. All of us, so the author implied, are potentially one or another of these things. It is just a matter of circumstances being right for us to develop that way. The proper circumstances to develop poltergeistism include being adolescent, preferably female, far from home, dull-witted, oppressed, and resentful. Dull-witted girls who are far from home and don't like it can achieve quite remarkable feats of poltergeistism. Water will fall from a clear sky, fires break out on tea tables, flat-irons and buckets fly through the air, hornets swarm, crops wither, beds turn somersaults, mirrors leap from walls, and treacle climb out of jars, while the young lady who is doing it sits brooding in a corner, not stirring hand or foot.

I say nothing yet. It is unscientific to jump to conclusions. It is uncharitable to give way to prejudice. I will wait till flames spout from my teapot or a flat-iron bounds from its shelf and knocks me senseless before I conclude that circumstances have been right for Evie to develop her particular wild talent. I don't think I shall have long to wait. Unless Evie's sirstifficket is renewed, she will come under the Conscription of Labour (Female) Act and be called on to work. That, as Mrs. Moor herself says, will be the Great Divide. And if I am not greatly mistaken, catching the eight-thirty train every morning will be just that ripening touch needed to develop Evie's talent to its fullest.

Meanwhile, to complicate things yet further, I am growing attached to Mrs. Moor. She is like that horse of my grandfather's who was such a nice, good-hearted beast, nothing wrong with it at all until it broke its loose box to matchwood and disabled the sexton. My grandfather said it was thunder in the air.

POOR MARY

At the last minute Nicholas remembered flowers. He went out and gathered some primroses from the hedgerow, hardening himself not to notice the snap of their stems. It was one of his fidgets to dislike picking flowers.

The lane sloped away downhill. Here and there the leafless hedge was tufted with white where the blackthorns had come into bloom. It was like a black wave breaking into lips of foam. Down in the valley a white plume of steam rose up, its summit catching the pink light of sunset. It was still hanging there when he heard the train go on. And he knew that his wife, shouldering her pack, had handed in her pass and joined the nondescript civilian group waiting for the bus. The white plume thinned out, the train gathered speed, snorting on towards London. But Mary had got out at East Wickering, junction for Stoat and Saint Brewers.

I want to spend this leave at home, she had written; *unless you'd rather not. It's more than time I saw you in your hermit's cell.* If it had not been for the last sentence he would have supposed she wanted to spend her leave with her family.

'Flowers for the spare room,' he said to himself, setting down the spotted mug in the centre of the bureau. The bed,

POOR MARY

an old-fashioned double bed with brass end-rails and a white quilt, suddenly seemed a bed in which he had never slept. It looked like Wordsworth's bed. He must contrive that she saw the camp-bed first. For the last week he had spent his spare time preparing for her, scrubbing the floors, polishing the windows, putting away his clothes, his books, his papers, so that his dwelling might offer its most impersonal face to her inspection. Now that he had remembered flowers everything seemed ready. The food on the table was covered with a napkin to keep flies off it, the kettle was in a state to boil when he wanted it to, the watercress was keeping cold in a damp cloth. He snuffed at his fingers' ends, and once more washed his hands very carefully. He had been cleaning out pigsties all the morning. Then he set off to meet his wife.

He had not seen her since 1941. A conscientious objector, he had applied for exemption from military service. The day after the tribunal had granted him exemption provided he worked on the land Mary volunteered for the A.T.S. They had never agreed about war, so neither was surprised by the other.

'But as we are bound to argue,' she had said, 'and people will only laugh at you if you have a military wife coming on visits, I shan't come. Unless you are ill, of course. Then I will apply for compassionate leave.'

One of the things he had learned in four years spent as a farm labourer was an exact computation of time. So he met her where he had intended to meet her, fifty yards from where the bus had set her down at the foot of the lane. Though he knew she would be wearing uniform, it was a surprise to see that part of the uniform was a skirt. He had been similarly astonished on their wedding-day when apparently he had been assuming that she would come up the aisle wearing white satin trousers. Seeing the skirt, he also saw her legs below it and that they were fatter than they used to be.

'Hello, Nicholas!'

'Hullo, Mary!'

She smells of metal, he thought, as I smell of dung. We are subdued to what we work in. He had smelled her, he had seen her legs. He did not seem to have seen her face. He took her pack, and said: 'Look! There's a hawk.'

'I suppose they do a lot of harm to the crops,' she replied.

'Wood-pigeons are worse.'

She set off, walking with quick resolute steps. Marching, in fact. So why on earth should she know about hawks? The thought prompted an enquiry about the V-2, and they went up the lane talking of air-raids and air-raid damage. Just as there was a difference between their smells and a difference in their gait, there was a difference in their manner of speech. Her voice had grown rather common and twanging, it sounded uncared-for, and she jumped from one subject to another. She seemed to preface every remark with *Gosh*! and he to inaugurate every reply with *Um*. Listening to himself, he thought: Do I sound more like the village schoolmaster or the village idiot?

A melancholy tenderness that was almost entirely the April dusk suffused him. Blackbirds shot across the path from hedge to hedge, scolding at them; beyond the hedges lambs bleated and rushed away at a ghostly gallop. He had been working from six in the morning; he was tired and craved for tea. Yet each time that they paused for Mary to recover her breath he was glad to postpone the moment of reaching his house, and when the one chimney-pot reared

POOR MARY

into view above the hedge and beneath the evening star he said gloomily: 'Here's where I live.'

'It's nice. And all to yourself? Lucky bastard!'

'There are only two rooms,' he said defensively. 'The third one leaks.'

'Is it old?'

'Run up after the last war by a chicken-farming ex-serviceman. When he was ruined the farmer bought it. As he bought it very cheap, naturally he doesn't trouble to keep it in repair. So I sit in the kitchen. But I've got a chemical closet.'

It was strange to hear her feet on the floor of concrete slabs. Not strange to her, though, who had been living for four years in army constructions. The only strange thing to her would be to hear two pairs of feet instead of thirty. He moved the kettle forward on the range and lit the candles.

'Candles!' she said appreciatively.

'Because it's a party. Ordinarily I use an oil lamp.' His voice was still heavy with gloom.

'What queer squat candlesticks! They're clay, aren't they? Did you make them?'

'No. I bought them at a sale. They're called corpse candlesticks. The idea is that you leave them by the body all night, you see, and the rats can't knock them over.'

'I wonder you don't use them every night,' she said. 'Have you got any other cheerful curiosities?'

She had taken off her cap and unbuttoned her tunic. The candlelight softened the contest between her natural high colour and the too tawny make-up she had applied to it. Seeing that he was looking at her, she said: 'Isn't it calamitous how fat I've grown? It's that army food, incessant gorges of starch. Gosh! Those puddings! Enough to make any girl look like a prize ox.'

'When I first came here I was covered with spots and boils,' he said consolingly. 'I thought I'd caught it from the pigs, till I discovered it was my water well. Now I boil it.'

'I'd hate to have to do with pigs.'

'They're clean animals, really. It's just that they are overcrowded, and dirty feeders.'

'Sounds like the A.T.S.'

He cut more bread, reflecting that he would need to bake again on the morrow. Habit, of course, and mass-feeding, and the goaded appetite of the disciplined: though that would not account for the scatteration of egg-shell, the jam spooned on to a salted plate, the wide periphery of crumbs and cigarette ash. Nerves, he thought. Poor Mary's nerves are strained. His own strained nerves obliged him to sip his tea as though it were Napoleon brandy and frown at an iron-mould on the cloth.

'Lovely bread, Nicholas.'

'Soda bread. I bake it myself.'

'You seem to have a lot of time. Don't you ever do any work?'

'Fifty-six hours a week. Sometimes overtime. Pigs on Sunday. But it fits in somehow, and I don't dislike it. And the alternative would be to have a woman in.'

He had not meant the implication and she did not perceive it. Staring round her as though on a foreign country, she said: 'And the polish on everything, too! You're wasted, Nicholas. You ought to be in the army.'

'Yes, sergeant.'

But, more concerned than he had been over his own maladroit remark, she flushed, and refused to eat anything more, like an abashed child.

POOR MARY

'Walk round and see the rest of it. Here's your room.'

'Pretty flowers.'

Glaring at the bed, he remarked: 'I've got a bed in the third room.'

'But that's the room that leaks. You said so.'

She had turned round from the mirror, and it was as though the mirror had given back to her her former countenance, at once innocent and domineering, the face of the girl-child intent on the doll's tea-party.

'It doesn't leak in dry weather,' he said. 'I expect the cat's there now. She comes in and out by the window.'

'Cat? Why, you used to hate cats. You said they tortured birds.'

'So they do. So I do hate them. But I must needs find this animal in a gin, and dress its paw, and the damned beast has adopted me. It's a female, too.'

'Life's harder in the country, I expect,' she said. It was for such slanting ironies that he had first loved her: for that, and for smelling of geraniums – and for the chivalrous quarrelsome disposition which had kept her at his side before his exemption was assured, saying hopefully that he might need someone to scrap with the authorities. But unseeing, she went on to undo it by saying: 'You know, a lot of people are awfully interested when I tell them my husband is a C.O. You'd be surprised how many feel the same way. All these murder cases, you know. Everyone's dead against the death sentence.'

'It doesn't surprise me very much,' he said. 'I was in the train the other day, I had to go to a dentist. And there was a bomber crew in the same carriage, and they were talking about a murder. They all agreed that it was wrong to take human life. I asked one of them why, and he said because you can't know what it is you're meddling with.'

'Exactly! I've heard dozens say the same thing. I'm beginning to think so myself. I think they ought to abolish it. I expect they will after the war.'

'They'll abolish war, my dear. Belligerents always abolish war after a war. It's harder to part with a death-sentence. And impossible to give up hunting and shooting, because hunting and shooting make us what we are. Have a cigarette?'

'I don't think you've grown any pleasanter,' she said. 'Is that an owl? Let's go back to the other room.'

In the other room the clock was ticking, the kettle was boiling. Three hours earlier the bed had not seemed his own, now his kitchen was not his either, but some sort of institutional waiting-room where two people had made an inordinately messy meal. At last, irked beyond bearing, he rose and began to clear the table and then to wash up. The hot water in the bowl, the feeling of the crockery, dried and still warm as he stacked it on the dresser, the resumption of his ordinary evening routine began to console him. He moved to and fro more nimbly, preparing for the two breakfasts he would get in the morning, pouring the remains of the tea into the bottle he would carry to work with him – he had grown to enjoy cold tea – rinsing out the teapot and standing it on its head, throwing out the slops and bringing in the kindling for the morrow's fire, winding the clock and putting the cat's saucer down on a sheet of newspaper. Now, had he been by himself, he would have raked out the fire and gone off to read in bed. Instead, hospitality constrained him to say: 'Have you brought a hot-water bottle?'

She did not answer. With a kettle in one hand and the

wood-basket in the other, he glanced at her. Her head was resting against the back of her chair and her eyes were shut. But she was not asleep. She was openly and abjectly crying.

He built up the fire and put on the kettle. This, whatever it was about, would mean more tea. Then he patted her shoulder and said: 'Poor Mary!' She put up her hand that was so plump and so demonstrably manicured, and clung to his wrist. She's going to have a baby, he thought. The cat in the gin that had clawed him to the bone, clawed and clung, had been within a few days of giving birth. He had made her a nest in the wood-house, but she had limped off to hide under a gorse-brake. The kittens had grown up and gone their wild way, and now she was pregnant again. But for poor Mary there was nothing but some sort of nursing-home.

She clung to his wrist and rubbed her head against his arm. Moulting, he thought, still clinically remembering the cat. She was going to have a baby, no doubt of it. It accounted for everything, for her nerves, for her legs, for her appetite, for her arrival. Poor Mary! Patriotism had not been enough, she had had no hatred in her heart for anybody, and so she was going to have a baby. The fortunes of war. Some get killed, some get maimed, some are got with child. There ought to be a pension from the War Office. And in that dreadful uniform, too, those pitiable skirts turned up. I hope to God, he thought, I shall not have to meet the father – one of those strenuous noodles who think badly of the death sentence as like as not. I'm damned if I will. And the next instant he was thinking: My poor Mary, I hope it wasn't a rape. Meanwhile his indifferent body was complying with the schedule of his daily life, and he felt himself to be growing more and more sleepy, and knew that unless he spoke he might yawn.

'If you'll let go a minute, Mary, I'll make some tea.'

She let go. The hand that had been so strong fell on her lap and crept into the other hand. Presently it moved again and pulled out a khaki handkerchief, and she began to mop her eyes and snort back her tears.

'This damned war! It's this damned war, Nicholas.'

He groaned assentingly.

'Now that it's nearly over, how I hate it!'

With an effort he refrained from pointing out that it was only in Europe that the war might be said to be nearly over.

'If they'd let me fight, as I wanted to, I might be killed by now. If we'd stayed in London and I'd driven an ambulance or a pump I might be killed by now. As it is, I've never been so healthy in all my life.'

'You don't look well,' he said. 'I noticed at once that you looked tired. And you got frightfully out of breath walking up the hill.'

'Eat! My healthy army fat! When I come out of the army, Nicholas, I shall come out healthy, hideous, middle-aged, and without an interest in life. And there will be hordes and hordes of me, all in the same boat. Gosh, what a crew!'

Giving up the hypothesis of a baby, he realised how much he was relinquishing. Once it was born, she would have been happy enough.

'We shall all be in that boat, dear. Besides, you're a sergeant, aren't you? That's something. You'll soon get thin, once you're out in the rough-and-tumble of civilian life. Once you're thin, you'll take hold, you'll get interested in something or other. Probably you'll fall in love, and make a fresh start.'

The kettle was boiling. He began to prepare for more tea.

POOR MARY

'Fall in love? Fall in love?' she cried. 'Not again! You see, I did it.'

He paused, kettle in hand. Would nothing rid him of these turbulent kettles?

'And he was killed? I'm sorry, Mary.'

'He wasn't killed. He chucked me, and now he's married to another bitch.'

'And that's all?'

'And that's all.'

He glanced towards the clock. It felt like midnight, but it was only half-past ten. If he could give her something stronger, some whisky, some rum. A little rum, now, in her tea. . . . But a pigeon-shooting party last week had cleaned out the *Red Lion* of everything except aniseed cordial.

'Sugar?' he enquired.

She looked at him.

'I'm sorry. I'm sorry! I asked you that only three hours ago, didn't I? I am an insensate clod.'

'That's all right, Nicholas. Actually, I never take sugar in tea. You could have had all mine, you see. Think what you've missed. Actually, why I came back was to see if you'd ever want to live with me again. Not that I thought it likely. Why should you? Anyhow, it's plain you don't. So that's over. What good tea you make.'

She drank in gulps, swallowing violently, swallowing tea and tears.

'You were always domestically inclined, weren't you? It will be a comfort to me, yes, really it will, to think of you being so happy and tidy and self-contained, with your cat and your corpse-candles and your books and your flowers. Did Robinson Crusoe have flowers on his table, as well as his old cat sitting up to it like a Christian? I can't remember.

Perhaps when we are both very old I may come and spend the afternoon with you on your island. And you can make me some of your nice tea, and ask me if I take sugar with it. But of course I'll give you ample warning. I won't be a disquieting footprint. I did warn you this time, you know.'

She had risen. She had picked up her cap and her pack and her cigarette-case and her lighter and her lipstick and all her bits and pieces.

'I think I'll go to bed,' she said. 'I've got rather a headache,'

'Yes. We'll go to bed.'

Leaving the room all anyhow, he thought, as he stared at her submissive military back in the doorway. Whether it made things better, whether it made them worse, it was the only thing he could do, the only way he could comfort her. They would lie in the Wordsworthian bed, their smells of dung and of metal would mingle, her shoulder would feel like greengages and her hair would get in his mouth, and she would be silent. It was one of her graces that she was silent in bed. And afterwards, when she had gone to sleep, he would straighten himself and lie on his back, letting the day's fatigue run out of his limbs as the fleas run out of the body of a shot rabbit. And probably his last waking thought would be of the alarm clock, poised to wake him at five-thirty, and of the limpid innocent morning in which he would go out to his work.

THE COLD

The Cold came into the household by Mrs. Ryder. At first she said she had picked it up at the Mothers' Union meeting; later – it was the kind of cold that gets worse with time – she attributed it to getting chilled through waiting in the village shop while that horrible Beryl Legg took over half an hour to decide whether she would spend her points on salmon or Spam. Never a thought for her child, of course, who by now should be getting prunes and cereals. Whoever the father might be, one would have expected the girl to show some maternal feeling – but no!

The next person to get The Cold was old Mr. Ryder, the Rector's father, and he immediately gave it to old Mrs. Ryder. They did not have it so badly, but at their age and after all they had gone through in London before they could make up their minds to evacuate themselves to their son's country parish, one had to put them to bed with trays, just to be on the safe side. Dry and skinny, they lay in the spare-room twin beds like two recumbent effigies on tombs, and chattered to each other in faded high-pitched voices. Segregated from the normal family life they had re-established that rather tiresome specialness which sometimes made it difficult to realise that they were really dear Gerald's parents. It is very nice to be cultivated, of course, but somehow in wartime it does jar to labour upstairs with a heavy supper-tray and hear, beyond the door, two animated voices discussing Savonarola; and then to hear the voices silenced, like mice when one throws a shoe in their direction, as one knocked on the door and called out brightly, 'Supper, darlings!' and to know, as clearly as if one had seen it, that old Mrs. Ryder was stubbing out one of her cigarettes. That jarred, too, especially as she smoked such very heavy ones.

From the old Ryders The Cold descended to the third and fourth generation, to Geraldine and her two boys. Thence it leaped upon the Rector, 'Leaped' was indeed the word. He had set out for the funeral looking the picture of health, he returned haggard and shivering, and so terribly depressed that she had said to herself: 'Influenza!' But it was only The Cold – The Cold in its direst form.

'No!' exclaimed Mrs. Allingham, indefatigable secretary of the Women's Institute. '*Not* the Rector?'

'If you had been in church on Sunday you wouldn't need to ask.'

For the indefatigable secretary was a matter for regret on Sundays, when she was more often seen taking her terriers over the Common than herself to Saint Botolph and All Angels. Such a pity! – for in every other way she was an excellent influence.

Recovering herself rather too easily, for it showed that such recoveries were nothing to the rebuked one, Mrs. Allingham went on: 'All seven of you! For I can see you've got it too. You poor things! My dear, what do you do about handkerchiefs, now that the laundry only collects once a fortnight? Can I lend you some?'

THE COLD

'Stella washes them.'

'Your marvellous Stella! What would you do without her? I hope she is still standing up.'

'I can't imagine Stella failing us,' said Mrs. Ryder with satisfaction.

In the sixth autumn of the war Mrs. Ryder was a little tired. She was feeling her age. Her last tailor-made was definitely not quite a success and, say what you will, people do judge one by appearances: she could not help noticing that strangers were not as respectful as they might be; though no doubt the unhelpfulness of Utility corsets played its part in the decline of manners. In the parish, too, there was much to grieve the Rector and the Rector's wife. The old, simple, natural order of things was upset by all these changes, the grocer's son actually a Captain, as much a Captain (and indeed senior in captaincy) as dear Geraldine's Neville, the butcher's wife in Persian lamb, the resolutions at the Parish Council only to be described as Communist, and the girls, her own Girls' Club girls, behaving so shockingly that she often wondered what the mothers of these poor American soldiers would think if they only knew what their sons were exposed to. But she had Stella. And having Stella she had all things.

No one could pick holes in Stella. There were no holes to pick. Stella was physically perfect, not deaf, nor halt, nor imbecile. Stella did not wear glasses and did wear a cap and apron. Stella was functionally perfect, she did not dawdle, she did not waste, she did not gossip, she was clean, punctual, reliable, she was always cheerful and willing, she scrubbed her own back kitchen and mended the choir surplices; and though of course her wages were perfectly adequate, no one could say that the Ryders bribed her to stay with them. Stella stayed through devotion, she could have got twice as much elsewhere. Finally, Stella was a good girl. In a time when manners and morality had gone down alike before expediency, when householders snatched at trousered and cigarette-smoking evacuees if the evacuee would 'help with light domestic duties,' when even the houses that ought to set an example employed girls with illegitimate babies and glossed over the capitulation with pretexts of being compassionate and broad-minded, Mrs. Ryder continued to boast the ownership of a virgin, a strong womanly virgin who wore skirts, fastened-up unwaved hair in a sensible knob, and said, 'Yes, ma'am.'

Naturally, one took care of such a treasure. Stella's cold was given quite as much consideration as any other family cold and dosed out of the same bottle. In the worst of the epidemic Mrs. Ryder said that if Stella did not feel better by midday she really must be sent to bed. For several evenings Mrs. Ryder and Geraldine washed up the supper dishes so that Stella might sit quietly by the stove with the surplices instead of shivering in the back-kitchen; and when Stella's cough persisted after the other coughs had died away Geraldine went in specially by bus to look for blackcurrant lozenges and came back with some wonderful pastilles flavoured with horehound.

But it was a long time before Stella's cough could be distinguished from the other coughs by outlasting them. The Cold was such a treacherous type of cold. When you thought you'd got rid of it, it came back. Like beggars, said old Mrs. Ryder (for they were downstairs again, one could not keep them in bed indefinitely). Like dandelions, said her son. Geraldine said that she believed it was nutritional.

THE COLD

Of course one ought not to complain, the food was marvellous really, more marvellous than ever if one thought about poor old Europe; but still, it wasn't the same, was it? She had met Mrs. Allingham, and Mrs. Allingham had enquired, of course, about The Cold, and had said that in 1918 everyone had just the same kind of cold, it was quite remarkable. What did the Grand-grands say? Did they have colds in 1918? 'We had much better rum, and more of it,' said old Mrs. Ryder. She looked at her husband very affectionately; he stroked his beard and looked back at her, and so they both avoided seeing Mrs. Ryder catch her breath like one who holds back a justified reproach because experience has shown that reproaches are vain. The Rector, even more imperceptive, remarked that it was very kind of his parents to make poor Stella a nightcap, he hoped it would do her good. He had seen rum do a lot of good when he was a chaplain in Flanders. Stella was a good girl, a very good girl. They would be badly off without her.

For some reason Mrs. Ryder and her daughter now began discussing how tomorrow they really must polish the stair-rods and the bathroom taps. They would make time for it somehow if Mrs. Ryder did the altar vases before breakfast and Stella took the boys with her when she went to the farm for milk. If the boys wore their rubber boots, the slush wouldn't do them any harm.

John was five, Michael was three. You couldn't really call them spoilt, they were just wartime, lacking the influence of a father about the house. But not spoilt. Besides, Geraldine liked boys to behave as boys; it would be too awful if they grew up like Neville's ghastly young brother who would sit for hours stroking the cat and turning off the wireless whenever it became worth listening to. A dressing-room had been made over as their play-room, but it was bleak up there, and naturally they preferred the kitchen. If anyone spoilt them it was Stella, who didn't seem able to say no to them. And if they were rather fretful just now, it wasn't to be wondered at, it was The Cold.

The doctor's sister, a rather uncongenial character with independent means, used to refer to Mrs. Ryder and her daughter as Bright and Breezy. They had a great deal in common she said, but Geraldine had more of it, and was Breezy. Geraldine now had more of The Cold. Her sneezes were louder, her breathing more impeded, her nose redder, and her handkerchiefs more saturated. Throughout The Cold Mrs. Ryder had kept on her feet: as a daughter-in-law, mother, grandmother, and wife to a Rector, she could not do otherwise; but Geraldine had not merely kept on her feet, she stamped and trampled. She scorned precautions, she went everywhere and kissed everybody, just as usual. She did not believe, not she! in cosseting a cold. What are colds? Everyone has them, they are part of English life. Foreigners have things with spots, the English have colds. She made having a cold seem part of the national tradition, like playing cricket and Standing Alone.

And so, when they had all got rid of The Cold and even Stella only coughed at night, Geraldine seemed to be breaking the Union Jack at the masthead when she woke the echoes of the kitchen with a violent sneeze, and asserted:

'I'm beginning another cold. And what's more, I can tell it's going to be a snorter. So watch out, one and all!'

'I do hope not, Miss Geraldine,' answered Stella.

THE COLD

It was rather touching the way Stella still called her Miss Geraldine - as if to Stella the passage of time were nothing, a tide that flowed past the kitchen threshold but never wetted her feet.

'No jolly hope!'

Geraldine went out. Presently she could be heard telling her mother about the new cold. Mrs. Ryder sounded unenthusiastic; she said she only hoped it would not last so long this time, as otherwise it would spoil Christmas. Stella went on rubbing stale bread through a sieve for the wartime Christmas pudding. It needed a lot of breadcrumbs; in fact, you might as well call it bread-pudding and be done with it; but Mrs. Ryder said the children must be brought up to love Christmas. They stood on either side of the table, rolling bread-pills and throwing them at each other.

The recipe for the wartime Christmas pudding which needed a lot of breadcrumbs also called for grated carrot. When she had finished the breadcrumbs, and put them on a high shelf where she hoped the children might not get at them, Stella went into the back-kitchen and began to clean carrots over the sink. If you rub stale bread through a fine sieve for any length of time, you are apt to develop a pain between the shoulders. She had such a pain; and the change of climate from the kitchen which was hot, to the back-kitchen which was cold, made her more conscious of it. When she had cleaned the carrots she went back to the kitchen. The two little boys were still there and Mrs. Ryder had been added.

'Oh, Stella, I came in to say that I thought we would have onion soup tonight, as well as the fish-cakes, Mrs. Hartley thinks she has another cold coming on.'

'Yes, ma'am. I wish to . . .'

Mrs. Ryder swept on. 'And, Stella, of course I know how busy you are, but all the same I think it would be better *not* to leave the babies alone in here. When I came in I found John playing with the flat-irons. Of course they were cold, but they might have been hot. Perhaps a little more thoughtfulness . . . With such young children one cannot be too thoughtful.'

'Very well, ma'am. But I wish to leave, ma'am.'

'Beddy-bies, beddy-bies!' exclaimed Mrs. Ryder. 'Come now, John, come, Michael! Kiss dear Stella good-night, and off with you to your little beds. Now a nice kiss . . .'

'Don't want to,' said the child,

Mrs. Ryder seized a child under either arm, waved them in the direction of Stella's face, and conveyed them out of the room, shutting the door on them with a firm sweet, God Bless you, my babies!' Then, flushed with exertion, with difficulty withstanding the impulse to go with them, she turned back, hoping that her ears had deceived her and knowing too well that they hadn't.

'I wish to leave, ma'am.'

'Stella! What do you mean?'

'I wish to leave, ma'am.'

There she stood, grating carrots as if the children's Christmas were nothing to her.

'But, Stella . . . I *trusted* you. After all these years! Why, we all look on you as a friend. What has happened to you?'

Could it be, could it be? Stella was short and the kitchen table was high and anything may be happening behind an apron. In a convulsion of the imagination Mrs. Ryder rehearsed herself saying that one should not penalise a poor girl for a solitary slip, that kindness, a good home, the

THE COLD

example of a Christian home-life which means so much, etc., etc. A harlot hope raised its head, and at the same moment she heard Stella say quite idiotically:

'I think I'm catching another cold.'

'Good heavens, girl, is that a reason for going? I've never heard such nonsense.'

'It's nothing but one cold after another – cold, cold, cold, work, work, work! It's not a fit place for me. Both my aunties were chesty, and if I stay here I shall go the same way, I know it. What's more, I'm going tomorrow. I don't mind about my money, I'm going tomorrow. I want to get away while I've still got the strength to.'

'In wartime,' said Mrs. Ryder, in her sternest Mothers' Union manner, the manner only unfurled for urgent things like War Savings Rallies and Blood Transfusion Drives, 'in wartime, when our boys are shedding their blood without a moment's hesitation . . . and you are positively running away from a simple cold in the head. I cannot believe it.'

Without a spark of incredulity she banged the door behind her.

There was the Rectory hall. There were the coats and the children's rubber boots and the umbrellas, and the brass letter-tray, and the copper gong, and the stair-rods ascending. There was Gerald writing in his study, and Geraldine gargling in the bathroom, and in the sitting-room the two old Ryders chattering like love-birds. Here was her home, her dear (except for the old Ryders), her dear, dear home, where everything spoke of love and loving labour: the happy, busy home that was – Mrs. Allingham's own words – a beacon to the parish.

But now . . .

Not Stella? Not your marvellous Stella?

The words seemed to dart at her from every side, stabbing through the unsuccessful tailor-made into her ageing flesh. Tomorrow the Sewing Circle met at the Rectory. Only self-respect withheld her from running back into the kitchen to throw herself on Stella's mercy, to beg, on her knees, even, to beg and implore that Stella would change her mind, would stay, would at any rate stay to see them over Christmas. Self-respect was rage and fury. Presently they died down. But she remained in the hall, knowing that any appeal to Stella would be in vain.

Tomorrow the Sewing Circle met. They met at three in the afternoon. Stella would be out of the house before then. *She must be!* Mrs. Ryder thanked God that self-respect had stood like an angel between her and a fatal false step. 'Stella has gone. Poor Stella! . . I could not keep her.' A few such words, and a grave grieved silence, nothing that was not true, strictly true; and the Sewing Circle might draw its own conclusions. Cooking, sweeping, scrubbing, doing everything that for so long Stella had done, she could still hold up her head.

ENGLISH CLIMATE

As Gunner Brock opened the door of the recreation hut a volley of rain came in, and a cat. He shut the door and turned to look at the cat. It was a new ginger, he noted. Cats came and went on the anti-aircraft site, and this annoyed Gunner Brock, who had a tidy mind and felt that cats should be permanent. One grievance flicked him into voicing another. 'Perhaps you'll have got those books changed by the time I'm back,' he said to Gunner Ives who was sunk deep in a chair, reading.

A dozen exhausted volumes sagged on a shelf by the door. Their subject-matter did not so much express the eclecticism of the Welfare Officer who had brought them out from the library a fortnight earlier as the fact that he had chosen them after lunching protractedly with a friend.

'Not till I've finished *The Wide Wide World*,' said Gunner Ives, who was a Marxist. 'Just listen to this. . . .'

Gunner Brock fidgeted with one foot and then the other and finally interrupted him. 'I've got to catch my train,' he said.

'Well,' Gunner Ives said, his glance still drawn irresistibly towards the paragraph he had been reading. 'So long. Have a good leave.'

'Thanks,' Brock said, and went out into the rain.

It was a five-mile walk to the station, and the last mile and a half he hurried, but he needn't have done so; the afternoon train was nearly twenty minutes late. He found a seat, and began his journey of nineteen hours and five changes. The railway track ran within half a mile of the anti-aircraft site. Through the streaming window he saw briefly the huts, the smoke from the cookhouse chimney, the searchlight and the locator in their canvas hoods. It looked as though some demented fair had set itself up on the heath and now waited for the arrival of customers.

By midday tomorrow he would be home. At midday tomorrow it would still be raining. He would spend the afternoon having a bath, wallowing at full length, hearing the chirp of rain in the gutters and the gentle wallop of the bath-water running down the overflow pipe. There he would lie, reading. And downstairs would be Mother, rattling the tea things, Edna coming home from her office then Dad. At seven Mother and Edna would go off to the Y.M.C.A. canteen, splashing so bravely through the wet. How on earth did women support life when there wasn't a war? What would Mother do when this war was over and the canteen was closed and she was left with but one son (if that, indeed) instead of those dozens of 'my boys,' towards all of whom she felt like a mother? A retired colonel, however fire-eating, takes up gardening or plays golf or bridge or busies himself with local administration or rings migratory birds, for men are flippant, variable, easily amused, But to a woman's iron energies what appeasement can peace bring?

Left to themselves he and Dad would wash up and get supper. The cat, the fixed and proper family cat, would rub round their legs. Once again he would feel that profound sensation of being indoors - a far more intimate sensation than that of merely being at home. Gradually, he would adjust himself to small rooms, unechoing floors, passages, stairways, the complexity of a house. And upstairs his bedroom, close-fitting as a thimble, would wait for him: silently, privately, intensely, it would await the moment when he switched on the bedside lamp and shut the door after him. In that room he would slowly and luxuriously undress and luxuriously slide between the sheets and find the hot-water bottle, and lie for a breathing space listening to the rain, summoning his senses for that journey of the hand to the bookshelf. Which should it be? The fourth from the left was *Boswell's Life*, then the even ranks of the *Fitzgerald Letters*. In his fingers stirred a consciousness of how that bookshelf would feel: the orderly row, the smooth backs, the sharp corners - a world away from that heap of flaccid derelicts by the door of the recreation hut.

Waking at a burst of light and cold morning air as three schoolboys, smelling freshly of soap and early rising, climbed in over his legs, Gunner Brock saw that the weather had cleared. The sun was rising into a sky full of wind and movement. Presently he changed into the last of his trains. It was a stopping train, and the last two hours of his journey enforced the sense of home-coming, for the new passengers had the familiar local accent and intonation and talked of people and of places that he knew. At the stop before Dumbridge a woman got in who said: 'Why, I do believe it's young Mr. Brock, isn't it?' and told him how wonderful his mother was, doing so much yet always ready to take on more, and Edna was wonderful too, the woman added. All this was dulling to the edge of arrival. He seemed to have been arriving for hours. As he walked down the Station Road towards the High Street home seemed to him primarily a place where he could put down his traps.

Turning into the High Street, he experienced a momentary impression that there had been an air-raid. Heaped on the pavements were bedsteads and fire-irons and kettles; Boy Scouts and Girl Guides were pushing hand-carts laden with bundles of clothes; on the wine-merchant's doorstep was a parcel of parchment-bound ledgers neatly fastened together, and from the house beyond an old woman came out who carried a bird cage and a large tolling hand-bell. The Union Jack flew from the church tower. Stretched across the street, banging and bellying in the wind, was a wide calico streamer: DUMB . . . NATION . . . AGE . . . 'DUMBRIDGE NATIONAL SALVAGE WEEK.' Mid-way up the street was a whippet tank, so flimsy, so out-moded, that for an instant he supposed that some citizen cherishing it as a garden ornament had now relinquished it for salvage, but of course it was there to show the good people of Dumbridge what could be done with their iron bedsteads. Beyond the whippet tank was a long meandering trail, a dingy caterpillar whose meaning became clear to him as a woman's voice behind exclaimed: 'Just look at the book mile! Where on earth have they all come from?' 'What a clearance!' replied her companion.

At first he thought he would turn into a side street and so avoid this *auto-da-fé* of disgraced books laid out ready for the junk collectors. But he was too angry to spare himself, and walked on, countering his distress by reflecting on the kind of books Dumbridge could muster up: *The Scarlet Pimpernel, Hints to Fly Fishers, Anecdotes of European Courts,* and volumes of poetry called *Tally-Ho* or *By Quiet*

Waters. 'If I see a copy of *Jessica's First Prayer*, I'll pinch it for Ives,' he told himself.

So inevitably he began to look, to loiter. *Montaigne's Essays* – good Lord, who would have thought Dumbridge could produce them! *Paradise Lost* – that was not so surprising. *Letters of Queen Victoria* – oh, poor Ives! *The Collected Poems of Edward Thomas* – now who, he wondered, owning that and reading it too, for it had the unmistakable warmed look of a well-read copy, could have cast it out into a book mile? He picked it up. The moment it was in his hand, as though some electricity leaped from the book to the man, he knew whose copy it was. He did not need the confirmation of the flyleaf: *Edwin Brock. April, 1934*. He put it back and walked on, as though walking on would annul what had happened. But the book mile kept up with him; in a moment he would be compelled to open his senses again, to walk slowly, to trail his glance from cover to cover, waiting for another recognition. What tomfoolery! He would go back and rescue it. It was his book.

A voice said: 'Edwin Brock, I do declare!' It was Mr. Cheeseman, chemist and town councillor of Dumbridge and an old family friend. 'Delighted to see you, my boy! I thought it must be you from the way you were studying those old books. You were always one for books, weren't you? Well, what do you think of it? Pretty good, eh?'

'Is there really a mile of it?'

'Well, between you and me, no. But it goes as far as the Boer Memorial. And every inch of it a gift, you know.'

'People bring their books, do they?' Edwin asked. 'And add them on?'

'Some do,' Mr. Cheeseman said. 'On our opening day you should have seen them come running out of their houses. Of course, by now it's beginning to dry up and we have to help out the look of it by books that have come in as ordinary salvage. But it's all genuine salvage, genuine Dumbridge Borough salvage, whoever puts it there. As for the old garden hoses and the brass door-knobs and the aluminium, you'd never believe it. Why, people have even brought out their medals!'

My *Fitzgerald's Letters* must be here somewhere, Brock thought; the old *Bevis* I bought when I was thirteen, and dropped into the river, and dived for; and my Nonesuch *Swift*.

'And every scrap of it good for something,' said Mr. Cheeseman with reverence. 'Every scrap of it useful at long last, You can tell the Army that we're doing our best for you. Well, here we are at the Memorial. And you can see it comes right up to here. I'm going your way, as it happens, so I'll walk with you. Mill Street looks a bit naked, doesn't it, with the railings gone?'

'Yes, it does a bit.'

'There's your mother waiting for you,' Mr. Cheeseman said.

She was standing on the doorstep, some knitting in her hands. When she saw Edwin, she waved the knitting and then added some more stitches.

'Here's my boy!'

Her first glance was for his sleeve. No stripes – and as he had foreseen, her face fell. Then, just as he had also foreseen, she reassumed that air of resolute buoyancy, the expression which in old days he and Edna had called Mother's Mrs. Greatheart, and began to tell him how well he looked, how much broader he had grown, and that she had actually got a duck for dinner, though of course it was only a small one.

'I explained to Mr. Hawes that you were coming back on leave,' she said, 'and he swore to do his utmost. People are so wonderfully kind! Oh, and that reminds me, Mr. Cheeseman, I can't manage Thursday, because I am at Report Centre in the morning, and then I shall be packing Prisoners' Parcels instead of poor Mrs. West – it's so sad for her that she gets these incessant colds just now – and after that I have the canteen, of course, and then the Working Party, and then the canteen again. Besides, I must keep a morsel of time for my Edwin now he's here.'

She laid her hand on his disgraceful sleeve and continued to discuss dates with Mr. Cheeseman. Edna appeared. She looked extraordinarily tired, shabby, and sterile. 'So you managed to get off for the duck and Edwin,' said her mother.

Indoors, there was a delicious smell of roast duck and a smell of daffodils. The table was spread with a damask so white that it seemed to sparkle, and by his place was his old mug and two bottles of beer. Edna went to wash her hands.

'My darling!' Mrs. Brock said to her son. 'My ducky! How I've been longing for this!' And for that moment she was quite genuine, and looked old and careworn and at the same time girlishly excited and vulnerable.

'Edna looks rotten,' he said. 'What's wrong with her?'

Instantly his mother began to bridle.

'I daresay she's tired. We're all a little tired, you know. And then, poor Edna, it's rather depressing for her not being allowed to join up in the A.T.S. But Mr. Ransom won't release her. And as I tell her, even if she has to stay in a civilian job, she's freeing someone else, so really it's just the same thing.'

'Better money, anyway.'

All through the meal it was like that. A devil spoke, not he, snubbing every advance, deriding every brag. And the poor old woman, gallant and obtuse, came back every time for more punishment. Even the duck he could only praise by saying that one didn't get that sort of food in canteens, and a mention of fire-watching provoked a belittling enquiry as to how many bombs had fallen on Dumbridge—none, as he well knew, having fallen. Yet he had not meant it, and even now did not mean it. Walking beside old Cheeseman, he had settled with himself that it was no use scolding over spilt milk, that there was nothing for it but philosophy. One was always being philosophic in the army, so why not be philosophic at home too, where at least there was peace and quiet to be won by keeping one's temper? But suddenly there was nothing left but to know the worst, and pushing back his chair he ran from the room.

When he came back Edna was carrying out a trayful of dishes. His mother was sitting by the window. Her knitting was on her lap, but for once she was not knitting. She was looking at a pot of newly opened daffodils and blinking, as though their pure colour hurt her eyes.

'What's happened to my books?' he cried. 'What have you been doing with my books?'

She turned to him, and it intensified his fury to see that her expression was one of relief. 'Your books, darling? I brought them down here, to keep dry. All the good ones – your prizes and the encyclopaedia.'

'Oh!' he said. 'Then why did I see so many of them in that damned book mile of yours?'

'Oh, those were only the old things. Edna and I went through them most carefully, I'm sure. And one must do something,' she added, losing her temper because she was afraid; 'we poor civilians in a poor old town that doesn't even get a bomb on it. Surely you wouldn't grudge a few old books for national salvage! Think what it means to the country!'

'Why didn't you burn them,' he said, 'and get some fun out of it, like they do in Germany?'

'Burn them? *Burn a book*? Why, for months now we've been lighting the fires with gorse and shavings. There's no paper burned in this house, I can tell you. Every scrap of it goes into salvage. Burn a book? Why, your father's even given up his shaving calendar!'

Edwin began to laugh. He laughed on and on, like a machine, for each idiot peal deferred the moment when he would have to decide between keeping his grudge or going to retrieve what he could from the book mile.

His mother went to the door. 'Edna!' she called. 'Edna, take your mack. It's coming on to rain again, a regular downpour. Such a pity, on Edwin's first afternoon, too!' And returning she knelt down stiffly before the grate, saying that on such a wretched afternoon they really must have a fire.

MAJOR BRICE AND MRS. CONWAY

In May 1946, Major Brice, of the U.S. Army, revisiting London and liking it no better than before, drove himself into the country on a vernal impulse to re-examine a Mrs. Conway who in 1944 had been briefly his hostess and his mistress – and more to his taste in the second category. Her house had been cold, her bathroom had been gaunt, her table had been ill-spread except when he spread it, and from sundown to sunrise he had been pestered with black-out regulations. That was how he had discovered her more satisfactory aspect. For while he lay reading in bed, the only place where he could escape from the draughts, she had burst into his room, wearing of all things a steel helmet – she had been out on some civilian nonsense or other – saying furiously that if he was afraid to go to sleep in the dark he might at least exert himself to draw his curtains properly. As one throws a cover over canaries when they make too much noise, he had switched off the light while she was still in mid-career. *Oh*! she had said, startled into primness. A minute later she and her helmet were scattered on his bed.

And really, that was the thing he most warmly remembered: her startled *Oh!* so inadequate and female, her lips, fresh with the outdoor cold, and the genuine satisfaction of having silenced them.

That was in February or early March. Ten days later he had gone off to a battle school and after that to battle itself. 'Give my regards,' he had said, 'to your English spring,' Every dreary acquaintance of hers and her incessant sister-in-law incessantly had remarked to him that really he should see Ludworth in an English spring.

Now, as the lanes became familiar and the name he had known by ordnance map and hearsay appeared on the fingerposts – Abbot's Woolcombe, Little Poakers, Chelbury Regis – he was seeing it. There was too much of it, he thought, and all of it too close. Hawthorn hedges blocked his way like snowdrifts, the small, steep pastures were bruisingly vivid with buttercups, and when he paused to study yet another fingerpost at yet another junction of floral rat-runs, the noise of the birds was deafening as musketry, and the smell of the may-blossom made him sneeze. She had been much the same, he thought: her lust too lusty, her abandonment without sensibility; and all, like this landscape, in such a small way; for there had been no perspective of love between them, no basic tenderness, scarcely a farewell, and no letter-writing. She had bestowed herself as the English sell bread: unwrapped and unanalysed.

As the house came into sight he thought: Perhaps she is away; and the surmise was followed by a distinct sense of relief. He wanted her to be away. But for all that he drove in between the stone gateposts and got out, leaving his bag in the car, and rang the bell.

The door was open, he could see into the house. It was as shabby as ever, so shabby that one could not see that it was two years the shabbier. After a while, since no one answered the bell (no one had ever answered any bell, for the only house-servant was stone-deaf), he walked in and went into the sitting-room. Nothing was changed yet everything was different. Presently he saw why. The hearth on which she had kept so inadequate a fire was blazing with sprays of beech and laburnum, with white irises and fat crimson paeony blossoms. The faded green walls, the sheep-faced family portraits, the exhausted upholstery, were shadows in a garden; for trophies of flowers stood everywhere, and through the open window the branches which had rapped with wintry fingers on the pane extended into the room – mock-orange and clematis and sagging roses.

Except for the birds yelling outside, all was silent. When he could bear it no longer he turned on the wireless. Out came a talk on the cuckoo. He twiddled until he found some dance-music, and made it as loud as possible. That always used to fetch her, then.

It fetched her now. She went by outside the window, wearing a blue dress. He whistled her. She made an almost imperceptible turn of the head, but did not pause.

When she had not come in he began to feel somehow alarmed. He switched off the wireless and heard her steps go swiftly along the passage. Then a door shut. That was all. He snapped on the wireless again, and the small action transmuted his feeling of alarm into anger and resentment. This was their English hospitality!

Unheard, she was in the room, wearing a green dress and saying: 'Do you mind if I turn this down a bit?' just as she used to do. Then she turned it off, just as she used to do, and advanced on him with her ugly, inattentive smile, the smile of a street urchin and not a woman's smile at all, and held out her hand, and said:

'Hullo! how nice to see you.'

Her voice expressed nothing beyond being in her own house and addressing someone who had entered it. But for all that she had stayed to change her dress. Her hand was quitting his when he took a firmer hold of it and kissed it. It was pretty much like kissing a lizard – a lizard with some ill-fitting rings on.

'Are you over here for long? Do sit down and tell me all your adventures. Did you enjoy the war?'

Aching to slap her face, he settled back in a chair, crossed his legs, lit a cigar, and said:

'Well, it was interesting. I suppose it would have been even more interesting if one had known it was in the nature of a last performance.'

'Do you think so?'

'Well, there aren't going to be any more wars like that. All that's a back number, now.

'Oh, of course. You're thinking of your new bomb.'

'I'm not the only one who's doing that'

'And do you know all about it, Terence?'

'No. We don't let it out quite as freely as that.'

'What a shame! Never mind, perhaps you'll be allowed to drop one. On London, for instance. You'd love that.'

'I mightn't feel too badly about it,' he said. 'But I wouldn't be doing it, anyway. They'll probably come over by rocket.'

'Better and better,' she said. 'Why, in the next war you Americans won't need to put yourselves out at all.'

'No. We'll just be sending you parcels. As usual.'

He looked at her green dress. It was ugly, made of a poor stuff and coloured with a poor dye. She had looked better in the blue one. Being a man of thoughtful character, he reflected: suppose she went and changed into an uglier dress because of me? If she imagined it enhanced her green eyes, she was wrong. It put them out.

'As a matter of fact,' he said, 'I just came down to look at the village church.'

She laughed.

'Suppose you have some tea first.'

'Oh, tea!' But because she had laughed and for a moment had looked easy, he added: 'Well, I'd like to eat another of those things like sponges. Crumpets.'

'But one doesn't eat crumpets in May!'

She spoke with no more malice than a school-teacher, and nothing she had said before was comparable as an insult.

'Of course not, of course not! It's their mating season.'

She waited a moment or two, and said smoothly:

'You're looking very well, Terence. Did you come over by air or on a food-ship?'

He threw his cigar at the paeonies and got up, just in time to see her walk into the room wearing a blue dress.

'Mary, this is Major Brice. This is my daughter, Terence.'

Mary Conway was not a beauty, she had no style, she had nothing beyond the temporary advantage of being twenty years younger than the mother she so exactly resembled. So why should Ruth Conway sound so jubilant about her? She could not possibly know of his mind's slight misadventure with a blue dress.

'Major Brice has come down from London to see the church, darling. He hadn't time to see it when he was quartered here in 1944.'

'I suppose you were frightfully busy?'

'Frightfully.'

Twenty years ago Ruth Conway was just as obtuse, no doubt. But now, he reflected, she wasn't. Such a situation had possibilities.

'After tea you must show it to him.'

'Oh, yes, I'd love to. Do you like architecture, Major Brice?'

'I'm fascinated by your British architecture.'

'He's seeing all he can in the time,' remarked her mother.

'I suppose you are going back quite soon?'

'We Americans are always in a hurry, you know. We haven't got your background, we haven't got your sense of repose.'

She turned to her mother and said: 'Would you like me to do anything about hurrying tea?'

'Don't think about tea,' he said. 'I know how things are over here. I'd hate to take the jam sandwiches out of your mouths. It's just the church I want to see.'

'Make sure he signs the visitor's book, Mary.'

'I'm crazy about your old village churches. We have no churches in the States, you know.'

'I expect you come from the Middle West,' said the girl. 'You ought to visit New England. There are some very nice churches in New England. They are made of wood and painted white, and they look exactly as if Sir Christopher Wren had designed some rather grand bathing-machines for Queen Anne. They can be moved about on rollers, too, which is more than you can say for our churches here. You really ought to go to New England if you are so fond of churches.'

'Don't the New Englanders speak with quite an accent?' asked the son of Vermont.

'Yes, they do, rather. It's supposed to be an English accent really. In some of the backward places in Lincolnshire the old people still talk like that.'

'Your mother didn't tell me you'd visited our country.'

'I was sent there in 1940 to be out of the way. I was there for two years, and I came home with a collection of the wildest hats, and such an accent that Daddy sent me to school all over again to be scraped.'

With a picture in his mind's eye of how Ruth Conway must be enjoying herself, he glanced round to confirm it. She was kneeling before the hearth. So she had knelt before, puffing at the fire with a pair of wheezy bellows and sometimes even dimly apologising for the absence of central heating; but now she was tranquilly rearranging her paeonies. His week-end bag, he remembered, was still in his car. He was in two minds whether it shouldn't remain there.

BOORS CAROUSING

It was still raining, it was half-past two in the afternoon. Mrs. Gainsborough had gone home, and would not be back till she came at half-past six to see about his dinner: he had his house to himself and the long afternoon before him.

No one would come interrupting in, the rain would see to that. Though country neighbours too often look on a snow-storm or an easterly gale as prevenient to a rousing walk and a call round about tea-time, this was summer rain: it would keep them at home, disapproving - irrationally, since the rainfall of an English summer is higher than the rainfall of an English winter. But they were not governed by reason.

He walked into the hall and took his telephone receiver off its stand. It began to utter the soft, duteous growl it would keep up till Mrs. Gainsborough came and replaced it. He stood listening to the only noise in the silence of his house. A heavenly and nourishing silence. No little footsteps on the stairs, no little smears of jam on the stair-rail. Magdalen and her brats had torn themselves away that morning. True, in the loving moment of riddance he had sketched an invitation for Christmas; but Christmas was a long way off, and by then, he hoped, his brother-in-law would be out of his job in Army Education and enforcing his natural dislike of intellectuals. All through his lovely empty house rang the noise of the rain, singing in the gutters, lisping against the window-panes, plashing on the flagged walk; and in his mind's ear he heard the most melodious rainfall of all, *l'eau qui tombe dans l'eau*, the rain falling into the swollen river that washed the foot of his garden and tugged at his Chinese willows. To look through the windows of a Georgian house at a Chinese view.... He sighed with contentment at his lot and went back to his library.

With a whole afternoon before him in which to write, it would be slavish, he thought, and sinning his mercies, to begin to write immediately. He would read for a little first. The act of reading, the effacement of mind in a kindred mind, *l'eau qui tombe dans l'eau*, puts one in the best frame for the act of writing. He would read for a little, then he would settle down to write; and seriously, working on his philosophical novel where he aimed to apply the narrow brush of Jane Austen to a Tiepoloesque design; for the charms of philosophy are usually obliterated by a style of revolting romanticism, all tufts and vapours. With Magdalen in the house he had found it almost impossible to get on with the novel; he had written short stories, a prey to human nature – which is poison and dram-drinking to the serious artist.

Half an hour later he put down his book, saying *Damn!* A knock on the front door had resounded through the house. Sitting motionless, he listened, and presently there was another knock.

'Blast these people who can't use the bell!' he muttered. Life in the country had taught him that there are two kinds of visitors: those who ring the bell and those who knock. Those who ring the bell are at least semi-educated and can be relied upon, after three or four rings, to use their wits and go away. Those who knock are the poor and humble, accustomed to being kept waiting, accustomed to being ignored. With the pertinacity of the down-trodden they are capable of knocking for an hour on end.

A third knock sounded, no louder than the first. After an interval, no longer or shorter than the previous intervals, there was a fourth knock. Exclaiming: 'And in five months' time it will be the carol-singers!' he rose and marched off to open his door.

'Oh, Mr. Kinloch! I see it's you, Mr. Kinloch. I am so sorry. . . .'

'Do come in.'

'No, no, I wouldn't interrupt you for the world. I just came to ask you – such a silly question, really. Do you think it will go on raining?'

'Undoubtedly, I should say. Do come in.'

'I said to myself, I'll just run up and ask Mr. Kinloch. I felt sure you'd have a barometer. I'm Miss Metcalf, you know.'

She was wearing a sou'wester, and the rain poured off it, and from under the brim and behind the raindrops she peered at him - like an elderly mermaid, he thought, who had taken to country life. Her name was Metcalf, and she was a maniac. So far, so good.

'Miss Metcalf,' she repeated. 'I live down by the river.'

Dort oben wunderbar. He repeated his invitation to come in

'I don't know if you've noticed how the river is rising. All this rain, of course. I'm so worried about the rabbits.

There are eight young ones.'

He said that probably their doe would look after them.

'But she can't. She's in the same boat. At least, it's a coop really, a sort of coop.'

'Dear, dear!' he said. 'But I wish you'd come in. You are getting so needlessly wet.'

She stared at him desperately.

'It only needs lifting. If it could be lifted on to the table – for I always keep a table in the garden, it's so nice in summer and one can put things on it – everything would be all right. But it is rather heavy, and the rabbits get so nervous and rush about like a shipwreck. . . .'

'I'll come at once,' he said, dimly and gloomily realising an appeal to his manly strength.

At his gate there was a moment of awkwardness, for he turned to the left and set off briskly towards the village. She followed him tugging at his sleeve.

'It's the other way, Mr. Kinloch. I'm Miss Metcalf, you know. I daresay you thought I was Miss Hancock. *She* lives by the church.'

They turned about, and splashed down a lane and across a sopping meadow where an indeterminate track led into a grove of willows and alders which was also, apparently, a rubbish-tip for the village, since some old iron bedsteads and disused oil-heaters glowered rustily among the tree-trunks. Beyond this, suddenly and surprisingly whitewashed and neat, was Miss Metcalf's dwelling, like a bandbox abandoned on the river's brim by someone who had committed suicide. And the river, just as Miss Metcalf had said, had risen enough to be washing over its banks and round a rabbit-hutch. He clasped the hutch – it was revoltingly cold and slimy – and lifted it on to a table.

BOORS CAROUSING

'It seems a pity,' he said, for somehow he had to overcome her pelt of thanks and apologies for having troubled him, 'to keep such a handsome mahogany table out of doors.'

'Oh yes, Mr. Kinloch, I often think so myself. But what am I to do? There is no room for it indoors and it belonged to my father. He was the rector, you know.'

So that was who she was! He had often heard her story and no doubt he had heard her name as often; but the two had become disconnected in his memory. Miss Metcalf's father had been the Reverend Thomas Metcalf, sometime Rector of this Parish and now resident under a very ornate and informative tombstone, which did not, however, mention that he had drunk himself and his fortune out of existence, which was why poor old Miss Metcalf lived where and how she did and was a trifle eccentric, you know.

But it seemed to him a charming place to live, if one did not object to being flooded from time to time and kept oneself uncompromised by rabbits. Her view was better than his own; for one thing it included his house, and at exactly the right distance to be seen at its best. Fortunate Miss Metcalf, who could gaze down the river all day at his south elevation, while screened from the world by her thicket of willows, alders, and old bed-steads! No one was likely to come knocking at her door. A time might come – a time might come too easily, if the housing shortage continued and he could no longer fend off impertinent enquiries as to how many bedrooms he had and whether he did not feel quite lonely all by himself in such a large house – when he might be very comfortable here. He did not suppose she would live for ever – and surely she and her rabbits would be much better off farther – so to speak – inland.

Meanwhile Miss Metcalf had become somewhat sprightly and was asking him in for what she called 'just a wee drappie.' It was now too late to refuse, so he followed her under a trellised porch that was like Niagara, and past what he believed to be a mangle to her parlour. Anyhow, he was pleased to, for he wanted to see the inside of her place.

There was this much to be said for it, it was totally unrestored; and with a very small expenditure and the right kind of fixings one could make the room very agreeable indeed. He noted the alcoves on either side of the hearth, their shelves now sagging beneath cloth-bound divinity and The Badminton Library, but worthy of his Montesquieu, and the latticed windows, so very jessamy, and the delicate original fire-place hidden behind that appallingly burly anthracite stove. One could make of it just such a room as de Quincey enjoyed those winter evenings in – omitting Margaret and the ruby-coloured laudanum. Of course one would have to put in drains and electricity and that sort of thing. Meanwhile he sat compressed between a portentous sideboard and a portentous table with an oil-lamp in its centre, and opposite him sat Miss Metcalf, backed by a harmonium and offering him cigarettes. No wonder she kept tables in the garden. He had never seen so much furniture, and all so frightful, in his life. The room was icily and cleanlily cold, and smelt of honest poverty. How on earth she cleaned it, how on earth she scrubbed the encumbered oil-cloth. . . .

Miss Metcalf remarked that she would have a little one too, to keep him company.

Yet the room did not look damp, it was just because she

kept no fires.

'How I wish I had a siphon! If I had known all this was going to happen, I would have gone to the grocer. Say When.'

He said. But would to God he had accepted it neat! For this was pre-war whisky, relict of the Reverend Thomas Metcalf's deep cellar, strong and smooth as silk. Fortunately she had obeyed his saying of When with instantaneous accuracy. One could see she was a drunkard's daughter, and well-trained.

'Personally I should never be surprised to wake up and find myself floating down the river – away and away! This is such a treacherous time of year, don't you think, and how one dislikes seeing swallows on telegraph wires! Do have another! To keep the cold out.'

Yes, one could be uncommonly cosy here, listening to the river and the trees, hearing the oil-lamp purr (for sentiment's sake one might keep an oil-lamp and use it from time to time, though de Quincey evenings would demand candles), reflecting on one's deep ensconced solitude. No one would come to stay in such a house as this. They could not. He would turn the second bedroom into a bathroom.

'I often wonder where I should get to. Out to sea, perhaps. But even in mid-Atlantic I should remember your kindness to my rabbits. Beverens, you know. I could not bear to eat them.'

He glanced across the table. She also was keeping the cold out, and it had greatly improved her. Sister to the beauty of the young leaf is the beauty of the skeleton leaf, having the last skirmish of its vegetable blood before the winter sucks it into the mould. She had pulled off her sou'wester. Her cropped hair was white as thistledown, and when she laughed, a wrinkle appeared on her long sheep's nose, But was this the last bottle of Mr. Metcalf's whisky, or would it be possible, possible . . .? No doubt she was all filial piety, the daughters of abominable fathers always are; but five guineas would be more to her advantage: with five guineas she could light a roaring fire in that deserted Moloch's altar there.

'I see you are looking at that picture, Mr. Kinloch.'

The walls of the room were plastered with things in frames, and he was not consciously looking at any of them. But now he followed the direction of her glance to the picture above the mantelpiece. It was a large steel-plate engraving, luridly brilliant. *Kermesse*, perhaps, or possibly *Boors Carousing*.

'It is a very fine specimen, I believe. And very valuable. My dear father thought the world of it.' Leaning across the table, her light whiskied breath on his cheek, she exclaimed, 'Sometimes I think I will take it down! But if I did,' she said, *'what can I put in its place?'*

'Why need you put anything?'

'Oh, I must, I must! Because, you see, if I took it down, there would be the patch on the wall-paper. The different-coloured patch where the wall-paper hasn't faded. It would always be there to remind me.'

'True.'

True, indeed. It would always be there to remind her. Absent or present, the boors would always be carousing. Morning, noon, and night Miss Metcalf would see those drunken, grinning faces, those paunches, overturned flagons, and wrinkled boots, those frank vomits and idiot rejoicings. Morning, noon, and night it would remind her of the Reverend Thomas Metcalf who had drunk himself to death and left her stupefied and penniless. Absent or present, it would taunt her with an inherited alco-holism, a desperate maidenly desire for strong drink.

Even at this moment, overset by her confidence, she had begun to whimper, and the first tears were rolling gaily down her flushed cheeks. In compassion and horror Adam Kinloch got up and made his hasty farewells.

Midway in the meadow he stopped and wrung his hands. The poor old wretch, the hapless elderly Iphigenia! Chance and the swollen river had brought her to his door, but only as another chance, and the swollen river, might have carried her past it. *Regrettable death of one of our oldest parishioners, Miss Metcalf, daughter of the late Revd. T. Metcalf, once Rector of Little Bidding. The deceased lady presumably fell into the river whilst attending to her rabbits, to which she was devoted. All those who knew her will feel her loss.*

All those who knew her! He began to walk on again, his hands in his pockets. All those who laughed at her, and hinted about her, and never went near her. There was nothing for it, he would have to pull himself together and be neighbourly to Miss Metcalf, take her for drives, ask her to tea, give her fur gloves at Christmas. Perhaps he could find a nice cheerful water-colour of some Welsh mountains to replace the *Boors Carousing*. But really the kindest thing to do would be to walk down with a bottle from time to time, and tipple with her. He would sit in her father's chair, and as the evening wore on, and the chairs creaked louder, she would scarcely distinguish him from the Reverend Thomas; all would be as it was, she would be a girl again, sipping from father's wonderful glass, and feeling proud to sit up so late like a grown woman. What a story she would make!

'You to the life!' he said aloud. 'Do nothing for her, but put her into a story.' The admission released him. He quickened his pace, he bounded up the steps to his door, he let himself in, he threw off his wet coat, he glanced at his wrist-watch. It was four o'clock. It was still raining. With a long sigh of relief he walked sedately into his library, sat down, and pulled a writing-pad towards him.

SUCH A WONDERFUL
OPPORTUNITY

The boy at the wayside garage said that it would take half an hour to do the repair properly. Why shouldn't I, said he, walk on to the village? There was a nice little public there – a nice little church, too, he added with impartial hospitality. A friend of his had read in a book that it had the smallest pulpit in England.

A charabanc was drawn up outside the nice little public, so I went on to the nice little church. Its coolness was quite as good as a drink. The smallest pulpit in England was certainly very small, and looked like an eggcup. It was beautifully unrenovated, and so were the high-sided Georgian box pews. When I had examined the pulpit and some fifteenth-century brass figures, I let myself into a box pew that had both a cushion and a prayer book in it, and began to refresh my memory of the Thirty-nine Articles of Religion.

I had got as far as Article XXXIII, 'Of excommunicate Persons, how they are to be avoided,' when I heard voices approaching and a clatter of buckets. Remembrance of things past told me that ladies must be coming to do the flowers for Sunday. I sank a little deeper into my box pew. Not that I was engaged in anything unlawful – what could be more proper than reading the Thirty-nine Articles? – but there is something about being hidden that inevitably gives one the sense that it would he better to remain in hiding.

There were two ladies, I saw, peeping out a moment later. Both of them were grey-haired, both sunburned in a gardening way, and the taller one seemed mysteriously familiar to me, as if I had met her a few minutes earlier; but after another peep at her I realized that she was one of those fifteenth-century brasses, made over to the feminine gender and wearing a somewhat more contemporary hat. The ladies marched up to the altar, stripped it of its vases, returned to the cool den under the belfry, where they had left their buckets, and resumed their conversation, which had been about the relative values of pig and horse manure. The fifteenth-century lady preferred pig – that is, if one knew how to manage it. I gathered that she was one of those who knew.

'Talking of transplanting,' she said presently, 'how's your Peony getting on?'

'Oh, not too badly. Wonderfully well, really, considering all things. Of course, it's a completely different climate. No real shade, and all those insects to contend with.'

'Food means more than shade,' said the fifteenth century decisively.

I supposed we were getting back to pig manure, but the reply made me revise my first impression. 'Peony says the beefsteaks are marvellous.'

'A good beefsteak,' observed the fifteenth century, 'a *good* beefsteak, properly grilled, with no nonsense about it, and served on a *hot* plate, would make up for a lot.'

SUCH A WONDERFUL OPPORTUNITY

'Just what her father says. As for plates, I really don't know. She hasn't said anything about plates.'

The fifteenth-century lady said one must hope for the best, and added that these large modern gladioli had no sense of devotion; it was impossible to make them sit quietly in anything but vats.

'Not that Peony complains,' said Peony's mother. 'Her letters are always cheerful, and she manages to make everything sound amusing. Even the picnics.'

'Picnics?'

'They picnic a great deal.'

'In the woods, I suppose.'

'Round cooking stoves, Peony says.'

'But I thought it was hot,' said the fifteenth-century lady.

'Yes, fearfully hot. But apparently it's a custom. Peony says it's not as bad as it sounds, because the food usually catches fire and the smoke drives away the insects.'

'I suppose that's why they do it. There's generally some practical reason for these local customs.'

'Either that, or something religious,' said Peony's mother. 'These asters are still full of earwigs.'

'Never mind. They'll have crawled away before the eight-o'clock service. Tell me some more about Peony. How does Nicholas like it?'

'Oh, he likes it very much. Of course, it's different for him. He's travelled so much, and then he's got his work.'

'It appears to me,' said the fifteenth century with virginal detachment, 'that men always have their work, just as the foxes have holes and the birds of the air have nests.'

Peony's mother laughed. 'I remember, my first time in India, how I used to envy Harry for being able to go off to his work looking so clean-shaved and calm, while I was left with all the real-life part of it. Scorpions and bandicoots and servants and the most awful holy men, who used to come and sit in the garden and could not possibly be asked to go away, because they were so holy. But, really, I wouldn't have missed it. It was such an experience! As for the bandicoots, they got so tame that they used to frolic all over Harry's bed. That's what I told Peony, the day she sailed. From this moment, I said, everything will be an experience. 'Treat everything as an experience, believe just one-half of what you're told, learn the currency, and you'll be all right,' I said. 'Fortunately, Peony rather likes snakes.'

They went up the aisle with their replenished vases and deposited them on the altar. Culling a few last earwigs, the fifteenth century remarked, 'Peony will do all right, I expect. She'll like meeting snakes, and the food will be good for her. It isn't as if she'd been brought up in a fool's paradise.'

'Oh, no! We're not worrying about her. On the contrary, I think it's a wonderful opportunity for her. Besides, one has to remember that she's really very lucky to be there. She's seeing a new country, and she's comfortable, even if it isn't always the kind of comfort she'd choose for herself, and she's got Nicholas to talk to, and the picnics can't go on all the year round, and she'll soon get accustomed to air-conditioning – it's shyness quite as much as claustrophobia. As long as she doesn't fall ill, she'll be quite all right.'

The fifteenth-century lady was now coming down the aisle. Peony's mother paused to give the altar a glance and a placatory little curtsy, before she followed her.

'No, no,' she said. 'I don't worry about her at all. It isn't as if Washington were one of those places in the really deep South, all swamps and moccasins. No, no! I'm glad she could go with Nicholas. It's bound to be an interesting experience for her, and in many ways I daresay she's better off than we are.'

They picked up their buckets and went away. I read on from the excommunicate Persons to Article XXXIV, 'Of the Traditions of the Church': 'It is not necessary that Traditions and Ceremonies be in all places one, or utterly like; for at all times they have been divers, and may be changed according to the diversity of countries, times, and men's manners.'

A BREAKING WAVE

In the bare landscape of the downs the house stood out plain as a bullseye. Below it the hillside hollowed itself into the curves of an amphitheatre. Zigzagging across the slope was the path made by the Butler children walking down to catch the school bus in the morning, walking back in the afternoon. Their feet had burnished the grass, and here and there had scuffed the thin turf off the chalk, so that the path looked like a strand of silk with a few pearls threaded on it.

It was because of the Butler children that Mrs. Camden was now walking up this path. As a rule she was glad enough to agree with her husband that parishioners who did not come to church would not want to be visited by the parson or the parson's wife. But the Butlers appealed to her as a special case. It was so enterprising of them to settle in that derelict house and send their children to the village school. 'Even if they don't come to church,' she had argued, 'they send their children to a church school.' Henry had replied by asking where else they could send them. Evading this, she had repeated that the Butlers were a special case. The truth was that the Butlers sounded unusual, and after seven years in a west of England country parish Mrs. Camden felt that the unusual would do her good. 'I shall make it clear that I'm not going there as the Parson's wife,' she added, 'but just as one woman to another.'

As an undenominational visit of womanly good-will her visit had been left rather late. The Butlers had been on their hill top for six months already. They must by now be sufficiently at home to feel that their home was their castle.

At this moment, she thought, they may be watching me approach and wishing I didn't. If the Butlers disliked being visited the oncome of a stranger must seem like a very slow arrow; for any approaching figure must be seen long beforehand, and with the certainty that it was directed towards them since it could not be directed to anything else. She had got thus far in her thoughts when a dog in the house began barking. If it had not been for her conviction that she was being watched she would have turned back; but it would look so very odd to come halfway and then retreat; so she went on, trying not to look at the house which was the only thing to look at.

The hollowed hillside was full of March sunlight. The air was windless, but cold. The appearance of warmth and revival was no more than a gauze laid over the uncomplying landscape. The greyish turf, the heaving downland contours, the sense of a close-lipped solitude extending on every side, evoked an impression of mid-ocean in which the house on the skyline seemed to be poised on the summit of a wave. The dog continued to bark, and Mrs. Camden continued to approach, passing a patch of newly-dug ground, a heap of builders' sand and a galvanized tank which lay on its side with a waterlogged teddybear in it. The Butlers' door was painted a gay green. When she knocked her knuckles clove to it, and she saw that she had left a mark on the wet paint. The dog snuffed at her under the door, and a high-pitched voice, impersonal as an oboe, said, 'Come in. He won't hurt you.'

The dog was a red setter, young and highly bred. Its brilliant coat emphasized the poverty-struck antiquity of the small stone-floored room within. Four doors and a flight of stairs led out of it, and except for a kitchen chair without a back it was entirely empty. She stood and waited, and the dog walked round her smelling her skirt. On the walls stains of ancient damp glowered through a coat of whitewash. A broken lath and tufts of cobwebby reeds protruded from a hole in the ceiling. Presently the dog's attention was distracted by a beetle, and it began to follow it round the room, diligently breathing on it. Mrs. Camden coughed, but to no purpose. She was counting ten before coughing again when a woman came slowly down the stairs. She was great with child and a tattered overall hung on her with classic dignity.

Good heavens, thought Mrs. Camden, is she going to smell me too? For the woman had now come close up to her, frowning slightly, and remaining perfectly silent. 'I am sure you must wonder who I am,' Mrs. Camden said. The woman continued to regard her without a trace of speculation. 'I am – I mean, my name is Camden. Mrs. Camden. I ought to apologise for being on this side of your door, but someone asked me to come in.'

'My father-in-law,' said the woman. 'He's in here.' The room they entered must have been the farmhouse kitchen, and now it was furnished in affected concordance with its former use. There was an oak settle, some stained deal chairs with patchwork cushions, a dresser displaying brass candlesticks and bakelite mugs. A modern shotgun lay on the old gun-rests above the hearth. An old man sat by the window in a wheeled chair with a rug over his knees, and the sunlight streamed into the room, obliterating the small fire under the cavernous chimney.

'This is my father-in-law, Colonel Butler. Father, this is Mrs. Camden.' Having completed her introduction Mrs. Butler lapsed into silence. Bowing from the waist, the old man excused himself for not getting up. Too profusely Mrs. Camden said, no, no, of course not.

'My legs are still there,' he said, glancing down at the rug, 'but they might as well be in New Guinea.'

Mrs. Camden said, 'Oh dear,' and bit back a parish-visiting impulse to remark that the wheeled chair must be a great convenience. While she was hesitating what to say instead Colonel Butler added, 'Or Tibet.'

'Tibet? Have you been to Tibet?'

'I don't think so.' His calm face became troubled. 'Emma! I haven't been in Tibet, have I? Emma, have I been in Tibet? Have I, have I? Emma, why don't you answer me?'

'No, father. You have never been in Tibet.'

Moving towards the window Mrs. Camden began to expatiate on the view, and this enabled her to turn round to Mrs. Butler with a suitable topic. 'I have always longed to live in this house myself. It seemed such a pity it should stand empty for so long.'

'We had looked everywhere for a house,' said Mrs. Butler.

'Yes? And then you found this? How thrilled you must have been.'

'It was all we could find.'

Her manner of speech and frowning attentive gaze might have seemed childish and rudimentary if they had not so patently been vestigial, the gawky remnants of an earlier candour and dutifulness. 'There's a roof,' she continued, 'But it leaks. There are no drains, the floors are rotten, and the well has rats in it.'

'Rats?' exclaimed Mrs. Camden, struck by the novelty of this last complaint.

'Dead rats.'

'But the situation,' said Mrs. Camden, falling into her parish-visiting tone; 'I'm sure the situation must appeal to you. Such a view! And such seclusion!'

Mrs. Butler flushed. Mrs. Camden became aware that her reference to seclusion might be construed as applying to the old gentleman in the wheeled chair. The old gentleman now intervened saying in a tone at once stately and airy, 'The house is well enough, but it's too high up. I don't like that because of these atom bombs.'

Unable to stop herself Mrs. Camden enquired, 'Why because of atom bombs?'

'One's so much nearer to them. Doesn't do, doesn't do!'

Mrs. Butler had now picked up a basket overflowing with ragged socks, and was thrusting her finger through one hole after another, as though measuring herself for a ring. Frustrated in her intention of finding a fellow-soul, Mrs.Camden tried to get what satisfaction she could from pitying a fellow-creature. Her life was already well supplied with pitiable fellow-creatures, but Mrs. Butler's claims could not be set aside, one must be sorry for any woman so unattractive, so plainly poor, with three children, and another coming, one might say, immediately, who had to live in a house perched like a piece of driftwood on an ocean billow with a crazy father-in-law and a well with dead rats in it.

Just now the crazy father-in-law struck Mrs. Camden as particularly regrettable. If he had not been there she could have got into a conversation about anaesthetics and breast-feeding, which might have made her visit seem more purposeful and rewarding. But there he sat, combing his beard with very thin and unnaturally taper fingers, so that in order to find something to say she had to look at the chimneypiece and ask, 'Does you husband shoot?'

'Sometimes. Mostly, he sets snares.'

They poached! Unfortunate creatures, they poached! In general she approved of poaching (both the Camdens belonged to the Labour Party) as being the nearest one could get in village life to Merry England and Robin Hood. But the poaching of the Butlers was another matter, For one thing, they were gentlefolk. For another, Mrs .Butler had no resemblance to Maid Marian.

'I see you are getting ready for a garden, I think you are so fortunate in being able to start your garden from the beginning. When we came here we inherited a garden so encumbered with Portugal laurels . . .'

The door burst open, and a man came in, saying, 'Emma, Emma! Where's the iodine?'

Spilling all the socks Mrs. Butler leaped to her feet. Her dull face was illumined with a look of such agonized despair that it was as though the devil had spitted her.

'Isn't it in the blue box? Oh dear, one of the children must have taken it! Where on earth? . . .' She searched about the room with a heavy fluttering movement, like a singed moth.

'Never mind. I'll give it a wash, and chance it.'

'Oh, but the soil! O Phil, you know they told us it was full of tetanus.'

Mrs. Camden produced a phial of iodine from her bag,

and then a clean handkerchief, and finally accompanied Mr. Butler to a very dubious basin in the back-kitchen, where she applied her first aid to the jagged cut in his wrist. She thought she had never seen a hand so deformed with cuts, scars, bruises, and chilblains, nor so white and well-shaped an arm, looking at his broken fingernails she recalled Colonel Butler's taper fingers. But there was nothing but satisfaction in Philip Butler's asseveration that he was a jack of all trades and master of none. Before she had finished tying the bandage he was opening cupboards and pulling out drawers to display his handiwork.

'Has Emma shown you round? No? But you must have a look at the place. Through here is what used to be the dairy. Just now we use it for a sort of rubbish-collection, but as soon as I can patch up the roof, and fix a better door, and stop the rat-holes it's to be a dairy again. We're going to make cheese from goats' milk. I mean to have a lot of goats, and do the thing properly. I've got a set of bells for their necks already. Now through here – I say, I hope you didn't twist your ankle – we really must clear these tins away, Emma? – through here there's a fine old pigsty. I only found it last week, when I was lopping the brambles. Well, I'm going to make a wire top for it, and keep snails. Snails make very good eating. And the place is alive with them, it's just a matter of collecting them and popping them into the snail-pen to grow fat. I'd like a fish-pond too, but water is the difficulty. But later on I mean to try my hand at making a dew-pond. Even if we couldn't keep fish in it, it would give us some soft water. The well water is so hard that Emma has a desperate job with the washing, it takes most of the family soap ration to get me a clean shirt.'

'You could get rain-water off the roof,' said Mrs. Camden.

A BREAKING WAVE

'Not till the roofs mended, and I can fix up some gutters. At present most of the rain comes indoors. By the way, Emma, that reminds me, do try to keep the children out of the end room. I haven't got round to fixing those boards yet, and I don't altogether trust the joists.'

'How the children must love this place.'

'Oh they do, they do! I suppose they're growing into young savages, but at the same time they're learning to make themselves useful. They pick up sticks – that's Emma's worst headache up here, worse than the washing, worse than the mud! It really is a problem how to find enough wood to keep fires going. And my poor old Dad feels the cold. But all that will be easier in summer.'

They turned the corner of the house, and the view extended before them.

'What a view! What a distance!' exclaimed Mrs. Camden.

'There's a rabbit,' said Mrs. Butler. 'Shall I get the gun?'

'I don't know. It's a difficult shot. Shooting down hill is always tricky. Besides, poor bunny! – he's enjoying himself. How do you think these fruit bushes are looking? I put them in last week. They don't look too good to me, but I daresay they'll come to something. Raspberries, gooseberries, black currants, three dozen of each. We ought to get enough home-made jam out of that, even for the children. Besides, there are always brambles. Here's our hen. The foxes got all the others, so now I am going to make a dovecot. Of course what one really ought to keep up here is a couple of falcons. Hawk, horse, and hound: that's what I aim to have in time.'

Mrs. Butler who had gone indoors now came out with the gun. She took a careful aim and fired. The rabbit rolled over, picked itself up, and ran.

'You aimed a bit too low, dear.'

She fired the second barrel,

'Nowhere near him! Never mind! Better luck next time.'

Breathing unsteadily she broke the gun, took out the cartridges, and put in two more. Mrs. Camden said again, 'What a view!'

'Yes, isn't it? Not a house in sight. That's what I like. Robinson Crusoe that's my idea of the good life.'

Turning to Mrs. Crusoe, Mrs. Camden remarked, 'I always think it's so fascinating to remember that this was once the most densely populated part of England. You know, there are ancient British villages and earthworks all over these downs.'

Philip Butler's face lit up. 'I say, Emma! That's an idea! That's what we'll do. We'll pick a site, and do some excavating. Yes, that's what we'll do next!' He was so delighted, and Mrs. Butler remained so unforthcoming, that Mrs. Camden had not the heart to tell him that amateur diggings were discouraged by the local archaeological society. Besides, she did not suppose he would get very far with it. Everything that she had seen about the house indicated that Philip Butler was a man of many beginnings and no completions. This conclusion was strengthened when a noise of tapping on the window behind them was followed by the crash of the window falling out from its frame. Colonel Butler, blinking in the pure sunlight, remarked through the aperture, 'There! Did you hear that one? It blew the window right off its hinges. I was just going to tell you that the fire's gone out again. That's all.'

'I suppose I shouldn't have trusted to the string,' Philip Butler said. 'Though it has lasted a long time. I've been meaning to get round to it for weeks, but there's always been something else.' He picked up the shattered window and considered it. Wonderful workmanship! I should think it's eighteenth century at least. Well, it wouldn't have lasted much longer anyhow. 'All right, father,' he added, 'I'll fix up some sort of shutter. There's that bit of corrugated roofing on the shed that got loose in the gale. I could use that. Emma would be thankful not to hear it banging any longer – wouldn't you, Emma?'

She was picking up broken glass, and did not answer. Colonel Butler peered out at them, looking like some abstruse hothouse variety of orchid exposed to the open air and fast becoming the worse for it. Mrs. Camden said she really must be going.

When she discovered that her host was determined to walk down as far as the lane with her she felt a twinge of social conscience. As though instantly aware of this, he said that he would get some sticks from the hedge. Emma would need more sticks. Now he wanted Mrs. Camden to tell him about mushrooms. During the autumn he had gathered all sorts of mushrooms and most of them had turned out to be edible, but some had not. Mushrooms led to wild flowers and a design of naturalizing opium poppies on the downs, opium poppies led to home-grown tobacco, home-grown tobacco to water-divining, and in the middle of water-divining the curve of the hillside reminded him to tell her about his plan for fitting out his children with roller skates and kite apiece, which would teach them the rudiments of managing the glider-plane he meant to buy as soon as he had finished paying for the house. By the time they reached the lane Mrs. Camden felt that Mr. Butler quite made up for her disappointment in Mrs. Butler. The readiness with which he blew up the tyre of her bicycle, which had deflated since she left the bicycle under the hedge made her think differently of his practical abilities: the crooked shelves, the window tied with string, the smudges of paint, the litter of half-baked projects, now seemed the expression of a courageous man battling with adversity. It was a pity that Mrs. Butler was not better fitted to live with such a man in the wilderness. But at least, she loved him. That moment of looking for the iodine had revealed a degree of love which Mrs. Camden, searching her mind for the right word, finally classified as *raw*. Yes, raw was the word. Raw, like a wound suddenly pulled open. A disagreeable analogy, and a disagreeable kind of love to bear one's husband, but that, undoubtedly, was how Mrs. Butler loved Mr. Butler.

Mrs. Camden had just settled this when the report of a gun ripped through the silence. Mrs. Butler must have seen another rabbit. Mounted on her bicycle Mrs. Camden was able to look over the hedge into the valley. She saw Mr. Butler roll over, exactly as the rabbit had done. But unlike the rabbit, which had picked itself up and run, Mr. Butler got slowly to his feet and seemed uncertain what to do next. A second shot rang out. Mr. Butler dropped rapidly, and began to move obliquely on all fours. Really, thought Mrs. Camden, it was too much! Of course with three children and two men to feed, one would take almost any risk to secure a rabbit: but Mrs. Butler was going too far. There she was, poised on the crest of the wave, and seemingly looking down into the valley at Mr. Butler travelling on all fours. A thread of light shot from the gun barrel, and now, good heavens! Mrs. Butler had reloaded the gun and raised it to her shoulder. Mrs. Camden, doing what she could, rang her bicycle bell. Like an unproportioned echo a third shot answered it. But she could not see what was happening, for the bicycle had carried her round the bend in the lane, and there, on the road ahead, was the school bus, pausing to set down three children who must be the Butler children.

Mrs. Camden dismounted. The children stopped and looked at her enquiringly. 'Are you the little Butlers?' she asked. One of them nodded. 'I – I thought you must be, I've just been visiting your father and mother.' They regarded her exactly as Mrs. Butler had done, as though they were smelling her. She listened, smiling at them, delaying them without alarming them. There were no more shots. I think you've got a lovely house,' she said. 'I wish I lived in it. I saw your dog, too. He's a beauty.'

There were no more shots. She re-mounted her bicycle, and saying, 'Goodbye, children! Goodbye!' rode on.

EVAN

His stepfather, in torments as usual at anything resembling a public appearance (and the platform of a country railway station is extremely public if it is the station of where you live), was in consequence talking too loud and too heartily.

'Well, that's all right. Your trunk is in the van, I've just seen it put it. You've got your suitcase, haven't you?'

'Yes.'

'Good! Don't forget it when you change at Market Beaton. And your sandwiches?'

'They are in the suitcase.'

'Hope they're good ones. Think I heard your mother mention ham. Lucky dog! She doesn't give me ham. Well, see you again at Easter. Hope you'll have a good term, and all that. And don't go catching mumps and measles if you can help it. But I suppose you're bound to.' Loyal to the English public-school system, Major Burroughs held as an article of faith the tenet that epidemics are peculiar to the Lent term.

'I've had measles. I had it last summer.'

'Yes, yes. Of course. So you did. Well, I'm sorry that holidays are over. Wish we'd had better weather, and you could have got out more. Dull work, hanging about indoors, reading, and amusing two small sisters. Very nice of you, to be so kind to Rhoda and Jenny. They appreciate it. So do I.'

'I think the train's starting.'

'Good Lord, so it is! Well, there we are. Goodbye, Evan, old chap. Sure you've got your ticket? Good, good! So long! See you soon.'

Dry-eyed and exhausted after this agonizing farewell, Evan pulled up the window, and then stumbled over the feet of the lady who was the only other traveller in that compartment. 'I beg your pardon,' he said.

'You didn't hurt me.'

He was startled. Though she was plainly not the type of lady who would say 'Granted,' he had expected a 'That's all right,' or something of that kind, in keeping with the impersonality of people in railway carriages. It was disquieting to be reminded that the feet he had stumbled over were sentient objects, attached to a being to whom he could cause pain. Her voice was not impersonal, either. It was warm and low-pitched, and seemed directly addressed to reassuring him. So he himself snatched up the conventional phrase saying, 'That's all right.' Spoken, it declared itself the wrong thing to have said – a pawn, when he should have moved out a knight. Becoming aware of a further threat in that the lady had no illustrated papers, and that he had none either, he began to look out of the window.

The lady at her leisure observed his long eyelashes. Long eyelashes being a beauty she herself regretfully lacked, this was always the first thing she looked for in a man or woman. The shade in the eye sockets embellished them as art would have done, but was natural – he was a boy of sixteen, or perhaps seventeen, who had outgrown his strength. Other things to admire were his small ears, and the well-shaped hands that grew like brown lilies out of his long narrow wrists. If due care had been expended on him, he would have been handsome. But care had not been expended, and whoever sent him to that haircutter should have been shot.

Meanwhile, the view from the train had shaken off the brief suburbs of the town and displayed a landscape of small steep hills and hanging woods. A brook ran counter to the train's course. It was in flood, and a hackle of foam rode on it. Evan had fished it during the summer holidays, and during the summer holidays before that, and before that. There was not an alder bush along its course that his line had not tangled in. He was tired to death of it, and of the woods where his family took picnics, and of the fields where they looked for mushrooms. If it had not been for the absence of illustrated papers on the lap opposite, he would have opened his suitcase, taken out the volume of Thomas Hardy's poems, and read himself into detachment. But to do so under her observation would appear uncivil, so he continued to look out of the window, and the lady continued to admire his eyelashes.

She saw them flick suddenly, and remain poised apart. Instead of just looking, he was now staring with all his eyes. His attention was so obviously arrested that she glanced out, too. She could see nothing to account for such rapt interest. The railway track had turned eastward into a landscape of shaggy, muddied pastures, hitched to the contours of chalk downs. On the horizon a roofless barn stood out against the sky. Beech trees had been planted round it as a windbreak; their boughs streamed in the wind like the skeleton of a wave. It was the image of desolation, so probably it was this that had caught his fancy. The young love desolation.

EVAN

Positively, he had flushed with pleasure, gazing at his gaunt and draughty Dulcinea.

But as Evan saw this same scene, the trees were heavy with foliage, and nothing stirred them but the occasional flight of a wood-pigeon, tumbling from one bough to another. At their feet were inlets of green moss, hot velvet in the sun, cold as ermine in the shade. Between the tree-trunks, as from a pillared portico, he looked out on the vast composure of a September day: the shorn fields, the ricks in the rickyards like loaves of bread on the baker's counter, the cattle grazing in the green aftermath meadows. He was alone there, with a day of flawless solitude before him, and he had never been there before, or known the epitaphs, as one does in a cathedral, but beset by no harrying verger or trailing sightseers; and the epitaphs had not a brag of virtue or regret or achievement among them, but were only names, or initials, or dates, with sometimes a heart, sometimes a phallus and sometimes a Union Jack scored in the chalk blocks of which the barn was built. His feet scuffed up the smell of leaf mould, and from a near-by field came the smell of a newly cut clover crop, steadfast, caressing and sweet as the sea is salt. He had spent the whole day there, a day so freed from time that when he disengaged his bicycle from an elder bush it seemed to him that the twigs had lengthened over the saddle and ripened their berries from red to purple since he leaned the bicycle there on his arrival.

The winter barn was swept out of sight, and with it went wish and motive to go on looking out of the window. Ransomed by remembered pleasure, he settled himself to sit comfortably, and stretched out his long legs. As he did so, he saw the lady hastily withdraw her feet. Catching his eyes, she smiled, and remarked, 'Still unhurt.'

It devolved on him to offer some ensuing politeness, and as she was not dressed as if to enjoy a ham sandwich or Hardy's poems, he asked if she would like the window opened.

She shook her head, and a smell of alembicated summer brushed his nostrils. 'I don't like fresh air unless it's warm.'

Just as the unhurtness of her feet had been presented as a matter of mutual concern, the lady's views on fresh air had a quality of being confidential. If confidences do not repel, they beguile. He said, with morosity, that he was travelling from one blast of fresh air to another, since at home his stepfather was always opening windows and at his school windows were never shut. This remark, too, was no sooner said than he regretted it – by an ill-considered knight's move he had exposed his queen. But the lady ignored home and school alike, and asked him what he had been looking at with such pleasure a few miles back. Out of his reply, it was the smell of the clover field she took up. They talked about scents, about fruits, about summer, about cats, and all the things they spoke about seemed an aspect of the lady, and in praising them he was also praising her.

They made no reference to their fellow-men. Even stories of eccentric aunts, the natural standby of the becoming-acquainted English, they avoided. The instinct that presides over the matings of wild animals and teaches birds the choreography of their courting dances warded them away from the evocation of what might re-imprison them in their incompatible realities: a boy going back to school, a woman returning from an interlude of country air and dieting to her stern career of courtesan; the one in terror of his inexperience, the other dreading the first folly of the over-ripe. After a stage in which they devoured every detail of each other's appearance, each had become almost unaware of what the other looked like, as though the nuptial darkness had closed about them. In that darkness they fell silent, lost in a watchful, dreamlike attentiveness to each other's existence.

But with a sigh of responsibility she glanced down at her wrist-watch and knew that there would not be time. If she did not hurry, they would not even kiss, and she was too far gone in passion for hurry and scheming to be anything but a vulgarly exorbitant purchase of something not meant for the market. Buildings darkened the outlook, sheds close on the railway track flashed by, and then others went by more slowly, and the train ran into a station and came to a standstill. From overhead, a voice of inhuman refinement bellowed through an amplifier, 'This is Peasebridge. This is Peasebridge. Change here for the London train. Change here for the London train. The train for Wittenham, Clewhurst and all stations to Market Beaton is now at Platform Four. Passengers for London will – 'Under cover of that voice she gathered together her gloves, her handbag, her wrap of moleskin. 'I must say goodbye. I am so sorry. Will you help me down with my things?'

He helped her to alight, lifted the luggage from the rack, and got out after her, the luggage in either hand, and set it down on the platform,. Raising his voice above the amplified voice, and ignoring its information, he shouted, 'Porter! Which platform for the London train?'

'Due in here, sir, soon as this one goes out . . . Thank you, sir, I'll be back when the London train comes in.'

'Well, that's very pleasant and easy,' he said, looking down on her affably. From the moment they were on the platform his whole manner had changed. It seemed almost as though – but it could not be! – he were feeling an immense relief at the prospect of getting rid of her.

'Thank you for getting me that porter. I hate scrambling with my bits and pieces.'

'You won't need to. I shall see to all that.'

'But the London train comes in after yours has gone on. He said so.'

'Yes. But I'm coming to London.'

'That you're not!' she exclaimed, the motherliness and vulgarity of the class she was born into coming suddenly to the surface of her manner. Squaring her shoulders, she looked shorter and almost stout.

'Yes, I am,' he insisted.

'Show me your ticket, then.'

'The ticket is out of date. I've changed my mind, and I am coming with you.'

'I never heard such nonsense. And suppose I don't want you?'

'I'll chance that.'

'A boy of your age – I heard your father seeing you off, to your Eton or Harrow or whichever it is.'

'As it happens, he is not my father.'

'No, no! Your grandson, of course.'

'And I am coming with you.'

'You're doing no such thing.'

Though she knew that every contradiction put them on more of an equality and strengthened his claim to insist, she was too flustered to use her advantage of sophistication. They stood on the platform, wrangling like man and wife.

His train was getting up steam. All along it, doors were shutting, and now only the door from which they had alighted still hung open. The guard slammed it to.

EVAN

'Guard! Guard! Don't do that! My son hasn't got in yet. He can't miss the train, he's got to go back to his school.'

To obliterate the look of triumph that she knew she must be wearing in his sight, she threw her arms about him. 'Goodbye, my darling!'

Awkward as a schoolboy, he let himself be embraced, he let himself be released, he let himself be jostled into the moving train. His face, as he turned it away, wore the same expression of frozen abhorrence that it had worn when she saw it first.

Horrified at the deed, she asked herself what else she could have done. If he had come with her, what sort of life could he have had? If after a night he had returned, it would have been to all the rows, inquiries and indecencies that the old keep up their sleeves to abase the young with. As it was, he would lick his wound and forget her. Sooner than she would forget him, she told herself, trying to adjust the weight that lay on her heart. The London train was signalled, the porter had reappeared and was looking invidiously at her suitcases – or, rather, at one of them. Large and shabby, it stood out among the rest. It was Evan's; he had set it down among hers, and it had been overlooked.

A DRESSMAKER

Madame Cleaver, late of Bond Street. Modiste and Dressmaker. Evening Gowns, Tailor-Mades, etc. Ladies' own materials made up. Re-modelling a Speciality. 29 C, Mill Lane. Dumbridge. By Appointment.

Though these last two words, 'by appointment', suggested something mysteriously grand and official, as though Madame Cleaver had been appointed by Royal Letters Patent *Modiste and Dressmaker* to the ladies of the Lord Lieutenant of the County, they meant in fact that she preferred intending customers to write beforehand – and were generally read as such. As for the Bond Street boast, there was this much truth in it: many years before, she had worked in the sewing-room of a real Bond Street establishment, hemming and felling acres of hand-made underclothes for the trousseaux of country-bred brides, whose mothers went to Langridge & Harmony because their grandmothers had done so. Later, she returned to her native town, where she married a Dumbridge man, a knacker, and bore him two sons. He died, and the business passed to them. The elder married, the younger took a religious turn and went into an Anglican friary. He was her

A DRESSMAKER

favourite son, and she was more widowed by his departure than by her husband's death. Yet she lived on in her old home, being useful where she had formerly been essential; for though she knew her daughter-in-law wished her away, she could not think how to comply with that wish. One day as she sat turning a grandchild's overcoat it occurred to her that she might be doing much the same work and getting paid for it. She drew out her savings, rented a small flat in the centre of the town, and put her first advertisement in the Dumbridge *Weekly Echo*. Within a week, it had brought her three customers.

To sit undisturbedly at her task, hearing motor horns and the voices of strangers instead of the lowings of wretched animals brought for slaughter, made her feel so stately and competent that she never doubted but that work would come and that she would be equal to it. When she received her first commission for a tailored suit she felt no particular trepidation; and when the suit was finished and the customer went away delighted with the fit and charmed by the little piping that gave such an elegant finish to the lining, she was not particularly elated. By studying the fashion papers and somewhat enlarging a good paper pattern she had managed it, just as by studying the cookery book and taking pains over the flavouring she had managed the far less congenial exploit of making black puddings for her husband. Mrs. Jameson's tailor-made brought three more commissions within a month. It was a pity that they were all for suits. Wool is not a very interesting subject. But after the third suit came a most enjoyable dressing-gown – purple velours with angel sleeves; and the following year, when the Bishop visited Dumbridge for a confirmation, Susie and Moira Jameson,

Anne Nobbs, and Dawn Pulliblank were dressed for the occasion by Madame Cleaver. Such dresses, with their pin tucks, their organ pleats, their little touches of hand embroidery, were a real pleasure to make; nor would her skill be wasted on a single appearance before a bishop, since afterward they could be secularised with coloured sashes and scoop-out necks and gone to parties in.

She would have liked to make more dresses for young ladies, dresses that could be dainty, light-hued, silken, and a little fanciful. Unfortunately, the young ladies of Dumbridge preferred to buy what they admired on the improbably ideal contours of the dummies in Wadman's windows, or Sylvester's, or in that new shop on Cornhill called *Au Paradis* – odd that this should be the French for 'paradise', when as a rule words became French by adding an 'e', not lopping one off. Her few youthful customers were poor, or prudent, or both; they wanted a skirt to go with a jumper they'd knitted themselves, old coats refurbished, bargain lengths, never long enough, made up. And though her clientele of matrons had come to include several ladies who required something handsome for a formal occasion and would pay anything in reason for it, they preferred colours that would not show the dirt, and styles that would not create remark. As for those evening-gowns that still haunted her advertisements, in the course of ten years she had not made as many, and of these, five were black, because black does not go out of fashion. But clouds have silver linings; and if Miss Hartley, in black velvet with her real guipure, resembled, try as you might, nothing so much as a first-class railway carriage for royal mourners, she was atoned for by Mrs. Jelks, who twice sang the contralto solos in the Dumbridge and Westpool

A DRESSMAKER

Choral Society's yearly performance of Handel's *Messiah* – once in shades of heliotrope, once in electric blue. Mary Cleaver attended on both occasions, of which the second was by far the most fulfilling. Like the note of a trumpet, the electric blue dominated the scene, more shimmering than the violins, more imposing than the organ. Bright, and never to be forgotten, was the vision of Mrs. Jelks, her bosom swelling, her skirts unfurling, rising in a torrent of electric blue satin to sing *He Was Despised*. But all this was a long time ago, and would not come again, since Mrs. Jelks was now singing elsewhere. In Ealing, to be exact, for her husband, a bank manager, had been transferred to the Ealing branch.

At first sight, there was no hint of promise about Mrs. Benson. She did not come by appointment. She did not even ring the street bell. Somehow wandering her way upstairs, she knocked. A certain class distinction attaches to those who knock, and Mary Cleaver, busy just then with a gusset, did not open her door immediately. Admiting an unusually tall woman in a whitey-brown mackintosh with a parcel under her arm, she saw that here was a new customer – but, from the look of her, a customer who would want only a remodelling, of which, at the moment, Mary had more than enough.

'Are you Madame Cleaver?'

The voice was low and slightly gruff, the manner grave and unsmiling. They made it evident that if this lady knocked it was with no acknowledgment of social inferiority, and that if all she came for was a remodelling the dressmaker might still feel aggrandised by her coming.

'I want you to make me a dress.'

'For afternoon wear? Certainly, Madam. Pray come in.'

'My name is Benson, by the way. Mrs. Benson.'

It seemed a casual way to introduce a married name.

Mrs. Benson sat down and began to untie the string round her parcel. The sight of her hands startled up an old woe in the dressmaker's heart. When her younger son became a friar, the thought of his poor bare un-sheltered feet in sandals had cost her many tears. Mrs. Benson's hands, still parched with last summer's sunshine, with the enlarged joints of those who develop chilblains in the cold months after Christmas, with the unvarnished nails of those who have grown disheartened and let themselves go, reminded her of Reggie's feet.

'I've got the stuff here. Your advertisement said that would be all right.'

'Of course, Madam. Ladies naturally prefer their own choice.'

Probably some sort of lightweight tweed, or a wool jersey. She would need the comfort of wool, poor lady, as she went up and down, to and fro, in a draughty old house with stone floors. Her hands proclaimed such a life – married, maybe, to one of those gentlemen farmers who were making, or not making, ends meet by Jersey cows, battery hens, foreign pigs; a hard life, somewhere away on the downs, far from Dumbridge and civilisation. Whatever the material, it must be good of its kind. No cheap draper would use such quantities of the best tissue paper.

The tissue paper rustled to the floor. Mrs. Benson unfolded a silvery-blue brocade, the colour of a winter sea; the colour, too, of her eyes, though until the brocade was unwrapped they had not seemed to be of any colour at all.

'An evening gown, Madam!'

'Do you think there will be enough?'

A DRESSMAKER

'Oh, ample, Madam. I don't know when I've seen a lovelier brocade.'

Mary Cleaver went down on her knees to it, as though before a shrine. Piously revelling in its intact beauty and abundance, she longed to get her scissors into it, to transform it into something really stylish. She brought out her fashion books. Mrs. Benson turned the pages like a polite child, but without the concentration one would expect of a lady making up her mind on the grave matter of an evening gown. When she spoke, it became clear that her mind was already made up. She knew exactly what she wanted. It was as though the dress were already shaped and tacked and she were describing something before her eyes. And though she seemed ignorant of the commonest dressmaking terms, it was impossible to misunderstand her.

'Yes, Madam. I quite see. What one might call a classic. Now, about the trimming? Some silver lace, perhaps, put on in a formal design. Or do you think it should be sequins? Sequins catch the light so gracefully, I always find.'

'I've brought that, too.'

She displayed a shell-pink net, criss-crossed with silver, and a brown net of coarser mesh veiling it.

'Like this. I don't know whether you'd call it a scarf or a drapery. Over the left shoulder – not bunched, though; almost floating. And tied in a large bow with long ends on the right hip.'

'Quite unusual.'

'Yes.'

She took off her raincoat and stood up to be measured. She stood unnaturally erect, as every woman does who is being measured. But in her case, the difference it made was astonishing. Six foot to an inch when she doesn't sag, thought the dressmaker. A minute later, she was thinking that Mrs. Benson's bust was too low, and should have been supported by a firmer bra. It was a curious thing; she couldn't really account for it. Here she was, with an evening gown, fallen from heaven, as it were, when she had been expecting a remodelling, or at best a light-weight tweed; and instead of feeling thrilled and delighted, instead of warming her fancy at this rich blaze, she was picking on every opportunity to be censorious. This was no frame of mind in which to undertake an evening gown.

The loveliness of the blue brocade mitigated her doubts as soon as she was left alone with it. And when Mrs. Benson came for the final fitting, and stood arrayed before the cheval glass, Mary Cleaver had no doubts at all. The dress was downright beautiful, a picture! Even that queer trimming was justified, clouding Mrs. Benson's shoulder and bosom like a vapour, emphasising that milk-white skin. If only the poor neglected lady could have left off at the wrists and at the base of the neck! But with such a gown, she would of course be wearing long gloves, and on the occasion for wearing it a facial and a perm would help surprisingly.

'Where would you wish me to send it, Madam?' Mary had a vision of herself entering the Dumbridge Central Post Office with an arrestingly large parcel addressed to Mrs. Benson, The Ritz, Picadilly, London.

'I'll call for it next market day.'

So might a servant girl have replied.

A week later, she called for it, saying, still like a servant girl, that she would pay now – only she paid with a cheque, and a bold strong signature: *Georgina Benson*.

A DRESSMAKER

Small-town dressmakers, dentists, chiropodists, hairdressers – people whose trade lies in individual contacts – practise, from motives of discretion, the secrecy sworn by priests and doctors. Mary Cleaver did not speak of her new client; she did not even mention that she had been making an evening gown. The ambition had been satisfied. The blue evening gown had expanded in her charge like some shining exotic flower; then the flower had been picked, and paid for, and carried away. She would not see it again, and those who saw it would not know it was hers – at least, she supposed not. Mrs. Benson did not seem a particularly acknowledging lady; she was not like Mrs. Jelks. Considerations like these presently accumulated into a slight sense of grievance. Having decided that Mrs. Benson would not come again, the dressmaker found that she was glad of it. It had been too much of a responsibility to handle that expensive brocade, to carry the burden of it unencouraged by any words of appreciation. Her other customers did not think it beneath them to consult her taste, to be guided by her knowledge of what was chic and becoming. With Mrs. Benson, it was more as if a possessed dummy had come to her for clothing, a dummy whose narrow mind knew what it wanted and knew nothing else. Had Mary Cleaver known the word 'arbitrary', she would have used it; as it was, she said to herself, 'Rather too hoity-toity.' And besides, the discrepancy between the shabby lady and the sumptuous apparel shocked her sense of decorum – her sense of decency, even. How could one be sure that Mrs. Benson would have her hair properly permed and tinted and remember to buy new shoes, and to hide those battered hands under kid gloves? When Mrs. Arthur Nobbs, arriving by appointment, asked her opinion as to what would be both suitable and practical for the Nobbs Seniors' golden wedding and afterward for sherry and television gatherings, and was so tractably persuaded to renounce an old-gold taffeta in favour of a neat floral-patterned crepe – the compelling factor being that taffeta cannot stand up to watching television, it rends at the seams – Mary Cleaver felt as if she had woken up in her own bed after a nightmare.

The tacking threads were not out of the neat floral pattern before Mrs. Benson was back again, for another evening gown. This time it was a satin, mahogany-coloured. The skirt was to be draped to show a lead-coloured petticoat, the trimming to consist of a few lead-coloured bows. Three sets of bows had to be made before Mrs. Benson was satisfied with them. It was a cruel gown to make, and would be even crueller to wear. But it was what Mrs. Benson wanted. She said so, standing in front of the glass, intent and motionless. It was as if she would stand there for ever, like a tree in a landscape, like an effigy of dark marbles in a church. It needed several recalling fidgets to dislodge her from her dream.

This was in early November. Five months later, she reappeared, and once more it was an evening gown she wanted. Winter had done its worst to Mrs. Benson, but had not tamed her ambition. She brought billows of glistening white gauze, splashed with vermilion and rose and lemon yellow, together with a wide ribbon of mignonette green for a sash – 'like an azalea bed', she remarked. Mary was about to ask if Mrs. Benson was fond of gardening – many ladies were, and looked the worse for it – when Mrs. Benson went on, 'And after this, there is something else I've been thinking about, something quite different.'

A DRESSMAKER

'A spring tailor-made, Madam?' Mrs. Benson's daytime appearance made this a natural assumption.

'For sad evenings.'

The word 'sad' has secondary meanings. It can be used for cakes that have failed to rise, for overcast weather. Mary supposed that the next dress she would make for Mrs. Benson would be for those dusky, clammy evenings when one almost lights a fire but instead puts on a shawl, and she was glad to think that for once Mrs. Benson was facing realities. Mrs. Benson was doing no such thing. The silk she brought, patterned in arabesques of brown and mulberry and a curious dead slate-blue, was fine as a moth's underwing. Held against the light, it was almost transparent, like a film of dirty water.

'You'll have a slip underneath, of course, Madam. What shade were you thinking of?'

But for once, Mrs. Benson had not got it all planned and settled. She stared at the stuff as people stare at slowly running water, and said nothing.

'It's really quite a problem to know which tint to bring out. Perhaps something quite a contrast . . .'

To aid her decision, since the decision was apparently going to be left to her, Mary Cleaver began to pass the silk through her hands.

'Oh, Madam, look here! I'm afraid it's past making up. It's been left in its folds so long it's quite perished. Look, here's a fray, and here's another. Right across the breadth, you see. I couldn't in honesty undertake it; it would fall to pieces before you'd put it on. What a pity, Madam, what a pity!'

Her concern was professional and genuine, though mixed with some anxiety as to how Mrs. Benson would take this blow.

'So it is. It's been left in its folds too long, just as you say, and now it's perished.'

Her tone of voice was airy, serene, a little singsong; false, because the situation demanded a false detachment from a true misfortune. She's taking it so well, thought the dressmaker, abashed to have been in doubt as to how Mrs. Benson would take it. But the gentry are brought up that way, generations of them, taking snuff one moment and having their heads cut off the next. She stole a respectful glance of compassion at this heroine. Mrs. Benson had repossessed herself of the silk, and with an expression of gleeful malice was poking holes in its ruined web. Mary Cleaver blinked and looked away, and afterwards tried to convince herself that what she had seen was nothing out of the common, and not in the least horrible. But though nothing more upsetting had happened than the natural decay of a curiously patterned silk, and the silk's lady taking it lightly and as a lady should, Mary Cleaver somehow felt, somehow even hoped, that Mrs. Benson would not visit her again. And though they met once more, the meeting was accidental.

*

It was in August of that same year. The holiday season had begun, and the weather had broken. Dumbridge was crowded with holidaymakers, who came up from Westpool in search of something more diverting than its wind-beaten esplanade and sodden bathing tents, and swarmed in and out of the shops, listless, irritable, and impeding as wet wasps. Mary accordingly did her household shopping early in the day, while the pavements were still passable and the produce unfingered. But on this particular afternoon she

A DRESSMAKER

was overtaken by a craving for cucumber sandwiches. She had edged herself through the clot of people who were sheltering from a thundershower under the greengrocer's awning, she had bought her cucumber and was making her way out, when she heard a sudden fusillade of titters, exclamations, and guffaws.

'Look at her! I ask you! Did you ever see such a scream? Well, of all the sights! Going to the opera, ducks?'

Other voices, further along the street, took up the View Halloo, and a child cried out, 'I don't like her! I don't like her!' and began screaming.

Two nuns came into the shop, one saying to the other, 'We must get whichever's cheapest.' The crowd made way for them, and through the gap thus created Mary caught sight of Mrs. Benson on the opposite side of the street. She was walking slowly along, looking neither to right nor left. There were people on that pavement, too, but they were silent, and shrank back as she passed them. She was bareheaded. She wore her old mackintosh. Below the mackintosh the blue brocade dress hung glittering to the ground and trailed after her.

Mary jostled a nun, elbowed the gapers and jeerers aside, and ran across the street. Old Mr. Bethel, the glovemaker, had come out of his shop and stood wringing his hands. Seeing Mary, his face cleared. 'That's right, you go after her, Mrs. Cleaver! I kept her in my shop as long as I could, hoping that someone would come. You're a good woman, God bless you, you'll know what to do. She's the Honourable Mrs. Benson, poor thing!'

As Mary caught up with her, Mrs. Benson began to walk faster, paying no heed to Mary's breathless civilities.

'What a dreadful day, isn't it, Madam? I don't know

when I've seen a worse August. Shocking for the harvest, too. Fortunately, I brought my umbrella. It really doesn't do to go out for a moment without one's umbrella, with the weather so changeable.'

Making conversation with a dry tongue, and attempting to hold the umbrella over a woman so much taller than herself who persisted in ignoring the attempt, Mary bobbed along beside Mrs. Benson. All very well for Mr. Bethel to say she'd know what to do. Knowing is one thing, doing quite another.

'Dear, dear! Another of these puddles! The Town Council lets everything get into such a state, I don't know what we pay rates for, I'm sure.' But Mrs. Benson had set her brogued foot straight into the puddle.

Grieving over Mrs. Benson's hem, Mary forgot Mrs. Benson's head. The umbrella tilted, caught and unloosed a lock of hair. Three holiday girls, looking silly enough themselves, God knows, with transparent showerproofs over their seaside nakedness, tittered. But Mrs. Benson laughed outright, a spontaneous, carefree laugh.

'Now what have you done to me?' she asked, smiling down on Mary's distress.

'Oh, Madam, if you'd come home with me, I could set you to rights in a minute. And if – don't think me impertinent ! – if you'd stay for a cup of tea, if you would overlook . . .'

'I should be delighted, I adore going out to tea.'

She had emerged from her madness like the moon from a cloud. Shedding romance and serenity like the moon, she drank three cups of tea and ate all but one of the cucumber sandwiches, talking of the price of vegetables, and the convenience of gas fires, and of Venice, and Madrid, and

Brighton. Discovering that Mary had worked for Langridge & Harmony, she told how she used to go there as a little girl accompanying her mother, to sit watching the fitter and wishing for a little black velvet pincushion to bob at her waist.

'Miss Dent. I expect you knew her.'

'Only by name, Madam. I was a sempstress, making underwear.'

'Oh, then no doubt you made all my mother's nightdresses. She was intensely particular.' She glanced down at her draggled blue skirts. 'I'm afraid you won't think that I am intensely particular.'

On the plea of a stitch in time, Mary got Mrs. Benson out of the blue brocade and into a borrowed skirt and pullover. The skirt was too short, the pullover too wide, but the mackintosh covered these defects. Then she accompanied Mrs. Benson to the bus depot, saw her into the bus, and stayed till its departure.

'Goodbye, goodbye! Please ask me again.'

The blue dress had been left hanging on the dummy. On her return, Mary's first impression was of something invincibly beautiful and sumptuous; but in fact it was past praying for, mud-stained and cockled with wet from hem to knee. This much was the day's doing, but not all the ill-usage it had suffered. Mrs. Benson must have walked over heaths in it, and through thickets. Burrs and sharp grasses were embedded in it, strands of silk had been clawed out by brambles, the delicate net was in shreds and tatters, and dry holly leaves had collected in one loop of the bow, as in a last year's bird's nest. She sponged and pressed and mended it as best she could, made sure of the address from Mr. Bethel, and posted it. Mr. Bethel's mood had hardened.

He hoped there was no money owing.

No acknowledgement came, and her skirt and pullover were not returned.

*

When the Street bell rang and the man on the threshold said, 'Are you Mrs. Cleaver? My name is Benson,' she could only just stop herself from replying, 'Yes, I know.' Some months had gone by, and she was certainly not expecting him, but she knew him instantly, because in the husband she recognized the wife. It was not merely that he was tall and gaunt and weatherbeaten, and spoke with the same mumbling aloofness. There was a deeper, more inflexible likeness, as if through the years of their married life they had been enforcing that look of fatigue and devil-may-care patience on each other. In silence he followed Mary upstairs and into her sitting-room, where the cat gave one glance at him and went out with a blank face, as though he smelled of fever.

'I'm here as my wife's man of business,' he said. 'I know you did some work for her. Does she owe you anything?'

'No, nothing at all. I hope Mrs. Benson is well.'

'She can't have paid you for that last job, I think – a dress that came by post.'

'It only needed a few repairs, and that was settled in advance. Mrs. Benson owes me nothing.'

He pulled out his pocketbook, and cancelled an item in a list.

'I suppose it was because you were cheap.'

'I beg your pardon!'

'I'm sorry. I didn't mean to be rude. But the cheques she made out to you are for very small sums compared to the

A DRESSMAKER

bills she didn't pay. Well, if you're sure it's all right, I'll be going. Goodbye.'

'I hope Mrs. Benson is well,' she repeated.

He turned back with a movement of his shoulders that was at once exasperated and fatalistically acceptant. 'Mrs. Cleaver, did it never occur to you that my wife was not in her right mind?'

'Oh, no! I never thought of such a thing.'

'Not even –' he broke off, gave her a furious glare, and continued – 'not even when you met her trailing through Dumbridge in an evening dress? Yes, I know all about it. I got it out of Bethel. And you were very kind to her, and I am very grateful. But why did nobody tell me?'

As though recognising the futility of this question, he put on an air of cross-examining composure. 'When did she first come to you?'

'A year ago. Almost to the day.'

'Exactly. By then the others must have been dunning her, so that she was afraid to go back to them. She'd been buying things all over the place – London, Bath, Cheltenham. How was I to guess?' His cross-examining mask had fallen off, and now he was the man in the dock. 'How was I to guess? She always looked so shabby. And when I begged her to get herself something new, something fit to be seen in, she'd put me off with not wasting money. But all the time, she was getting these fantastic fineries.'

'One could see she was used to the best.'

'I never saw her wearing them, but the milkers did, and the farm hands. She used to go out early in the morning and wander for miles. How was I to know? I was at work then, packing mushrooms to go off in the van. If she was late with breakfast, I supposed she'd overslept. I knew nothing till the morning they pulled her out of the river and brought her home dripping in white satin. Couple of days later - Sunday - she went off again, walked over the downs to Epworth, and turned up at the Wesleyan Chapel in a yellow ball dress. But one can't keep one's wife under lock and key.' It was to himself he was talking, reiterating a familiar, hopeless rationalisation of his calamity, as an animal in a cage trap turns round and round, unable to remember where it got in, unable to find a way out.

'I had her certified.'

'Oh, no!'

So might a farmer speak of a cow. *I sent her to the knacker.*

Hearing Mary's exclamation, he seemed to catch sight of her. Frowning, and quickly averting his glance, and exaggerating his mumbling aloofness of manner, he said, 'They say she'll recover in time, with rest, and proper meals, and warmth, and all the things she didn't have at home. That's what they hope. Meanwhile, I'm trying to clear things up, deal with the debts, deal with those wretched garments – for she mustn't see them again. They'll make an expensive bonfire. I don't know whether you'd be able to do anything with them. Sell them on commission, you know, or buy them outright. I'd be thankful to get something for them, however little.'

'I'm afraid you are quite mistaken.'

Shock, disapproval, compassion for the woman she had succoured, mortification because that same woman had only resorted to her when she could go nowhere else, injured professional pride, and a belated, violent realisation of the horror she had felt at her husband's trade

– all these elements, jostled together, exploded in Mary Cleaver's wrath.

'Yes, Mr. Benson, quite mistaken! I am a dressmaker. I have earned my living as a dressmaker for the last twelve years, and this is the first time anyone has insulted me by taking me for an old-clothes woman. Good morning to you!'

The door slammed to behind him. He was out on the landing, in the company of several empty milk bottles. He noticed them sharply, and thought, these people seem to drink a lot of milk. By the time he reached the street he was shaking with rage, while at the same time waves of self-pity swept over him. Such was his state of mind that he had to spend several minutes looking in at the saddler's window. Leather to leather. Leather suffers long, and is tough. He had endured worse things than being stormed at by an elderly dressmaker standing on her dignity.

A QUEEN REMEMBERED

It was New Year's Eve and so long ago that I cannot remember the date of the year. We had finished our dinner and were drinking coffee in the upper room when we fell to making New Year's resolutions – a calm process, since we had often made them before. We must keep a register of books we'd lent, and consult it in order to reclaim them; we must tidy the garage, throw away all the old paint-pots, buy some new wastepaper baskets, invite the Harrisons to a meal.

'One thing we must do,' said Valentine with decision. 'We must buy some peat blocks. We always talk about peat fires. We never have them. This year we will.'

'But where from? Coal merchants don't sell peat blocks. Peat just means azaleas in Dorset.'

'Yes, there's another thing we must have. When does one plant azaleas?'

'Not till the frost is out of the ground.'

'Good. That leaves tomorrow. Tomorrow we will drive into Somerset and buy a load of peat.'

It was stimulating to have a New Year's resolution which could be put into effect at once. On New Year's Day we emptied the hold of the car, studied the road map, and drove towards Sedgemoor.

We had learned from other pursuits of the attainable that in the West of England it does not do to ask point-blank for information. It is proverbial that if a stranger in a car halts to ask a pedestrian the way to such-and-such, the pedestrian cups a deaf ear, puts on a grieved, thwarted expression, and walks away; or replies, after the question has been repeated several times, that he really can't say, he is a stranger himself. In neither case is this true. The cupped ear catches every word you say, the stranger is a hardened inhabitant. It is you, not your inquiry, which is of interest. As they don't like to appear inquisitive they learn what they can about you by observation. Only when you have acquired a certain mossiness as a familiar object can you expect to be answered. Knowing this, we entered a roadside inn called the Volunteer and asked for bread and cheese and two half pints of draught beer. There we sat, waiting for the moss to grow and seeing from the window how incoming customers stopped for a good look at our car.

A bold spirit addressed us. 'Come from far?'

'From near Dorchester.'

'Ah.'

'We are looking for somewhere where we can buy peat. Do you happen to know –' There was a disclaiming silence. I went no further.

A voice at the back of the room said, 'What about Bert Gary?'

We said nothing. We had not been addressed.

'Or young Damon?'

'Maybe he might. But he's in Bridgwater on Fridays.'

'Always is. With his lorry.'

'What about his mother, though?'

Opinion seemed pretty evenly divided as to whether Mrs. Damon might or mightn't.

All this time a peat fire was noiselessly burning on the hearth, filling the room with its smell of mouldered summers.

Valentine now struck like a falcon. 'Where does Mrs. Damon live?'

Startled into compliance, the customers of the Volunteer directed us to Mrs. Damon's house, which we couldn't miss if we turned to the left a couple of miles or so short of the old pumping station.

'Your hair smells of peat already,' said Valentine as I got into the car. 'Peat and beer.'

It has always seemed to me that skies are coloured by the soil beneath. We had begun our journey under the sharp forget-me-not blue of chalk, Now we travelled under a web of smokey bronze and cobalt, The road was ditched on either side and pollard willows grew along the banks. It was a landscape in which it was impossible to judge distance. Its measure was duration, not miles. We had driven for a long way before a huddle of bricks and timbers told us that we should have turned off to the left a couple of miles before. We drove back and took the turning into a narrow track. Like the road we had left, it was straight, ditched, willowed, and featureless, except for being deeply rutted. Encouraged by this assurance of young Damon's lorry, we drove on and on. A hen crossed the track,

'Where there is a hen there is a woman,' I said, 'It can't be far off now.'

'It looked to me like a lost hen,' said Valentine. I replied that it couldn't be lost unless it had a home to stray from.

We had branched from hens to the dubious efficacy of scholastic logic when Mrs. Damon's house started up behind the willows. The ruts led us over a plank bridge into a yard with some sheds standing about in it. They looked casual and dilapidated. Not so the woman who came out of the house. She was tall and thin. She held herself erect and wore a long white apron. Her grey hair was fastened in a neat knob.

She was Mrs. Damon.

I explained. She listened to me and looked at Valentine, This was nothing out of the common. I continued to explain and Mrs. Damon continued to look. Seeing that I was getting nowhere, Valentine also began to explain. Mrs. Damon came back to real life, smoothed her apron, and asked how much peat we wanted. As much as we could get into the car, Valentine said. Mrs. Damon glanced at the two-seater. With an air of indulgent gravity she opened the peat shed and hauled out a sack, remarking that we would get more in if we packed them by hand, Together we packed the peats into the hold and behind the seats, and Mrs. Damon's apron remained as white as ever, and her lips fluttered as she kept her count. All this took some time, as she and Valentine were both determined to get in as many peats as possible. When the last blocks had been fitted in, we stood back and surveyed each other, as fellow-workers do. Suddenly Mrs. Damon said to Valentine, 'You don't come from hereabout, do you?'

'From Dorset.'

In that sombre, brooding landscape Dorset seemed far distant; but not distant enough to satisfy Mrs. Damon's conjecture. 'Not born there, though?'

'No, I was born in London.'

'That's what I thought. Whereabouts in London?'

'In Brook Street.'

'Just so, Runs into Park Lane, doesn't it? The moment you got out of the car, I said to myself, "That's the West End." It was something I never thought to see again.'

'So you're a Londoner, too?'

'Not born. But I was in service there for twelve years. The best years of my life. It was a wonderful place - two in family and seven servants kept. Porchester Terrace. Then I went too far on Armistice Night, and had to marry him, and came down here. And here I've been ever since. I suppose I wouldn't know London again if I saw it now.'

'The Park's much the same – though if you saw some of the riders in Rotten Row they'd be a surprise to you.'

'Never is what it used to be – that's what they say about Jobling, she was the housekeeper, used to talk about her first place. There was a golden fountain in the hall, and when the family had their dinner parties and receptions it was turned on and sprayed out eau de cologne. But that was in the old Queen's days.'

'Did you ever see her?'

'No. But I've still got my Diamond Jubilee mug they gave at the school treat. All these years I've treasured it. And I've left it in my will that it's to be buried with me.'

A moist wind had risen and swayed the willow boughs. Mrs. Damon's hens were gathering round her. It was a strange place in which to be hearing about golden fountains, I thought. Mrs. Damon was talking on.

'A good Queen, if ever there was one. And over and above, she was a good woman. And the faithfulest of widows. I never look at my mug but I think of her driving to the Albert Memorial. Every afternoon she drove out in her closed carriage, with a lady-in-waiting or a princess beside her drove from Buckingham Palace along Knightsbridge as far as the Albert Memorial. And there the carriage would stop, and she'd look at it – look at it with all her heart and soul. And then she'd signal and be driven back, hiding her face behind a white handkerchief with a black border. There's love for you. There's faithfulness.'

'Yes, indeed.'

We paid, and drove away. After a pause, I began:

> And out of his grave there grew a rose,
> And out of her grave a briar . . .

Valentine took it up:

> And ever they grew and ever they grew
> Till they could grow no higher.
> And twined themselves in a true lovers' knot
> For all folk to admire.

Forgetting our errand, forgetting our route, we marvelled at this encounter with the authentic voice of balladry which had installed Lytton Strachey's Victoria, Victoria of the sneers, among the Good Queens of legend: Eleanor of the Crosses, Queen Anne of the lace, Berengaria who sucked the poisoned wound, Philippa whose great belly shielded the burghers of Calais. Talking of these, speculating about Mrs. Damon, we lost our way twice over in the gathering dusk before we reached home.

FLORA

A footpath branched off the track across the heath and vanished like a wild animal among the bushes. One would not have supposed it led to a dwelling – one might not have noticed it at all, if one's attention had not been arrested by a white plastic rubbish bin. This assertion of civilisation made the surrounding landscape more emphatically waste and solitary. But the footpath, twisting past thorn brakes and skirting boggy hollows, led to a house, the residence of Hugo Tilbury, D.Litt., F.R.S.L., named by him Ortygia. Edward, who knew the way, walked ahead. It seemed a never-ending way; I had plenty of time to muse on the donnish associations of the name and why it carried overtones of retirement, but it was too late to ask. Edward disliked conversation on country walks, alleging that one cultivated voice would scare every bird, beast and butterfly within hearing.

He came to a pause under a group of tattered conifers, and said, 'There it is.' Before us was a neat red brick cottage with a single chimney and a water butt. In front of it was a plot of dug ground, with some cabbages growing unwillingly in the peaty soil, fenced with wire netting against rabbits. The cottage looked unwilling, too – as if,

FLORA

being so up-to-date and rectangular, it felt demeaned by its situation and wanted neighbours.

Ortygia's door was open. Edward knocked on it, and a reedy voice said, 'Come in.' We entered a room containing a bicycle, some gardening tools, several pairs of gum boots, a pile of neatly folded sacks, two pictures standing face to the wall, a narrow, painted wardrobe with a mirrored door, and a fish kettle. Everything was clean and orderly, as though it were made ready for an auction. From this strange ante room we went into a sitting room, where Mr. Tilbury rose from a wooden armchair and said, 'Ah, Edward.' He was a short, sturdy old man with bushy eyebrows and a trimmed beard. Turning a bright, unseeing glance on me, he took my hand in a firm grip and remarked that Edward had brought me, and that I was Flora – or was I Dora? He hoped the walk had not tired me. I praised the surrounding expanse of heath. 'A protective custody,' he said.

Motioning me to another wooden chair, he began to talk to Edward. They talked. I sat. Their talk had the embowering intimacy of two experts, so I felt free to study the room. It was clean and bare as an empty snail shell – Mr. Tilbury's shell. There was a fireplace filled with fir cones. Each of the walls had a door. As two of the doors were above floor level I supposed they were cupboard doors. A highly polished sham-antique oak table was planted on a central mat, brushed and threadbare. A fair-ground vase, assertively pink, stood on the window sill with some heather in it.

I was sufficiently tired by my walk to feel chilled, and from feeling chilled, to feel intimidated. To rouse my spirits, I began to nurse rebellious thoughts. Mr. Tilbury, so perfectionist in clean bare surfaces, probably ate his dinner off the floor if he ever dined. There was no whiff of nourishment in the air, and the chimney pot, as I now recalled, had no smoke coming from it. Perhaps he was an exquisite epicure, and behind those cupboard doors kept caviar, foie gras, artichoke hearts, ranks of potted delicacies from Fortnum & Mason. This was too much to suppose: I decided that what he kept in his cupboards was skeletons – skeletons on strings; that when we had gone away he would fetch them out and make them dance to their Daddy, their heels clattering on his bare boards and that before he put them away he would polish their sallow bones.

Meanwhile he and Edward were talking about calligraphy with never a sensual thought in their minds. Taking a sharp pencil and a piece of scribbling paper from his pocket, Mr. Tilbury drew the terminating twiddle by which one could infallibly distinguish between the work of a French and a Burgundian scribe, and when Edward said yes, he saw, Mr. Tilbury put it back in his pocket. It was then I noticed that there was no wastepaper basket in the room.

Yet a wastepaper basket, however much Mr. Tilbury might dislike its disorderliness, would seem an essential adjunct to calligraphy. Professional scribes (French, Burgundian, what you will) must sometimes have spoiled a copy – duplicated a word, misplaced a twiddle. With parchment, this was easily put right, they scraped off the error with a sharp penknife. But when progress drove them onto paper, they must have wanted to discard a faulty page – crumple it up and throw it away. Into what, if not a wastepaper basket? When did that essential adjunct to calligraphy come into use? I ransacked my memory for works of art recording it: Saint Jerome in his study – in his numerous studies – Petrarch sonneteering, usurers calculating . . . Nowhere a trace of the wastepaper basket, not even among the Pre-Raphaelites. I forgot my place and broke into the conversation. 'When was the wastepaper basket invented?'

Edward emerged from calligraphy, laughed, and said, 'God knows.'

Mr. Tilbury, too godlike for such an admission, impaled me on a glare and said, 'That would take too long to answer, young lady.'

I realised that I had foxed them both.

Some time later – it seemed like hours – Mr. Tilbury opened one of his cupboards and took out three pony glasses and a bottle labelled 'Ketchup.' Ketchup contained a home-made sloe gin. He filled the three glasses with a steady hand, impartially. We drank the stirrup cup and took our leave.

When we had gone a little way, Edward asked what I had made of old Hugo. I praised his sloe gin, adding that it was magnanimous of him to give me a fair share of it, since it was plain he disliked women, more especially young women who went about with young men as though they were married to them but weren't. He disliked anything he couldn't be sure of, Edward explained. The Hunter's Moon, which follows on the Harvest Moon, had risen, blackening and brightening the path. I could not believe it was the path we had come by earlier. Nothing was the same, till we came to the rubbish bin, implacably itself even by moonlight. On the track across the heath, where we could walk side by side, it was as though we were freed from a constraint to remember the afternoon's visit. We planned how we could contrive a spring holiday in Portugal. Edward hoped that Mrs. Hooper of the Fox Inn would give us something hot for supper.

Yet that night he reverted to Mr. Tilbury, speculating about why he had secreted himself and his learning in that comfortless Ortygia. Some shock, some personal disaster, some scandal must have driven him there, for in conversation old Hugo revealed a livelier past, when he was sociable, knew all sorts of people, went to the opera, supped at the Café Royal (still fashionable in those days) had a top hat. It couldn't have been a religious bolt; Hugo had no more piety than a ferret. It couldn't have been money: Hugo didn't mind what he spent on something he wanted; he was poorly off for wants but not for means. And when it came to his private fortune of scholarship, he had none of the usual expert's niggardliness; from the day Edward, following the clue of a savage retort to an ass showing off in a learned periodical, had tracked him to his den on the heath, Hugo had been a most generous teacher.

Exhausted with so much exercise and open air, I kept on falling asleep and re-awakening with a sense of guilt that I should have taken such a dislike to the old man who had given Edward so much pleasure. In one of my wakenings I heard Edward say, 'I could never repay him for all he has done for me – even if I could bring myself to give him my Kepler letter.' He gave a deep sigh. The letter by Johannes Kepler was his dearest possession. He had found it in a Birmingham auction room, in a folder labelled 'Letters Various and Curious'. Mr. Tilbury had approved and authenticated it, and though no such vulgar word as 'stroke of luck' had been spoken, Edward felt himself considerably advanced in his mentor's esteem. I was going

FLORA

to suggest he might tell Mr. Tilbury that he meant to leave it to him in his will when the sigh was followed by a contented yawn. Edward was asleep.

*

Five months later Edward was killed in a car crash. He died intestate. Had I told his mother that he would have wished the Kepler letter to go to Mr. Tilbury, my word would have counted for nothing, so I waited for the hour of his funeral, let myself into his flat, and stole it. It was not so easy to part with it. Not that I needed anything to remember him by, but his hand had warmed it, he had made the parchment case that held it. Eventually I brought myself to write to Mr. Tilbury, telling him of Edward's death, that he had meant to give him the Kepler letter as a token of gratitude, and that I would prefer to bring it rather than risk it in the post. The reply was brief and businesslike: he was sorry to hear of Edward's death, and would expect me on March the 10th at 4 p.m. I took a taxi from the local station to the Fox Inn, where Mrs. Hooper exclaimed and sympathised, and gave me a drink out of hours against the cold, saying that the wind on the heath would perish a Londoner.

It was an east wind, shrill and searching – a spring-cleaning wind, I thought. From time to time, it tore rents in the cloud cover; shadows hurried over me, a distant stretch of grass suddenly became a brilliant watery green. As I turned into the path, I looked at my watch. It was quarter to four. Everything was going to plan. The path that had been so much changed by moonlight was as much changed by bursts of sunlight; leafless thorn brakes were silver-plated with litchen, bramble patches had a smouldering richness of purple and russet.

The door of Ortygia was closed. There was a push-button on it. I pressed the button, and a bell – the kind of bell that works by a battery – responded with a loud jarring sound, so instantly that I flinched, as if it had spat in my face. No-one came. I waited and rang again, and again, for a third time, and a fourth. The door faced east, and the spring-cleaning wind pinned me to it; when I gave it a push, I found it was barred. It was the 10th of March, I had arrived at the hour Mr. Tilbury had appointed, and I did not recollect that he was deaf. If not deaf, perhaps he was dead? If so, he must be newly dead, for his patch of ground was freshly weeded; some plucked-up nettles blown against the wire fence were barely wilted. He had weeded, gone indoors, secured his door against the wind, opened a cupboard for a drink of sloe gin, had a heart attack, fallen dead, or palsied with one eye closed in a ghastly wink. That would be very awkward. I looked in through the sitting room window. The heather had been removed from the fairground vase, and a fire of fir cones and neat billets of wood burned in the grate. Otherwise, the room was exactly as I remembered, except that Mr. Tilbury was not in it. He was not in the water butt either – a frantic supposition, but by now my imagination was keeping my courage up – for he could not have bolted the door behind him before going out to drown himself in his water butt and in any case, he was not the sort of man to act without due consideration. So I went back to the door, rang the bell again, knocked, whistled, shouted his name, felt increasingly silly, wondered if I would go away – and waited on.

At twenty to five I decided I would wait till five, return to the Fox Inn, and from there ring up the police. Mr.

FLORA

Tilbury, I would say, had asked me to be at his house at four o'clock without fail, as I had a valuable parcel to deliver. He did not seem to be there. I was afraid something had happened to him. Etc. A flicker of amusement warmed me at the thought of loosing the police on Mr. Tilbury who, if he retained any consciousness – perhaps he was just drunk, lying comatose with a bottle of ketchup beside him – would resent this incursion on his private life. If dead, there would be headlines in the local papers – mysterious death of Woodmell Heath* hermit – and later a respectful obituary in *The Times*. If drunk, local merriment. Either way, he would give pleasure.

Meanwhile, I had my errand to attend to. I was about to make a last attempt on the bell when I heard a sound of life overhead: a loud, irrepressible sneeze, and another, and another – the sneezes of a man in perfect health but with imperfect control of his bodily reactions. I laid the Kepler letter on the doorstep and walked away.

A moment later I heard the door open. There was no need to look back; my mind's eye showed me Mr. Tilbury, D.Litt., F.R.S.L., dart out, seize on his prey, and carry it into his den.

I told myself as I hurried up the path that it was the insult to Edward that made me weep tears of rage. But it was also the insult to myself. Edward's was unscathed, safe dead, with his illusions intact, with his intention carried out, with nothing to revenge. I had been summoned, slighted, left to kick my heels in the cold, while Mr. Tilbury sat warming his malevolence; and no possible revenge was in my power. Attaining the rubbish bin, I gave it a kick. It answered back with a multitudinous light rattle. I took off the lid. Inside was an accumulation of emptied tins that had contained a brand of ready-cooked rice pudding know as 'Lotus'. The tins were spotlessly clean and as if a rat had licked them – a sturdy rat with a trimmed beard, a rat who in better days had supped at the Café Royale, a rat who for some reason, some personal disaster, some hounding scandal, had fled to a hiding place on the heath. Looking round on the darkening landscape I remembered his words: 'A protective custody.' Even so, I could feel no pity for him.

* Tadnoll Heath in the original MS, the most northerly outpost of Chaldon Herring parish.